S. E. Gilchrist can't remember a time when she didn't have a book in her hand. Now she dreams up stories where her favourite words are … 'what if' and 'where'? Writing as both S. E. Gilchrist and Suzanne Gilchrist, she loves combining romance with adventure and suspense across many different genres including science fiction/space opera, apocalyptic, and contemporary small towns.

For more information, visit her website:
www.segilchrist.com

Also by the Author

Writing as: SUZANNE GILCHRIST

Cowboy under the Mistletoe (Edge of the Outback Romance)
Dance in the Outback (Edge of the Outback Romance)
The Cowboy's Gift (Edge of the Outback Romance)
Under an Outback Sky (Edge of the Outback Romance)
Love's Sweet Challenge (Bindarra Creek Short & Sweet
Romance)
Take Me Home (Bindarra Creek A Town Reborn)
A Dangerous Secret (former title - Amulet of Death) (A
Bindarra Creek Mystery Romance)
The Mistletoe Wish (A Bindarra Creek Christmas Romance)
The Glitter or The Gold (Bindarra Creek Small Town
Christmas)

Writing as: S. E. GILCHRIST

SCIENCE FICTION/SPACE OPERA ROMANCE
Darkon Warriors series:
Legend Beyond the Stars
The Portal
Awakening the Warriors
Star Pirate's Justice
When Stars Collide
Bargain with the Enemy
Touring the Stars
The Slave Trap

Mars Academy Series:
Stranded
Cosmic Fire

Apocalyptic/Dystopian:
Paying the Forfeit
Storm of Fire
Don't Look Back (Warders of Earth)
Quest for Earth

CONTEMPORARY
Bindarra Creek Makeover (Bindarra Creek Romance)
Endangered Heart
Scent of the Jaguar (Deadly Forces series)
Cotton Field Dreams (Mindalby Outback Romance)

FANTASY/ANCIENT WORLDS EROTIC ROMANCE
Bound by Love
Bound by Lies

A DANGEROUS SECRET

A Bindarra Creek Mystery Romance

By

SUZANNE GILCHRIST

CHAPTER 1

Dear family,

Many happy returns, mother and may God grant you many more. Alfred and I are going strong. Do try and not worry. Tell father not to hire Roaming Jack for shearing this year. Too many bloodied sheep the last time he was on our farm. There is plenty of tucker although it is always the same. Nothing like your home cooking mother which I miss dearly. Like our tucker our days are the same. We rise at dawn, march from the barracks to Rosebery, no idea why and back again. There is bayonet practise and we exercise constantly. I suppose we must be in tiptop shape so we can fight the Jerries. Rumour is our squad will leave our shores in the next week or two. It will be bonzers to be on our way. I have taken up learning French, it may prove useful. I am sure we will be home by Christmas.

With love to all, I remain your affect. son and brother, Mitchell.

Exultation sizzled like an electric current through the man's veins as he stepped off the lowest tread of the rickety stairs and into the gloomy cellar. The old timber creaked underfoot, a thunderbolt of noise in the heavy silence. He paused, his breathing pulsing loud in his ears as he sucked in the stink of mould from years of neglect and damp. His excitement heightened, twisting hard in the pit of his gut and his palms tingled. All those years of study and chasing down every clue no matter how small had led him right to this moment, this place. Finally, he was close to achieving his life-long obsession.

He groped along the grimy wall, unable to find another light switch. Slipping his mobile out from his pants' pocket, he flicked on the torch app, then frowned. Layers of cobwebs clung to the ceiling. Mice droppings mounded in the corners. There were no prints in the thick dust underfoot.

No one had entered the cellar in years.

Not that he intended to give up and turn tail now. Everything he'd earned in life had been done the hard way which, in turn, had honed his ruthless nature into a brutal and unrelenting weapon. His prize was close – he knew it, and all he had to do was find the clue that would reveal the next link.

He paced further away from the only other light source, a single bulb positioned above the steep stairs, and pushed aside a curtain of sticky, filmy, web. Just as well cramped, dark places didn't bother him. That particular fear had been well and truly conquered years ago – a time in his life that had essentially gone down to the wire – either deal with it or be broken. He had too much innate stubbornness for that to ever happen. A cockroach skittered across the floor and disappeared beneath a broken sideboard. There were a couple of ancient beer barrels stacked against one wall. Three rickety shelving units stood crammed together, blocking any further passage to the right. He had hoped for at least an old tin trunk or a pile of bric-a-brac to examine.

Nothing. His elation faded. But there were still the old woman's private rooms to search. He'd turn the place inside out if he had to. All he needed was time alone.

A warm puff of air wafted over the back of his bare neck – a sudden odd intrusion in the coldness of the silent cellar. It felt like - *like a breath!*

Like someone was behind him.

His heart slammed against his ribs in a sudden gallop as panic flooded his mind. He stiffened. Whirling thoughts crashed in frantic union with his pounding heart. How could he explain what he was doing prowling about in the cellar? But wait – no one was home. He'd made certain they had all left before he began his search. Then who the dickens stood behind him in weighted silence?

The chill in the cellar increased sending goosebumps brushing over his skin in a flurry of icy strokes. He shivered as the freezing air sank into his bones. Should he attempt to explain? Or wait for the other to speak first? To his left, there was a flick of a tail as a mouse melted into the darkness as if desperate to escape impending danger. His hand tightened around his mobile. But…

A shadow rippled over the wall – *too late*.

A rush of air behind him – *too late*.

Agony splintered across his skull as lethal as a rockslide. His vision dimmed to blackness and he crashed to the floor.

CHAPTER 2

Clan McEwan,
At sea.
3rd July, 1915.

Dear mother and father,

I hope all is well at home. We have been at sea for almost three weeks and at first I was sick as a dog as the old tub rolled all over the place. I am tip top now and we are due to dock in some port or other soon. The tucker is not very plentiful. We only get enough jam and butter to last one meal. But there is enough feed for the horses. Most days, I look after Blaze and Smarty. Tell Matilda they are in fine shape. We had a wash day parade Friday. Shower day is every second day and our water ration is getting smaller. We do drills on the deck. I could do without all the marching as it is very hot. I have not got any letters from you or Alfred and Mitch for some time. What the deuce is going on. Silly beggars. They should have joined the 6th like me and not the 8th. Still I carnt wait to catch up with them in Gallipoli. How are things at home. Do not *worry too much, mother. The fellows are a good mob and keen as mustard to fight for our King. We will soon have the Turks on the run. I will close now as the light is fading.*

Love to you all from your affect. son, Gregory.

Two coffees and one bottle of water down and Natalie's brekkie *'date'* still hadn't arrived. Seated at one of the Cyprus Café's outside tables gave her a good view of Main Street and she craned her neck for the umpteenth time. However, there was no sign of a silver-haired man amidst the smattering of shoppers trudging along, all rugged up against the wintry morn. Shivering, she swallowed the last mouthful of cold coffee. The excess of caffeine smashed through her system, causing her already jittery nerves to overload. She couldn't stop the incessant tap of her foot against the pavement nor the continuous tugging of her hair. And that sick churning feeling in her belly warned she may well have made a fool of herself the previous evening. Maybe she'd been too eager – too easy to please? *What if I came off as desperate!*

That's what living without a partner for fourteen years did to you – eroded your confidence, turned your thoughts inward, and put you out of practice with the dating game. It didn't help that the first streaks of silver were threading through her hair, and at forty-one years old, she'd well and truly lost the bloom of youth.

Heat scalded her face as she sensed the not-so-covert

ogles and craning necks of Bindarra Creek's notorious gaggle of busy-bodies. They sat about two metres behind her bundled up in coats and jackets, at the table closest to the open door that led inside the Cyprus Café. Natalie had firsthand knowledge that these old ladies were fundamentally kind to their souls. However, their immense kindness was matched by their equally unwavering desire to meddle in other people's lives.

Puffing out a slow breath that she hoped would steady her racing heart, she willed her hand away from her hair and picked up her mobile to check the time. Yet again. Ten-fifteen a.m. He'd definitely said eight o'clock when they'd parted ways last night outside the Riverside Pub's bistro after having dinner together. It had taken every scrap of confidence she possessed to attend that meeting, and every scrap of courage to put herself out there in the app dating world in the first place. But she was tired of having no one to share the highs and lows of everyday life. Tired of having no one to laugh and cry with. Although she loved him with every fibre of her being, her sixteen-year-old son didn't quite fill the void left by her dead husband. Besides, it wouldn't be long before Noah would be off – living his own life and even though she'd made friends during the three years she'd lived in the small town, it wasn't the same as having a loving partner by her side. Once Noah was out experiencing the world, she would truly be alone. Most of all she missed the companionship – all of which had led her to linger at the café for the man she'd been matched with, to turn up.

She dropped her mobile onto the red-checked table-cloth and looked around for the waitress, but she'd disappeared inside the warmer café – no doubt to avoid the chill. She'd be inside herself if there had been any vacant tables. This morning, the yoga class had run over time. When she'd arrived, the café had been crammed full of pensioners and a few intrepid joggers.

Another blast of wind frosted her cold face. No way would she wait for her erstwhile date any longer. A tiny flicker of annoyance burst into life, dominating her previous thoughts of inadequacy and smothering her normally cautious nature. She was worth more than being stood up. She'd track down the wanker and tell him to his face how disrespectful was his behaviour. Fuelled by her rising indignation, she dug her credit card out of her shoulder-bag and waved it in the air.

"Are you waiting for someone?" Bracelets jangled as a wrinkled hand pulled out the vacant chair next to her, and an elderly lady with braided grey hair almost reaching her waist, plopped into the seat. Ms Edwina Lette. The leader of the gang. She dropped her scarlet yoga mat beside feet clad in a pair of muddy pink gumboots and brushed her fringe away from needle-sharp eyes. The puffer-jacket she wore made her scrawny frame appear plumper than normal.

Too late. Natalie should have bolted when she'd had the chance. The remaining two chairs grated as they also were dragged out when two other elderly women claimed them. Florrie Miller, the newly ordained Church of England vicar and Pamela Brown – both as lethal as Ms Lette but in very different ways. A quick glance over her shoulder revealed the less dangerous member of the nosey mob, Mrs

Beatrix Fukuka, was deep in conversation with Therese Morgan, whose white hair shone like a holy beacon when a shot of sunlight broke through the heavy clouds.

Pamela Brown picked up one of Natalie's empty mugs and frowned as she peered inside at the dregs. She tutted, her back ramrod straight. "All that coffee on an empty stomach is no good for you. Have the Greek scrambled eggs and avocado toast. I'll wave Thea over so you can order."

"There's no need… I was just leaving… " Her face hotter than a furnace, Natalie attempted to deflect their attention. She shouldn't have bothered.

Edwina interrupted. "Now, if you'd had a pot of tea, I could have read your tea leaves and told you when a handsome man will appear in your life. Or – perhaps he already has?" She winked as she leaned forward in a conspiratorial manner. "Tessa had dinner at the Riverside Pub last night with that lovely doctor, Emma Fahey. She told me all about how she saw you there with your new beau. A distinguished-looking fellow with silver hair, I believe. *And* he's our new guest at Fig Tree Lodge. Our only guest, if I'm honest but not a bad catch. I caught a glimpse of him yesterday morning when he arrived. Very tasty." She smacked her lips with gusto.

Natalie cringed. *Kill me now.*

A group of teenagers dawdled into view, laughing and jostling each other, school backpacks slung over shoulders hunched against the biting winter wind. One kid even dragged his bag along the ground with little thought to the damage being caused.

Natalie spied the familiar, tousled dark-brown hair of her only child. "Noah!" Her screech reeked of *'save me!'*.

Noah flung a startled glance toward her, his eyes widening as he took in the women flanking her on both sides. Ducking his head, he gave a half-hearted wave and slunk behind Drew Taylor, whose bright red hair was covered by a woolly beanie knitted in Bindarra Creek's high school colours. Natalie recognised it as one of the beanies his adoptive mother Abby had made a few months ago when she'd attended a Country Women's Association's craft session. "Sorry, Mum. Can't stop. We're late for class."

The group sent hunted looks towards the occupants of the table before picking up their lagging pace until they all but sprinted down the footpath.

Late! At after ten o'clock they were more than late, and Natalie made a mental note to question Noah when he got home from school. She gazed longingly at his rapidly retreating form, before girding her loins and turning to face her interrogators. "Morning again, ladies. I really enjoyed Tessa's yoga class this morning. What did you think of the new routine?"

With the unwavering determination of a killer shark circling its prey, Edwina ignored Natalie's feeble diversion tactic. "I do like a man who knows how to dress, and dimples in chins have always made me weak at the knees." She emitted a dramatic sigh and fanned her face. "A couple of years ago there was this Pom I had the hots for. A little younger than me but I always fancied myself as a bit of a cougar... "

Pamela interrupted her oldest friend with a rude

snort. "Nobody is interested in your fantasies, Edwina. Besides, at your age it's ridiculous the way you carry on."

"I'll have you know they are not fantasies."

"That's made me think of a theme for this week's sermon." Seemingly oblivious to her friends' snappy exchange, Florrie Miller rested her elbow on the table and cupped her chin. Her short, greying brown hair poked out from her woolly Sea Eagles beanie like tufts of straw. "Trust - how social media has impacted on our ability to trust others."

"Trust has nothing to do with it." Edwina jabbed Natalie in the ribs with a bony finger. "It's all about the sex. Nothing reduces stress levels like sex. In saying that, I'm not so sure about this new man of yours, Natalie. Only this morning as I was looking for my push-up bra, I had a premonition." She sank back in her chair and folded her arms, her narrow gaze pinning Natalie in place like a nail gun.

"A premonition? That's a new one. I'm surprised your dear-departed aunt Matilda wasn't whispering in your ear." Pamela Brown gave a haughty sniff, her narrow face settling into disapproving lines.

Edwina scowled. "Actually, it's been a while since Matilda's been around. She must be busy."

"What rubbish. This insistence on communicating with ghosts has to stop." Pamela rolled her eyes.

"I'm serious. But I must admit I'm getting worried."

"About your ghost?" Natalie could feel her mouth drop at the idea.

"Absolutely. She has never been absent for this long in

all the years I've lived in Fig Tree Lodge. Basically, that's most of my life."

Natalie shivered as another gust of wind scattered wet leaves down the footpath and swept over her bare arms. Her thick parka would have been a better choice than the short-sleeved tunic dress she'd pulled on after changing from her yoga gear. She'd hoped the emerald colour would heighten the green flecks in her hazel eyes. A pointless effort considering the man she'd intended to impress had failed to appear. "Maybe she doesn't like the idea of me cleaning out your attic."

"Honestly, Natalie. Don't encourage the silly old woman." Pamela Brown speared Natalie with a shrivelling glare.

"Ignore her." Edwina reached over and patted Natalie's hand before cradling it in between hers and turning her palm over. She squinted and mumbled something under her breath.

"There she goes, again. Doing that psychic act. It's heathen." Pamela waved a hand in the air as if she was about to perform an exorcism.

With a sudden hiss, Edwina dropped Natalie's hand onto the table. "Well. That was interesting."

Natalie gave a tight smile. She needed to get out of here or she would have wasted the entire morning doing nothing. Especially as there was still no sign of the man who only the night before had professed how happy he was that they had connected on the internet. "I really have to go." She made a show of checking the time again. "I've got to clean a couple of the caravan park cabins before the next check-in time this afternoon."

"In that outfit? It's so tight I would have thought you'd have difficulty bending sideways let alone using a mop and bucket." Edwina raised her eyebrows as her gaze travelled down Natalie's torso.

Heat scalded Natalie's cheeks. "I'll change into my uniform of course."

But Edwina had already moved on from the topic of clothes. "How much work is left in the attic? Did you find any more letters?"

"Not since the first couple between Gregory and Matilda that are dated not long after he signed up for World War I. I'm hoping to find more which will help flesh out your family history. When I was up there last Monday, I spotted a very old desk stuck behind a wardrobe. I want to take a good look at it, but I need to move the wardrobe out of the way first. I may need help doing so as it's one of those massive, solid timber pieces. I'm hoping to find a secret drawer or a box or something with more letters; even newspaper cuttings would be useful." At the reminder of what she'd discovered in Edwina's historic home's attic, excitement flared anew. She was positive this was the chance to make some real money which she needed sooner rather than later. Her fingers positively tingled to continue with her efforts in restoring the crumbling pages. Heaven only knew what other treasures she'd unearth amongst the dusty and ancient furniture.

"I think it's wonderful that you're going to write a history of Bindarra Creek, and in particular, the role Edwina's family played in the town." Florrie's nose quivered as she clapped her hands loudly.

Old Ted, wearing a moth-eaten woollen scarf wound about his head and neck and who was seated at the next table beside his equally ancient wife, Betty, dropped his jam and cream scone into his teacup. Betty, with her church hat planted over her wispy white hair, directed a glare at Florrie while her husband fished for his now soggy pension-week treat.

"Hopefully, with the vlog I'm doing on my progress and the publication of the book, it will fire up some enthusiasm for tourism again. After all these lockdowns I imagine the town could do with the money visitors bring." Natalie gave a rueful shrug and spread her fingers wide. "I've never written anything before in my life. I may make a complete hash of it."

"Nonsense. You're perfect for the job." Always the peacemaker, Florrie Miller was quick to reassure.

Natalie wasn't one hundred percent convinced – not that she was going to let that stop her. It had been a long time since she'd finished her education and helping her son with his homework really didn't count. Writing a book was a totally different kind of beast, but it wasn't as if she was taking up something as risky as sky-diving. Sitting alone in a room and scribbling away was the kind of safe job she could tame. She had to – an opportunity like this only came around once. There was no way she could pass on the notion that she might make decent money. Money that they desperately needed for Noah's future. Plus, she was hooked. Hooked on delving into the past and especially those heartbreaking years of the Great War.

From the little she'd managed to read so far she'd

gained the sense that something of momentous importance had occurred in the town around that time. A family tragedy perhaps that wasn't connected to the war like so many had suffered in that era. Regardless, what fired her imagination was the lure of delving into the everyday lives of people who had lived and died over a hundred years ago. How different Bindarra Creek would have been in those days. How different the world! A time when life was simpler – it was all about survival and working on the land. The world would have been fresh and shiny, so much to explore and discover. No mobile phones, no internet, no technology to connect you instantly to other communities or countries. A time when letter writing was an art form, almost a way of life for many. The thought of these possibilities had sparked interest and colour in what was her normal humdrum life. More than that, she could see a shiny future for herself and Noah if the book sold well. It would be a future where she wasn't watching every dollar they spent and one where she could afford the operation her son needed.

"I shall pray the poor woman has finally found peace." Florrie turned a speculative glance toward Natalie. "Now, dear, your thoughts about the whole internet dating thing would be appreciated. I can use your experience as the foundation for my sermon."

Natalie shot to her feet, sending her chair flying. "Maybe some other time, Florrie." Flushing, she plucked the chair back into position before scooping up her yoga mat and the gym bag. "If you'll excuse me."

Leaving the elderly ladies whispering to each other,

she rushed inside to the counter and paid for her drinks. As she strode past their table, she kept her footsteps brisk, giving the impression she was in a hurry. Well, she was – in a hurry to escape, plus she couldn't deny the faster pace would warm her stiff bones.

A wry grin tugged at her lips as she crossed Main Street and turned onto Wattle Tree Drive. If she was honest, she usually loved hanging with their gang and listening to their stories about their youth and the latest news on what was happening in town. News that was always peppered with anecdotes about a particular person's life. Not today – today she was on a mission. She walked past the doctor's surgery which occupied the corner block and slowed her hectic pace. Whether or not Ernest had slept in or really had avoided meeting her that morning, no way did she intend to arrive all hot and bothered. That would put her on the back foot; and she wanted to be confident and cool when she gave him a piece of her mind. Her earlier sense of outrage that had been momentarily smothered by Edwina Lette and her cronies, resurfaced. That bloke had a lot of nerve! Standing her up. Not even a text message. So what if she wasn't young, or a confident professional or a beautiful model type? She deserved better.

Her footsteps slowed as she approached the boundary fence of Fig Tree Lodge, the Lette family home and one of the oldest historical buildings in Bindarra Creek. The winter wind whistled through the Norfolk pines growing on the opposite side of the street, dissipating the last tendrils of fog that clung to the topmost branches. The sound was reminiscent of the wailing of lost souls. Natalie couldn't help shivering. Chiding herself for her fanciful thoughts, she buried her unease and stopped to pull out her comb to smoothe the tangles from her hair. Next, she checked her lipstick with a small compact mirror then dithered, staring at the massive fig tree that dominated the front yard of Fig Tree Lodge.

The tyre swing that Dodge, Edwina's grandson, had made dangled from a thick low-hanging branch and drifted slowly back and forth as if someone had only just jumped off. Tiny droplets of moisture from the early morning mist glistened on every leaf and blade of grass. Glorious purply-blue hyacinths flowered in clumps between the tree's snaking roots as well as butter-yellow jonquils. Delicate violets and white snowdrops peeked through other flowering plants she didn't know the names of. After several months of consistent rainfall, even in winter, the gardens were a stunning testament to the hours of work Dodge's wife, Tessa had put in under Edwina's careful direction. The now rich green lawn certainly made the Lodge picture-perfect in its new life as a Bed and Breakfast establishment. Over the past two and a bit years, the guests had dribbled away to nothing. Her 'date' was the first paying guest the Lodge had had since late last summer.

Usually, Natalie loved looking at the old house but for some strange reason, today was not one of those days. The front of the building faced west and thus the weak morning sun failed to lighten the dark shadows haunting the upper wrap-around balcony and lower veranda. A prickle of cold iced over her skin and she shivered. The wide double timber doors with beautiful stained-glass panels on either side stood closed. The bank of windows looked like blind eyes staring back at her. No lights glowed from inside. At this time of day, Tessa would be fronting Phoenix Antiques and Restorations. Dodge would be just coming off night duty as a security guard at the hospital. Their kids would be at school and day-care which meant the house would be deserted – apart from Ernest.

A little of her earlier confidence slithered away and her heart pounded uncomfortably hard against her ribs. She slipped her compact and comb back inside her gym bag and fumbled for the electronic key card Edwina had given her when she'd been awarded the cleaning contract. With one eye on the still gently swaying swing and the other on the dark windows, she forced herself to move forward onto the gravel drive. The crunching of pebbles underfoot were as loud as gunshots in the quiet street.

By the time she reached the main entrance, she couldn't believe her knees actually trembled. *Get a grip, woman!* She mentally slapped herself up the side of her head, but that sense of deep foreboding was dragging down her soul. With a clatter, the key card fell from her cold fingers onto the first step. It landed… in a small pool of ruby-red liquid.

That looked like… *blood?*

Timber creaked. Her gaze shot to the side veranda. Her hand covered her mouth, smothering her gasp.

The footsteps came closer.

CHAPTER 3

Fig Tree House,
Bindarra Creek, NSW.
10th July, 1915.

Dear Gregory,

The notice of your departure on the Clan McEwan has arrived. You must be somewhere over the Atlantic by now. The news from the war has been grim and Mother spends a lot of time crying over cups of tea. She asked me to write in her stead. The Herald reported a list of casualties two weeks past and she was grieved to see Mitchell has sustained a wound in a battle in Gallipoli. Colonel Hawker at Victoria Barracks sent a letter saying Mitchell is off to Egypt to recuperate. I tell Mother Mitchell is a stout fellow and I have no fear he will do just fine. Father says very little but you know that is his way. He is taking Mother to Tamworth for five days. That is sure to cheer her up. We received a brief note from Alfred yesterday. He tells us he is in the best of health and has dodged the Turks' bullets to date. You must give a full account of all your doings and the wonders you will see. Life goes on much the same. We are down to Old Dave after Will and Roy left for Sydney to enlist. Father works hard and I help him on the farm. I am up before the sun and oft it is after midnight before I seek my bed. I teach Sunday school and sing in the church choir and take much comfort that God will look over you, Alfred and Mitchell. The winter has been cold and I sorely miss your hunting skills. Hurry back so I can have rabbit stew or roast wild pig and yams again. I tire of mutton. Write soon.

Your loving twin, Matilda.

After more than twenty-five years of fighting for his country, Troy Davidson never dreamed his retirement would include breaking and entering. Yet here he was – creeping around a house in a remote country town. There was a soft 'plop' as if an object had landed in a puddle, then the sharp intake of breath. The unexpected sounds caused him to tense and bring his foot down on a loose floorboard much harder than he intended. He grimaced as the timber creaked beneath his weight for the second time in as many moments. So much for stealth. The house was supposed to be deserted but someone was definitely snooping around Fig Tree Lodge's front door. Although he couldn't deny that was exactly what he was doing himself. He laid a firm hand on Chip's head when she gave a low growl. The short red hairs on her back bristled into a stiff brush. Her muscles were bunched tight. Troy read the familiar signs. His protective dog was ready to attack. Not a good idea. That would draw too much attention. The last thing he needed was to be forced to explain his presence on someone else's property. Not to mention the hammer hanging from his belt.

There was also the set of lock picks in his pocket.

His muscles coiled. His every sense sharpened as he sought to discern the severity of the threat. Could be a door knocker or a neighbour. Still, he acted on instinct and shifted closer to the wall, flexing the fingers of his free hand. He'd be ready to land a punch if he had to.

He rounded the corner and came face to face with ... Natalie Wasson, the widow of his best mate. The woman he'd fallen for the moment he set eyes on her all those years ago. Feeling as if he'd been sucker punched, he drank her in, admiring how her dress hugged her curves and how the years had been kind to her complexion. It could have been only a few months since they'd last met, instead of years. Then the memory of John's funeral intruded, and reality smacked him in the face. Best mate's widow, remember?

When her astonished gaze fell onto his raised fist, he dropped his hand to his side. He watched with an interest he struggled to fight, as hot colour flooded her pale cheeks. Her hand pressed over her heart, bunching the material of her green dress in her fingers and drawing his attention to her breasts. All the air squeezed out of his lungs and the attraction he'd long denied stirred to life.

She seemed to gather herself. Her chin lifted and she banked her expression as she met his eyes. *"Troy!* You're the last person I expected to see. What are you doing in

Bindarra Creek?" Voice so cool she could have been addressing a delivery boy. Or a complete stranger.

Irritation flared along with several other emotions he'd rather not name – like guilt and shame and, heaven help him, something that had been snuffed from his heart for too many years. Hope. With an effort he dragged his eyes away from Natalie's lovely face and scrutinised the area behind her. She was alone. His hand left Chip's head and the dog surged forward, tail wagging, tongue lolling as if eager to greet her. Chip sure had good taste. "This is Chip."

"Have you had her long? She looks like a young dog. She's lovely. Who's a good girl?" Smiling, Natalie petted Chip on the head then rubbed her fingers along the dog's back.

"She's a little over two years old. I've only had her for six months. She was on one of those animal rescue sites. Don't know much about her background. But, as soon as I saw her, I knew she was the dog for me."

Chip panted in ecstasy and slobbered a few times over Natalie's arm. Natalie's smile faded as she straightened and her curt, "Well? You were telling me why you're in town" reminded Troy that he had yet to respond.

"Sorry, I was just as surprised to see you here." Liar. Knowing she lived in this small town had been the swaying factor behind his presence. "I'm visiting family." He jerked a thumb toward the front door. "My mother is Edwina Lette's cousin."

Natalie's eyes widened and she bent down to pet Chip again as the dog's tail wagged in a frenzy. "I had no idea."

"Small world." He shrugged and the movement set the hammer that hung from his belt swaying.

"Looks like you're here to do some repair work." Natalie gave a sniff and left off scratching behind Chip's left ear. "Which is odd as Dodge usually does everything around the house."

"You make it sound like it's a crime for me to be here." He planted his hands on his hips, liking how her gaze drifted towards his waist then lower before her lips flattened.

She frowned and stood on tiptoe to see past him. "Are you alone?"

"Yep. Just me and my dawg." He grinned when she rolled her eyes, looking exasperated.

A tiny tilt to the corner of her lips told him a different tale. One of the many aspects he'd liked about her was how they seemed to get each other's sense of humour without explanation.

"No, I wondered if you'd seen anyone else. Like another man." Her cheeks deepened to a darker pink. "Ernest should be around here somewhere."

Of course, she'd have moved on from John. Maybe she'd even re-married. He'd been a fool to hope otherwise. "Sorry." The clipped word sounded harsher than he'd intended.

She fell back a step and glanced from him to the door then stooped to pluck a keycard off the ground.

"Wait. Is that blood?" Troy crowded her, stepping right into her personal space, his attention fixed on the small rectangular card where the edge was stained a dull red. A minuscule droplet formed before dripping downward.

"I hope not. Could be anything. Sauce. Fizzy drink." The words rushed from her mouth.

"Just in case – make sure you walk around that spot."

Her wide gaze darted from his face to the small puddle. "Gosh Troy. You make it sound like we're at a crime scene!"

"It's probably nothing." But still, he took a couple of paces backwards until he was close to the wall, watching as Natalie skirted the possible blood. "Are you staying here at the lodge?"

"What? Oh, the keycard. No, I'm the cleaner." Avoiding looking in his direction, she plucked a tissue from her handbag and wiped the keycard clean before fussing with the panel inset beside the door.

State of the art security. Interesting. Troy lifted his head and spotted the tiny camera with its red blinking eye. It had been built into a wooden welcome sign adorned with painted green leaves, yellow wattle and a surprisingly good rendition of a kookaburra. Someone had gotten creative. Certainly, the old house bore little resemblance to the home of his memories. Even though he'd only been to Fig Tree Lodge a couple of times when as a kid, he'd come away with the impression of cracked brickwork, broken floorboards and peeling wallpaper. Someone had been busy as the exterior of the building had been restored to mirror its former glory. He had a feeling the interior was going to match the stunning pictures of meticulously renovated rooms on the website. Even if it had been Dodge who'd performed the majority of the work, it was obvious a decent chunk of money had been spent. Money that strictly speaking, was family money and not just the prerogative of Edwina Lette's to use as she saw fit.

There was a click, the door unlocked and swung open. They stepped into the wide hallway with its massive oak hat and cloak stand to one side and a beautiful timber staircase winding up to the upper floors at the end. Several doors led off both sides of the hall.

"Hang on a second." He caught hold of Natalie by her upper arm, holding her still while he listened. The only sounds were the hollow ticking of a grandfather clock and the soft pants of Chip who'd pattered in behind them. His dog thrust her nose into his free hand and snuffled wetly against his palm.

"You're making me nervous." With a short laugh, Natalie pulled away from him and marched down the hallway.

Trusting she knew the layout better than his fudgy memories, he followed, Chip trotting by his side but he kept his hands free. The house gave a spine-prickling *'off'* vibe he was well familiar with, and hard-won experience warned him to be on his guard. They entered a room towards the rear of the house. One glance was all it took to reveal the dining room was empty of people. There was no indication anyone had been in the room recently either as the long rectangular timber table lay barren save for a display of flowers in its centre. Natalie quickened her pace as if eager to widen the distance between them. The thought rankled. They passed into a massive kitchen which again was devoid of life. She stopped near an old-fashioned fuel stove and laid a hand on the side of the kettle while Troy circled the cutting bench.

His gaze arrowed onto the window where a cool wind whistled through the space where glass should have been. "Don't move, Natalie."

Glass crackled underfoot as he inspected the broken pane. The gap was sufficiently wide to enable an adult to pass through. Leaning closer, he noticed a fragment of cloth caught in the jagged edges rising above the frame. "Looks like someone gained entry through the window."

"What? Like a burglar?" Alarm heightened her normally pleasant tones and her voice grew louder with each word. "Ernest's car is still in the grounds. He must be somewhere in the house, too!"

Snagging her gaze, he shook his head while placing a finger close to his lips, satisfied when she gulped then nodded. He crossed to the door leading out into the back-yard, but the heavy steel bolt was secured in place. Whoever had entered the house had certainly not left via the kitchen door. That could mean one of three things; they had crawled back out through the window risking cutting themselves, or there was an open door elsewhere, or they were still inside the building. He refrained from turning the door handle. If there were fingerprints on the knob, no way did he want to smudge them and make the police's job harder.

Police. Bloody hell, that was a complication he could have done without but if there was a thief in the house, he *would* have to call them.

With Chip by his side, he moved to the walk-in pantry. After waiting a few beats until he was certain he could hear no movement, he opened the door and checked inside. Nothing appeared to have been disturbed. Another long look around at the tidy kitchen counters and shelves. He was satisfied that whatever the intruder was after, was not located in that room. Which only left... *how many rooms were there?*

He stepped over to where Natalie stood near the stove and lowered his voice. "Listen. I want you to remain here while I check the rest of the house. I'll leave Chip with you."

A scowl formed on her brow. Eyes spitting daggers, she muttered, "No way am I staying here alone. I'm coming with you. Look a... a friend of mine could be in trouble. He's a guest and was supposed to meet me earlier at a café. That's why I'm here. When he didn't show I thought I'd come and check."

Not a husband or boyfriend – a friend. Relief flooded through him, and he grinned. "You mean you wanted to give him a piece of your mind for not turning up on time. Good on you. Okay then, but once we leave this room, no speaking. Understand?"

"Lead on, Rambo. I assume you know your way around the house? Since you're a relative and all."

He met her narrowed gaze. Her mocking tone indicated that she didn't buy his connection to the family. That was her problem. He was speaking the truth – at least, about that aspect. "I was a kid the last time I was here, but I've got a pretty good idea of the layout. Most of these old homes are the same."

"Then what are you waiting for? Oh... " She dug into her bag then waggled her phone in the air. "I think we should call the police first. Or maybe even better, we wait for them to turn up. I'm surprised you haven't suggested it."

"I thought you were in a hurry. You did say you were worried about your… *friend*." He put a hard emphasis on the word *'friend'* and experienced a bitter twist of satisfaction as she blushed.

Her chin lifted. "There's no reason for you to be like this, Troy."

"That's true enough. I apologise." Reaching out, he gently placed his fingers on her shoulder for a split second and even that brief touch was sufficient for memories to cascade through his mind. Memories – and emotions he had no right to feel. His hand fell back to his side, and he half turned away. Not before he saw the sheen of tears in her eyes. Maybe she really was concerned about this friend of hers. If he'd been alone, he would have had no qualms about searching the house from top to bottom. But he didn't want to risk placing her in any kind of danger, no matter how small. "How about we call the cops, you wait here, and I check the house?"

"We've been over this already." She scrolled through her contents and pressed a button. A few seconds later, she whispered, "Abby, I'm over at Fig Tree Lodge and someone has broken into the house." She listened for a few moments before adding, "No, we can't hear footsteps or stuff being trashed…. I'm here in the kitchen with a distant relative of Edwina's… Okay… but…" Then sighing softly, she ended the call.

"Well?" He shot an impatient glance towards the doorway. Even now the thief could be exiting via another window or door. As he had made his way around the veranda, he recalled there had been several French doors opening onto the outside. Too many exits. Too many entrances for anyone else to burst into the house. Which meant leaving Natalie alone, even with Chip to guard her, wasn't an option. The need to move, to *do* something, made him antsy and he shifted his weight from foot to foot. He'd never been good waiting on the sidelines. His hesitation about what to do with Natalie was unusual to say the least. Yeah, back in his life for a matter of mere minutes and already she had messed with his head.

"Abby, she's a member of our local police and a friend of mine." Natalie stopped speaking as she'd thought better of what she'd intended to say next.

Troy's internal radar hummed into life. She was hiding something from him.

"Unfortunately, there's been a car accident on the Corella Road. A rollover. It's going to be at least another twenty minutes or so before someone can get here." Her lips trembled.

Inwardly cursing himself, Troy had to wrench his gaze away. Thinking about kissing her was… not… a… good… idea. Nor was pulling her into his arm and hugging her. He needed to get moving, give himself something else to concentrate on other than succumbing to his urge to give her comfort. "Look, we've been here… what? About ten maybe twelve minutes? I reckon whoever broke in, is long gone. We've heard no footsteps, no voices, nothing. If you're not keen on waiting here by yourself, then I suggest we go together and look for your… friend."

"I agree." Natalie slipped her mobile into her handbag before placing her gym bag onto the cutting bench. "I have a horrible feeling that something has happened to Ernest. Remember the blood we found?"

Bloody hell, he'd forgotten that drop of red. Dumb of him to have done so. Without a shadow of a doubt, having Natalie close by his side was screwing with his thoughts and dulling his normally excellent sixth sense of danger. Whoever the bloke was, he could be hurt. They were wasting precious time hanging about the kitchen. "Alright. Stay close."

With Natalie treading quietly behind him, Troy moved into the dining room and back out into the hall. Chip's claws clicked on the floorboards as she trotted next to him but once they stood on carpet their steps were muffled. They checked the formal living room where nothing appeared out of place then made their way to the library. When they entered, cold air rushed into the room. A pair of French doors were opened wide onto the veranda, the breeze lifting the gauzy curtains like a billowing bridal veil. Beside the open doors were three books that appeared to have been hurled onto the floor judging by the way two were upside down. Another had a few ripped pages hanging from between its covers.

He bit off an oath and paused to whisper in Natalie's ear, "Those doors weren't open earlier when I walked around the house. I bet our intruder has indeed left the building. Just in case, wait here. If anything happens, run to the front door and get outside." Using hand signals, he indicated to Chip to guard Natalie. He circumvented a couple of comfy sofas, three armchairs, and some beautifully carved coffee tables until he reached the other side of the room. He swept the curtains aside and stepped through. After circling the house via the veranda and seeing no movement on the grounds, he made his way back into the library.

Natalie had remained where he'd left her, and she was rubbing her hands up and down her arms as if she was cold. Which she probably was, given the chilly winter air that filled the room. Chip sat on her haunches, ears pricked. The short hairs on her back bristled. A low growl rumbled from her throat.

"Easy girl." He rubbed her ears. The growling stopped but she didn't move. "I didn't spot anyone about. We probably scared them away." He shrugged off his jacket and eased it over Natalie's shoulders.

Her cheeks pale, she shivered. "Thanks. I can't believe how cold it is now."

Troy speared a glance back at the doors, then shook his head. "You wouldn't believe it but it's actually colder in here than outside. Come on. The cops should arrive soon. Let's go find your friend."

"You think it's safe?" Biting her lip, she held back when he walked forward. "Sorry, I've just got this really strange feeling." Her gaze darted about the room like she was looking for something.

He rubbed the prickling hairs at the nape of his neck and imitated her. They were alone. No one else was there and yet he couldn't shake his own impression that they were being watched. His dog sure thought the same, judging by how rigid she sat and stared at the wall. Maybe there was a cavity behind one of those bookshelves, although his mother had never mentioned a secret passage or *'priest'* hole. Besides, who the hell would want to hide and spy on them?

"Come on," he muttered in a gruff voice and, taking Natalie's hand, pulled her out of the room. He snapped his fingers and Chip followed. As soon as they had put some distance between themselves and the library, the odd sensation abated. Something for him to think about later.

Natalie must have been as relieved as he was to leave the library because her expression lightened as they mounted the stairs to the first floor. Together they checked every room on the upper levels, not entering, merely pausing in the open doorway and listening. They found no one. They emerged from the last bathroom to find Chip growling and standing at the top of the stairs, looking down into the lower floor.

"Do you think they came back?" Natalie clutched his hand and gripped it hard.

He couldn't believe how crazy happy it felt to have her reach for him for protection. His chest swelled. He had to tamp down those inappropriate feelings and fight to focus. Now wasn't the time to start fantasising about *'maybe's'* and *'what-if's'*. "No idea. But let's check out the rooms below again." He motioned for Natalie to walk behind him as they started down the stairs while Chip padded ahead.

The second Troy heard it, his dog stopped in her tracks too. A moan. Barely a whisper of a sound. Stifled, as if… as if deadened by something thick and heavy, like carpet… or a mound of dirt.

It immediately transported Troy to his past life as a soldier in the Special Operations Task Group and an incident he never wanted to experience again. That moment when he'd regained consciousness only to find himself buried alive with the bloodied body of his dead mate crumpled beside him.

With nothing to be heard but the moans of the dying.

CHAPTER 4

Dear folks at home,

Glad to say your letters are to hand. The extra socks and tin of tea will serve me well and I will use the envelopes to send my news. Ta muchly. I also got two from Dot and a brief note from Mitchell - he is keen to return to the fight. Today the Turks are quite [sic] a nice change from shot and shell flying round. If we are lucky we may nap later. We sleep in dugouts at the bottom of the trenches which wind in and out of the hillside. For water we use the wells in Shrapnel Valley where we are allowed enough for tea only. At night we bathe in the sea. Firewood for cooking is scarce and we dodge bullets and step over rotting bodies as we search the hills. The 8th hold the worse position on our front only about 25 to 30 yards apart. The Turks charged us last night crying 'Allah Allah' over and over until just on daylight. We mowed them down with few *losses on our side. So far I have lost a good half of my troops mainly wounded thankfully. Keep an eye on Dot for me will you. Her last letter sounded quite down since news of Joe's death in May. Have any other men from town joined the force? Cold footed beggars if they dont. Take good care of yourselves and dont worry as we are alright.*

Love to all at home, Alfred.

The deep thump of pain in Ernest's skull intensified as a woman squawked questions and a man barked orders. What the dickens were they jabbering about? He needed them to ... *stop... talking.* It was killing him; each rise and fall of their voices were like hammer blows inside his foggy head. For the life of him he couldn't force a single syllable from his cotton-wool mouth. A shiver racked through him as the chill in his bones registered. Whatever he was lying on was ice cold. His shaking fingers groped over a hard surface and gritty dirt seeking some kind of clue as to his whereabouts. He couldn't focus. A breath that stank of dry dog food blasted over his face. Nausea rose; hot, acrid and demanding. Rolling his aching body to the side, Ernest puked over and over until his cramping gut was empty. He flopped onto his back and finally squirrelled open his eyes – one tiny slit at a time.

Agony slashed behind his eyeballs. He groaned as he slammed his eyes shut again. It didn't matter anyway – that one bleary glance told him nothing. Shadowy figures with a glow of light coming from somewhere. An open door perhaps.

He concentrated on slowing his hoarse gasps and racing heart. With each passing second a little more clarity seeped inside his brain. The frantic yabbering finally stopped. Footsteps, like heavy boots, crunched over the ground along with the pattering of smaller feet – maybe paws? – then faded. Were they leaving? He grunted, his legs thrashing as he tried to roll onto his side again. Pain crashed through him stealing his breath away. *Stay! Don't go!* But the words wouldn't push past his cracked lips.

"Ernest? Can you hear me? Try not to move. We've called for an ambulance. You're going to be just fine." The woman's voice had lost its panicked edge and he fastened onto the soothing tones like a leech.

She sounded familiar. More than that, she sounded… comforting, dependable. Suddenly a memory rose. Long, dark hair, soft hazel eyes and a gentle smile that had fired a warmth inside a heart that had lain dormant since the Ice Age. He knew her. Natalie. That was her name.

A hand closed over his and life pulsed through his veins at her touch. He struggled to raise his body off the floor.

She stopped him with a gentle push on his chest. "It's best you don't move. Not until the ambos have assessed you. That's a nasty blow to your head and we don't know what other injuries you may have."

Cautiously he prised his eyes open. This time the pain was less intense, and he no longer had the urge to pass out. His attempt at speaking resulted in a strangled croak.

He was making progress. His gaze shifted a tad to the right and his blurry sight steadied.

Natalie was crouched beside him. "I'm afraid we had to move you onto the stair landing. I think you must have tripped coming down the steps; they are quite old and my foot almost went through one of the boards." Shifting her gaze from his face she frowned at something beyond his limited point of vision. "You were in the cellar beneath Fig Tree Lodge. I came looking for you when… when you didn't turn up at the café. You're lucky we found you – rather it was Chip who led us to you."

Chips? Why was she talking about food?

Her hand slipped from his as she pushed to her feet. She busied herself, brushing dust and cobwebs from her dress. "Chip is Troy's dog. They've gone outside to wait for the police and paramedics. Shouldn't be long now but please don't move. I don't want you rolling off the landing and falling back into that cellar. It took us forever to get you up here." Her smile was quick.

He was grateful for her attempt at humour even if he couldn't appreciate it.

Police? Damnation but his head hurt. Come to think of it, his entire body pulsed with pain. Something slithered through his mind. He tried to grasp the tail end of the thought – or was it a memory? – but it disappeared like a lost tomb. Never mind, whatever it was would resurface when it was ready.

"Troy?" This time he did manage to speak. His voice came out hoarse and just that one brief word caused his throat to ache like crazy. What had happened to him? Could he be on an archaeological dig in Alexandria? No –

that wasn't right. Natalie had never been on any of his digs. He would never have forgotten that.

Natalie ducked her head and tutted over the state of her clothes as she swatted at her legs. A large ladder ran up her right shin and disappeared beneath the hem of her dress. There was a smaller hole over her bloodied left knee as if she'd fallen. "Troy? Oh, he's a... a relative of the Lette's."

Ernest was battered and bruised but there was nothing wrong with his hearing. Or his intellect which was gradually resuming its usual razor sharpness as the fog cleared from his head. He'd picked up on the change in her tone. For some reason, she'd just lied to him. Like his mother, like all the other women he'd known in his life. Disappointment left a sour taste in his mouth, adding to the metallic tang of dry blood as he swallowed. His gut churned and, raising his head, he dry-heaved, hating how helpless he felt. At the mercy of others. Fury flooded through him at his predicament. He had never shown any kind of weakness. Never. Not since his grandfather had beaten out every possible atom of what he had termed *'being a fop'*.

For one long drawn-out second, terror was a heartbeat away. Until Ernest wrestled the emotion that had flavoured his entire childhood to the ground and stomped it into oblivion. "Feeling... better."

With that he forced his body into movement and he sat up, ignoring Natalie's entreaties to remain where he was. No one else would witness him in such an ignominious position. He already felt as if he'd somehow given away his power to Natalie. And let's not forget the invisible Troy. Gritting his teeth, he battled the throbbing in his head. "What's… time? How… ?" His voice grated harshly as nausea rose. Again. But he had nothing left to eject.

Natalie dropped beside him and slung a supporting arm around his shoulders. "Lean on me, Ernest. I think it's a little past eleven-thirty."

Almost mid-day? Then…

"You've probably been down here since early this morning. Your skin is so cold. I should have come looking for you earlier." Concern etched her face and those lips that were so close trembled.

Maybe he'd been mistaken about her lying. Maybe she truly was a kind person. That very thought blew Ernest away because there had been very few kind people in his life. Suddenly the thought of losing her was untenable. Reaching over he grasped her hand tightly in his. "Don't leave."

Looking pleased, she smiled gently. "I won't."

The tramp of several feet heralded the arrival of others. Natalie, after squeezing his fingers gently, shuffled to the doorway where she directed a torch onto the landing. The pool of light did little to illuminate the cellar where Ernest had been found. He would have to come back later and try to remember anything that could give him a clue as to the perpetrator. In the meantime, he had better think up some kind of plausible explanation as to why he had been down there in the first place.

Aware of Natalie's proximity, he bore the next few minutes with as good a grace as he could muster while the two paramedics asked a bunch of questions he couldn't, and wouldn't, answer. They checked him over, scribbled notes on a form and muttered between themselves. Finally, one of them went through the doorway returning a moment later with a gurney. Once he was strapped on, they wheeled him through a house that suddenly seemed to be filled with people. One of whom wore the distinctive blue uniform of the New South Wales police force.

"I'll follow the ambulance to the hospital. Natalie, would you like a lift?" the policewoman asked as he was wheeled past.

He strained his eyes trying to catch a glimpse of Natalie but some tall, muscular joker with a dog blocked his view. His gaze fastened on a hammer hanging from the bloke's belt. Despite himself, a tremor shook his hands as he was loaded into the back of the ambulance. That had to be the *'Troy'* Natalie had mentioned. Some bloke who, unless his instincts deceived him and they rarely did, shared her past. The doors slammed shut and the vehicle roared down the drive. Judging by the sound of gravel spitting by, the vehicle was doing a hell of a lot of damage to the surface. Not that he gave a flying fig. At least he didn't have to suffer the indignity of sirens.

The next few hours were ones he had no wish to recall. The ignominy of it all! A lot of poking, prodding, whirring of machines and more poking. That time accompanied with the pricking of needles - blessedly and finally brimming with a decent painkiller followed by the sensation of his skin being stitched together. It wasn't until he was sequenced into a bed situated next to a window with a surprisingly nice view of the countryside, that he allowed himself to relax. The last of the nurses tucked him in tight then pressed a drink with a straw into his hand before she bustled off to torture some other poor sod. Gingerly, Ernest allowed his aching head to sink into the mound of pillows propping him up and fingered the bandage wrapped around his skull. He was wondering how he could reach his chart at the end of his bed without alerting any official when Natalie appeared in the doorway.

She hovered there, like a bird uncertain whether to take flight, before rushing over to his side.

"I'm glad you came." Still a grating rasp but at least he was able to form a complete sentence.

"Of course." She sounded a little surprised and a look of uncertainty flashed across her face.

He lifted the drink closer and took several sips of the liquid. It flowed thick like honey and soothed the dry crustiness of his throat. A few minutes later he felt as if he'd be able to speak like a normal person again. "I'm sorry I missed our coffee date. I was looking forward to seeing you again." Not bad. The tones were only a few decibels harsher than his usual fluid manner of speech. More of his natural self-confidence returned. Under lowered eyelids he watched Natalie while a million thoughts rotated through his mind.

A bright smile chased away her previous hesitation and after drawing a chair closer to the bed, she sat down. He'd definitely hit the nail on the head. When he hadn't shown this morning, she must have doubted his intentions. Now she looked happy that she'd been wrong. Something hot and amazing swelled inside his chest. He couldn't believe his search had led him to this small town in the middle of rural New South Wales – nowhere really – (and what a nondescript decrepit place it was). Where he'd also discovered something that had always been beyond his reach. Something that he would never attain. "Natalie… " The odd hesitation in his voice baffled him. Before he could continue, two police officers marched into the room.

The female, a sturdy blonde type in her mid-forties and with an air of *'don't give me any of your crap'* about her took the lead and fetched up beside his bed at least a good two strides faster than her much younger, male partner. "Mr… ?" She whipped out a notebook from one of the myriad pockets on her vest and hovered a pen over the open page.

Colour sweeping over her face, Natalie spoke for him. "This is Ernest Verne. He's a school teacher from Melbourne."

"Uh huh. I'm Senior Constable Taylor." The blonde tilted her head towards her counterpart. "This is Constable Donaldson. Mr Verne, what brings you to Bindarra Creek?" Her eyes as sharp as picks settled on his face and didn't budge. It felt as if she was peeling away his skin in much the same way he unearthed layers of sediment on his digs.

A bead of sweat pricked his underarm. He hoped nothing more tell-tale had formed elsewhere – like his face. This woman would notice a finch's dropping at a hundred metres. He knew, the moment the cop had walked into the room, she would be hard to fool. His cover story felt incredibly flimsy as he blurted out how he'd been matched with Natalie on a dating app and, after an exchange of emails, they had agreed to meet. If she asked for ID, he was royally screwed. His fake driver's license wouldn't stand up once she'd checked official records. There'd be more questions and more wasting time of which he no longer had the luxury. He had to finish what he'd started then get the hell out of this shabby town. But that would mean leaving Natalie behind and a pang of loneliness assailed him. The feeling was so alien he instantly buried it; inwardly cursing whoever had called the police. He strongly suspected the mysterious Troy.

Senior Constable Taylor made a noncommittal sound as she scribbled in her little book. "Let's move onto this morning. In your own words, Mr Verne."

Some almost primordial instinct made him glance to the doorway in time to see part of a tall, masculine figure move past. He strained his ears but failed to discern the sound of footsteps. Was the bloke listening around the corner? Just in case, he slid his hand over the base of his neck and lowered his voice. He didn't have to act, his throat hurt like the dickens. He had to be careful, he couldn't afford to give even the slightest hint of the true reason why he'd been investigating every unlocked room in the house.

"I rose early about fifteen minutes before six a.m. then attended the dining room where a cold breakfast had been laid out for me. Apparently, the ladies of the house were at a yoga class. Although I only partook of juice and a small fruit bowl, I rinsed my dishes under the sink." He turned to Natalie and smiled. "Old habits die hard. I couldn't leave a pile of dirty dishes for Ms Lette," he added smoothly, feeling smug when approval glowed in Natalie's eyes.

Senior Constable Taylor tapped her pen against the notebook.

Ernest returned to his tale. "I went for a brisk walk to the church and cemetery then returned to get ready to join Natalie for a coffee at a café on Main Street." He paused to frown and paste a pensive expression on his face. "I had just left my room; when I thought I heard footsteps which puzzled me as I understood the house to be empty."

"Footsteps?" Taylor's eyes turned as flinty as pebbles. Ernest kept his gaze steady and didn't blink as she added, "Are you sure what you heard wasn't Dodge, that is Ms Lette's grandson, returning from his security guard shift at the hospital?"

"Definitely because I looked out the window and could see that his car wasn't in its usual parking place beside the garage."

"Mmmm. What time do you think this was?"

"Seven forty sharp. I verified the time because I didn't wish to be late for my… er… meeting with Natalie."

"Right. Carry on."

Ernest cleared his throat. "Well, it's quite simple really. I began to check the house for an intruder. I was aware that time was passing, so it's possible I may have stumbled and fallen in my haste."

"Didn't happen. Why didn't you phone the police?"

He managed a shrug. "I didn't want to waste your time as I could have been mistaken about hearing someone. It's an old house."

Taylor stopped scribbling. "Doc said you have no obvious sign of bruises elsewhere on your body, just the injury to the top of your skull. That tells us, you didn't fall down any steps. What were you doing in the cellar?"

His breathing all but seized. He hadn't imagined someone standing behind him. "I told you, Senior Constable." He always ensured he gave full respect to any official when conversing with them by remembering their title or rank. The tactic usually tempered even the most hard-boiled. Although the policewoman in front of him gave the impression nothing short of a volcanic eruption would soften her. "I was searching for an intruder."

"Then you must have thought the noise you heard came from the cellar."

She was like a dog with a bone. Heat crawled up his neck and he gritted his teeth. "Possibly, there is a bit of a gap in my memory. I'm a little foggy as to exactly what happened to be honest."

Her lips flattened. "You should have called us, Mr Verne, and not gone searching yourself. A window was smashed which must be how the perp gained entry. Count yourself lucky all you got for your trouble was a crack on the head."

"But to attack Ernest in such a vicious manner." Natalie sat forward; her smooth brow wrinkled in concern. "Bindarra Creek isn't the sort of town that has a lot of crime."

"Not usually, no. Normally, just kids letting off steam or performing some minor thefts."

"Then something was stolen?" Ernest held his breath

as he waited for the officer to respond and willed his blood pressure to settle.

Senior Constable Taylor shared a glance with the male Constable before saying in a neutral tone, "We're still searching the house which, by the way, is off-limits until we've conducted our enquiries." She tucked her notebook and pen away, before folding down the flap of her pocket with a snap. "Senior Sergeant Morgan is fingerprinting the window and the kitchen. Ms Lette is not going to be happy when she sees all that black dust but hopefully a print will turn up."

"There were a couple of books on the floor in the library," Natalie offered.

"Yep. Spotted them and the library is next on Riley's to-do list. We're off to canvas the neighbourhood to see if anyone happened to spot anything unusual or someone in the grounds who shouldn't have been there. But you're right, Natalie. This act is something quite different to what we are used to, and I don't like it. If you think of anything else, Mr Verne, please contact the station." One more piercing glare as if she knew he was withholding information, then Taylor plucked a card from another pocket and handed it over. "When you've been discharged, come down to the station. We will require a written statement from you."

"Of course, you can count on me." Projecting what he hoped was the right note of a concerned *honest* citizen, Ernest smiled and nodded as the two police officers walked off. His gut twisted into a savage cramp as pain wracked over the top of his head. He winced.

Natalie tutted as she adjusted the pillows beneath him.

Obviously, any movement would cause him some grief for a while until the wound healed. He'd have to take it easy. Maybe even put his investigations on hold for a tad. Even as that thought entered his mind, another smothered it – what had been taunting him since the second he'd regained consciousness.

A memory. He'd switched on the overhead light before descending the stairs. That he was positive of – since he could recall seeing the number of dusty shelves and old barrels that had filled the cellar. Moments later, the light flicked off. The coppers were right – someone else had been in there and attacked him. More to the point who? Something about that picture was off – as if he'd forgotten an important detail. Something he'd seen? Or heard? The more he tried to recapture whatever it was, the more it eluded him and the more his head ached.

He'd been careful to shroud his research in secrecy, never discussing that part of his work with colleagues. What if he'd been careless? Slipped up somewhere? Could his attacker also be tracking down the same thing he was - his forty-year long obsession? The true reason why he was in Bindarra Creek?

The only thing he was certain of, was that he could trust no one. As usual and like every moment of his life journey, he stood alone.

CHAPTER 5

Hello old girl,

We lost our fifth horse two nights past. He injured himself and had to be shot. Put a damper on feeling glad to get off the ship I must say. But hoorah arrived in Alexandria yesterday and its wonderful. The harbour is full of sailing boats and I never seen so many people in the one place. Far more than Melbourne and thats saying something. I would like to explore the town but there was no time. We boarded a train and then sister – we passed through a lovely stretch of green called the Valley of the Nile where all around lies nothing but yellow desert sand. The natives live in filthy hovels and many have sores or are cripples and there are camels everywhere. When we reached Cairo we had to lead our horses for ten miles as they need time to recover from being on the ship. Night was setting in and it was past tucker time when we arrived at our camp outside a small town called Maadi. You would love Maadi as there are gardens everywhere and lots of trees. Today is busy with training and exercising the horses. It is hotter than home and tiny flies are a real pest. Because of the heat we may train at night. Soon we will be on our way to Gallipoli and I for one carnt wait. If I can arrange before I leave I will visit the pirimids. I will write again soon. Send mother and father my best.

Your affect. brother, Gregory.

Head lowered, Natalie put her entire body into it and scrubbed fiercely at the stubborn stain on the tiled floor of the local caravan park's ablutions block. She'd said she was ready. She'd put it out there into the Universe that now was her time. That she was open to more possibilities – anything that would help her only child. That she wanted more for herself than the role she'd fallen into and the safe path she'd chosen. She'd said that she was willing to step out of her comfort zone and for the first time since John had passed away, bring another man into her life.

By everything she'd read on the dating app and after that one brief dinner date, she'd hoped she'd found her ideal man in Ernest – sober, steady and settled with a stable and safe job. While there had been no pull of physical attraction, she had liked his thick mane of silver hair, the neatness of his clothes, his educated conversation and courteous old-world manners. It hadn't hurt that he was eleven years older. However, all it took was one look at Troy, one touch of his hand along with the sound of his deep voice and all those careful considerations flew out the window.

All those long-suppressed dreams and feelings had resurfaced, surprising her with their power. She couldn't resurrect the past. She wouldn't. Of course, there was Noah. Always Noah.

She scrubbed until her hands were raw and chaffed inside the rubber gloves. She scrubbed until her knees ached where she knelt on the cold tiles. She scrubbed so she couldn't acknowledge the ache in her lonely heart for all the 'might-have-beens'.

She couldn't acknowledge the raw throb of guilt.

Too much had happened since those heady days when she'd fallen in love with the handsome young soldier who fairly crackled with a restless energy that had both equally fascinated as well as terrified her. A man who'd reminded her too much of her father and his rash nature. In the end, it had been the memories of the pain her mother had experienced as well as all those childhood days which should have been idyllic. Instead they were fractured by the sound of arguments and fists punching through walls. She'd taken the safe path, by marrying John, the quiet-mannered and sensible best friend of Troy.

Finally satisfied the old tiles were as clean as possible, she packed up her products and left the block. After signing out of the office, she rode the bicycle she'd had since a teenager, to the shabby, two-bedroomed building she called home. She'd been lucky the park owner had agreed to time off yesterday so she could visit Ernest in the hospital. Although it meant working extra hours on Saturday, a day where she usually worked only two hours in the morning and had the remainder of the day free. In winter she could cheer Noah on from the sidelines at a soccer game. No such luck she'd make the game today. It was after three-thirty by the time she propped her bike against the side of the garage and trudged inside the rented, pre World War II built house. She spent the next ten minutes bringing in the load of washing hanging on the Hills hoist in the narrow backyard. Some items were still damp; there had been little warmth in the sun today. Later, she'd drape them in front of the fire. After a super quick shower, she changed into jeans, a loose pale green sweater, and pulled on her sneakers. Snatching up her mobile and a weatherproof jacket, she sent a quick text to Noah.

Sorry, I didn't make the game.

All good, Mum. Am on the sidelines today.

Her fingers hovered over the buttons. Noah hated when she made a fuss but still she had to ask. The doctors had told her to keep a health diary… *Coach's decision? Or is the pain bad? Any dizziness?*

The minutes ticked slowly by until… *Yeah, I'll be OK.* He ended with an emoji smiley face.

Her throat closed tight and her eyes burned for a second then she responded… *Home around 6. Will make pizza.*

How she longed to fling herself onto her bed, bawl her eyes out and rest her tired body, but she had her other job to do now. So instead, she closed the front door and hauled a backpack over her shoulders. In front of the house across the road, a car sat, engine idling. The driver had their back bowed as if looking out the passenger-side window. Stuffing her jacket into the wire basket she mounted her bike, rode along Wilgarra Avenue. She turned into a stiff wind that blew in bitter gusts along Main Street and stung her exposed skin. The next left led onto Mt Ingalls Road then she took another right onto Willow Tree Drive. The low hum of a car had her checking behind her. Instead of passing her, the vehicle pulled over to the side of the road and stopped. Her thigh muscles protesting, she pressed down harder on the pedals as she closed the distance to Fig Tree Lodge. Overhead, heavy dark clouds roiled over the north-eastern horizon. More rain. Not that they needed any more moisture. The ground was so sodden that every step squished up muddy puddles. Dampness seeped inside the soles of her sneakers and often washed wiggling leeches onto the path. A new pair of shoes would be nice, but they would have to wait.

The police tape barring entrance via the front door had disappeared. As Natalie rode around the side of the house, her gaze shot to where she'd seen the small spot of blood. If the police had taken samples for DNA testing, then hopefully the intruder would be caught soon. The idea that he or she was still wandering around had given her a sleepless night. Leaving her bike outside the kitchen, she approached the screen door and gave a short rap on the side of the building.

"Natalie! Come in, we're having a cuppa," trilled Ms Lette, waving madly from where she perched on a stool beside the island bench in the centre of the room.

After wiping her feet on a straw mat, Natalie entered the wonderfully warm kitchen to find the Lette family together for once. Next to Edwina sat her step-great granddaughter, Kaylee while her mother Tessa stood beside a counter with her nose buried in a pile of papers and a heavy frown on her face. Dodge, Tessa's husband and Edwina's grandson, stirred the contents of a large pot on the old fuel stove. Little four-year-old Matilda or Tilly as her family lovingly called her, stood in front of a plastic toy play stove replete with its own plastic pots and pans and even a small fridge. Every two seconds she switched her gaze from her pot and spoon over to her father then back again, religiously imitating his every move.

What a sweetheart. Natalie's heart swelled. There'd been a time when she'd longed for a little girl of her own. After Noah, there had been no more children for her. Another lost dream.

Edwina slipped off her stool and fetched another cup, then poured out steaming black tea. "Milk? Sugar?"

"A little milk, thanks." Smiling a greeting, Natalie took the proffered cup and sipped. She sighed as the liquid warmed her cold bones and the delicious scent of lamb stew hit her nostrils. The heat from the stove made the room cozy. She could have sat there the rest of the afternoon.

"Good to see you, Natalie." Dodge taste-tested his stew then shot a glance toward her. "There's plenty here if you and Noah would like to share dinner with us."

"Thank you, but I've promised Noah homemade pizza tonight."

Edwina snorted. "First nothing but coffee in your belly and now pizza. Doesn't sound healthy."

"I use a cauliflower base and load it with veggies. We'd love to come over another time." Natalie looked up to meet Edwina's eagle eyes. "I thought I'd do more work in the attic if that's okay with you?"

"Of course, dear. I had a feeling you'd be along today, so I've organised a surprise." Cunning glinted in those eyes of hers.

With several past occasions in mind when Edwina had had that same expression on her face, Natalie braced herself. It always paid to be vigilant around Ms Lette.

Dodge chuckled and turned around, pointing the wooden spoon at his grandmother. "Gran, give the woman a break."

"Pwush. She can take it. She's tougher than she thinks she is." Another appraising stare from Edwina before she reached out and crammed an entire cupcake in her mouth.

"Grannie! You know you're not supposed to have more than one a day!" Kaylee snatched up the plate and stomped over to the cupboards where she smacked the plate onto the counter with a clatter.

Crumbs flew through the air as Edwina spoke around a mouthful of cake. "If I can't eat cake and smoke, I may as well be in the ground."

Dodge added a pinch of salt to the pot. "Don't worry too much, Kaylee. I kept the sugar and fat down in that batch. So shouldn't be too bad, if the old girl has nicked more than she should."

"Old girl! I'm not old. I'm in my prime. Just you wait

my boy until you reach my age, then you'll understand you're never too old." Edwina placed her hands on the countertop and scowled.

"I surrender!" Dodge threw his hands into the air and over in the corner, little Tilly giggled and followed suit.

"Glad to see you know who's in charge. Now then, where was I? Oh yes. A surprise for Natalie." After taking a last noisy slurp of tea, Edwina pushed her empty mug aside. "Troy will be here soon to lend a hand moving some of that furniture out of the way."

Despite her best efforts, Natalie's heart kicked up several gears and something hot fluttered to life deep in her belly.

Thankfully, she was granted a reprieve from having to respond as Dodge argued, "I could do it, Gran. My shift at the hospital doesn't begin until eight o'clock."

"No way, son. Besides, you can't deny the bloke has some serious muscles." She smacked her lips and made kissy noises while Tessa smiled.

"Pity he's so old," mourned Kaylee then she and Edwina giggled together like a pair of schoolgirls, which of course, Kaylee was but it had been more than half a century since Edwina had seen the inside of a classroom. Although not related by blood, Tessa had told Natalie the two had bonded almost from the first moment they had met.

Wagging a finger, Tessa looked over with fake alarm on her face. "Eyes off, young lady. You are too young to be thinking about boys or men."

"Nothing wrong with looking – isn't that right, Grannie?" Kaylee said.

Dodge gave a dramatic sigh. "Like peas in a pod, those two."

"She does take after me." Edwina sounded smug. "As for you, young man, you need some time with your family – that is, if Tessa can tear herself away from those accounts."

Tessa lifted a pile of paper into the air and looked at Edwina. From outside, came the muted growl of a car trundling down the drive. "I'm not going to sugar-coat it. The situation is grim."

Frowning, Edwina jerked a thumb over her shoulder towards the kitchen door. "Let's keep that to ourselves."

"I'll be quick, and we'll talk more later. I know it will be tight, but Dodge and I will be okay. We'll work something out with our business." She paused and shared a smile with her husband. "However, I don't understand the details of the inheritance. It might be worthwhile getting a solicitor to check the will. Is it your father's?"

"No, the estate is tied up in some type of trust that my great uncle Mitchell set up in 1938, just before he died."

Tessa bit her lip and rifled through more paper. "That explains how your cousin has a share in Fig Tree Lodge. Maybe she can inject some money to tide you over until the tourists return to town?" She shared a glance between Dodge and Edwina.

Edwina was already shaking her head as she pushed to her feet and began to gather up the mugs and plates. "There's more than one cousin named in the will actually, apart from Janice, Troy's mum. Not that I've heard from the other two for years. Louisa married an American and moved to California. I know they had three kids but that's about all I do know. As for Elspeth – she took off travelling the world and apart from a postcard here and there, she never got back in touch. It's possible one or both of them may have passed away. It's been so long."

"It might be worthwhile locating them to see if they will help."

"I don't need any of them putting their two bits in and telling me what to do with this place. This is my home, not theirs." The plates rattled as Edwina placed them onto the sink. Turning around, she planted her hands on bony hips encased in a pair of flame-red leotards that peeped below the edge of her black and white diagonal-striped skirt. A pair of sheepskin slippers covered her feet and the tiger print fluffy sweater she wore would have looked fantastic on someone forty years younger. Somehow, no matter how outrageous her clothes, she always managed to pull it off.

Natalie wished she had even a smidgeon of the old woman's panache. A car door slammed.

"Tessa has a point though, Gran." Dodge settled the lid onto the pot and placed the wooden spoon beside the stove. Snatching up a washcloth, he wiped down the stove before crossing to the sink and running his hands under the tap. Little Tilly ran over to wrap her arms around his leg. Giggling, she placed both her small feet on top of his right one and hung on as he *'walked'* her about the kitchen. "If they have a stake in Fig Tree Lodge then they should be sharing the costs. From what Tessa tells me, you're the one who's been carrying the burden of upkeep all these years."

Edwina shrugged. "I get to live here rent-free. That was the verbal deal we made years ago."

Stopping beside the stove, Dodge gave a wry grimace as he ran a loving hand over Tilly's hair. "Not to mention all the free labour I've provided."

"Gonna send me an invoice, boy?" Edwina cackled and moved to perch on her stool again. She swung her legs to and fro, her toes kicking the cupboard beneath the bench. "Maybe I'll send you and your father one for all those years you lived here too."

"Maybe that's the problem." Dodge grinned and checked the contents of his pot again before swinging Tilly up into his arms. "You've been too generous."

Edwina puffed up her bony chest and smirked. "Sounds just like me." The mobile on the counter next to her trilled *'We are the Champions'* and her grin grew broader. "Speaking of eye candy… " She allowed the call to go through to voice mail.

"But you *are* generous, Grannie. You took me and Mum in, too. I love it here, I wouldn't want to live anywhere else." Kaylee gave her grandmother a hug which Edwina returned with a noisy kiss on Kaylee's cheek.

Outside, footsteps crunched over gravel. Natalie rose and took her mug over to the sink. Turning, she shifted closer to Edwina and lowered her voice. "What if that's why Troy is here? You said you've had little to do with your family. What if he's here to see how the Lodge is doing financially?"

"I got the impression that this isn't the first time you've met him."

Heat bloomed over Natalie's face and neck at Edwina's

scrutiny. "Years ago. Before I married John." She ducked her head.

"Like that is it? I thought so." Edwina crossed her arms.

Someone knocked on the kitchen door. Troy had arrived.

Her excitement at seeing him churned into a sick feeling as an unwanted realisation entered Natalie's head. The intruder hadn't been identified. Whoever it was had left no prints and had been savvy enough to leave no evidence apart from a broken window. When she'd come face to face with Troy on the veranda, there'd been a pair of work gloves dangling from his belt; along with a hammer. A hammer that could well have been used to smash glass.

Maybe there never had been an intruder; maybe the person who had broken into the house had been Troy. Maybe he was searching the house for his own ends – something to do with his mother's shared inheritance perhaps? What did she know about him really? Four crazy months when she'd imagined she was in love. There had been little time spent sharing their innermost thoughts and dreams. What she did know, was that he was a man of action. A man used to taking chances and who had pursued a dangerous, adrenaline-fuelled career. A man used to war and all its deadly consequences. The moment he appeared in Fig Tree Lodge, someone was attacked. What if he was the one who had hurt Ernest?

Dizziness assailed her and she clutched at a nearby chair to keep upright as with a smile on his face, Troy opened the screen door. He stepped inside the kitchen, his gaze sweeping the occupants as his dog panted happily at his heels.

Natalie bent over and murmured, "He could be here to persuade you to sell."

Steel entered Edwina's eyes and tossing her grey hair over her shoulders, she glared at Troy. "This is my home. The only way I'm leaving this house is feet first."

CHAPTER 6

Fig Tree House,
Bindarra Creek, NSW.
31st July, 1915.

Dear Alfred,

 How it warms my heart to read your words... [more details about the farm] *... After church last Sunday Dorothy spent the day with me knitting socks for you and your brothers. She is a sweet lass and made scones for our supper. Her talk was all about her plans for your shared future together. She hopes for at least four children which made me very happy. It will be wonderful to have babies to fuss over once more. To see you married in our local church is a dream that I cling to. I am to meet her at the markets this week where we will exchange our news of the war. Your father sends his best and bides you to take care of your feet. You and your brothers are oft in my thoughts and I pray each day the Good Lord will bring you home safe to me.*

 With love, Mother.

The words Troy had overheard replayed inside his head as he ascended the ladder, his muscles cramping with tension. It had taken all his control not to argue his mother's case and verbalise his outrage that virtual strangers had passed judgement on her without even asking for an explanation. Aunt Edwina had thrown down a challenge that stiffened his resolve to continue, a fact that, if he was honest, had begun to waiver after he'd met Natalie again. If there was one thing he valued more than anything else in this world – it was loyalty. His father had hammered that trait home often enough during his childhood. A life career in the Army had cemented it into the pillar stone of his character. After all, it had been loyalty that had made him keep his distance, shut his mouth, and walk away when the girl of his dreams had married his mate.

His head then shoulders breached the manhole, and he froze. His gaze took in the dim shadowy attic. His hearing was assaulted with the multitude pinging of rain on the iron roof – far too similar to a barrage of bullets. A rapid crescendo of drumming that matched the heavy thump of his heart and the white noise buzzing in his ears. His fingers pressed into the dirty floor while his toes curled inside the heavy boots he had planted firmly on the drop-down ladder.

A light hit his eyes. He squeezed them shut as he beat down on memories of blood, war and death.

"Is everything alright?" Natalie's voice came from out of the shadows and somehow pulled him back from the brink he teetered on.

He swallowed and snapped open his eyes at the touch of her hand on one of his. She'd propped the torch on its end, the beam aimed toward the roof, and had crouched down beside him. When had she moved? His breath hitched sharply, as heat slashed across his cheeks. Fancy freezing like a two-year old! He forced his eyes to meet hers but there was nothing but concern on her face.

"Give me a minute." Rising swiftly, she crossed to an old desk and turned her back. The zip of a lighter fired several times and then wavering light flooded the attic from six or so candles.

He forced himself to move and found himself standing, sweating and breathing hard, on the dusty floorboards. Without saying a word, she gave his fingers a gentle tug before scooping up the torch and aiming it towards the jumble of broken furniture crowding the far end of the attic. Finally, he found his voice, and with it the stunning realisation that his panic had vanished. "What a lot of junk. How did they get all this up here?"

"Originally the attic was used as servants' quarters. There was a staircase which was demolished, and the space converted into another room sometime in the nineteen-fifties."

"They just left all this stuff here?"

"Yep." Natalie tossed him a smile over her shoulder as she stepped forward. "Edwina didn't mention exactly how much work is needed?"

Bless her. She wasn't going to comment on his wig-out

moment. At least – not now. "Yeah, she was a little coy about the whole thing. Said something about moving furniture for you. But I don't mind helping while I'm in town."

"You're not here long then?" After setting the torch onto the desk, Natalie began shifting damaged timber chairs to one side and stacking them on top of each other as best she could.

"Mind you don't go lifting anything too heavy." In two strides he was by her side and taking over.

"Sorry, you were saying?"

"I asked how long you're staying in town."

He took a moment to wedge the chair he held onto the growing stack. "No real time frame."

"Don't have to rush back to the Army?"

Interesting how her tone held a touch of resentment. Troy straightened to face her. "I've been discharged. Thought twenty-seven years is enough to give my country."

"That's a huge change for you. You joined up after you finished high school, didn't you?"

"Yeah. Did my degree while I was in officer training."

"What are you going to do with the rest of your life?"

They stood there barely a metre apart and neither moved as they stared at each other. She was so close he could see the thickness of her dark lashes and the tiny laugh lines fanning out from the corners of her eyes. So close her soft breath stirred the cold air in front of him. The urge to draw her into his arms had the hairs on his arms tingling. His body stiffened. He dug his short nails into the palms of his hands so he wouldn't act on what would no doubt be a foolish move. As if in warning, the rain hammered like machine-gun fire on the roof above their heads. "I'm still working on it."

A couple of drops of water plopped onto his hair. Several more leaks appeared forming puddles on the grimy floor. The old house sure was in a dismal state. He forced a grin and bent to pick up the last chair. "At the moment I'm enjoying being a free man. We've been doing some travelling and camping around the state."

"The *we* being you and Chip?" Natalie smiled as from the open manhole came the definite bumping of a tail on hardwood and a soft yip. She wiped a raindrop from her cheek with the back of her hand.

"That goes without saying. Chip's a permanent fixture in my life now."

"Then no Mrs Davidson…?"

Was it his imagination or did she blush? "Never married. What about you? Ever tie the knot again after John?"

"No. It's just me and Noah." Her chin came up as her eyes narrowed. "And Bindarra Creek? What made you decide to come here?"

Bloody hell but she was tricky. Cushioning the real question she had wanted to ask with a bunch of all that pretend phoney interest in his life. How had he forgotten that about her? He rammed the last chair home and dusted his hands while mulling over the fact she didn't have a significant other in her life and why it lifted his spirits. "Since I was going to be in the area, Mum asked me to look in on Aunt Edwina."

"Aunt Edwina? Isn't she like your second cousin or something?"

He shrugged. "Old habit from when I was a kid. Besides, she hasn't told me to call her anything else. I'm here to do some white-water rafting down the Akuna River in the National Park. With all this wet weather, it's running strong and fast."

Her mouth turned down and her expression became fixed. "You always were an adrenaline junky."

"Hey! I don't take chances, just calculated risks."

She snorted. "Like that makes it any different."

"You haven't changed then. Never taken a risk. Never done anything remotely exciting." He couldn't help himself. He had to poke the bear. Had to rid himself of at least a modicum of the bitterness that dwelled deep inside. "Just lived a safe boring life with safe boring John."

"How dare you!"

He flinched as her open palm connected with his cheek. The sting brought him up sharp. He deserved it. Made him feel even more lousy about himself and his own decisions than usual. But he couldn't be a fake. He always had to be true to himself and others. "That was uncalled for, and I apologise. John was a great bloke and I know my career was a problem for you."

Natalie turned her back. "You have no idea." Her voice shook and sounded thick and heavy. Probably with tears.

Yeah. He was a total arse and truth be told, had never deserved a life with her anyway. "You made the right choice, Natalie. My job would have always come between us, and I couldn't give it up. Not even for you." He hesitated then asked the question that had all but burned him alive for years. "You never did give me a reason, only that you couldn't be an Army wife. Was there something more?"

"It's over and done with, Troy. I moved on from you a long time ago."

Ouch. That was telling him. She was right, the past belonged in the past. Now all he had to do was convince himself.

She stalked past the chair stack and fronted two massive-looking wardrobes. "Let's get this done. I want to be home by six to cook dinner for my son."

"Yes, ma'am. What's up first?"

"We need to move these two items of furniture so I can get to a kitchen dresser and a desk that's behind them."

"Whew! For a moment there I had a horrible feeling you expected me to somehow magically squeeze them through the manhole and onto the floor below." He grinned, relief sweeping through him as the distant expression on her face faded and she smiled in response.

"Not yet at any rate. Although you never know with Edwina."

Troy laughed. "I'll have to organise a crane to be on standby so we can take them out through the roof. Otherwise, we will have to dismantle them piece by piece." He moved closer and ran a hand over the intricate carving on the wardrobe doors. "Nice bit of timber though and a similar period to the antique sideboard in the dining room at home. I wouldn't mind having a go at restoring it."

"That will be Dodge's job should Edwina decide she wants to use the furniture downstairs." Even through the gloom, there was no mistaking the suspicious glare in Natalie's eyes as she stared back at him.

His amusement fled along with their brief moment of rapport. Maybe that was for the best. As soon as he'd accomplished what he'd come there for, he would go back to his own life. What that would look like now that his Army career was over, he had still to figure out. He set to, wiggling and shoving one of the heavy units, centimetre by centimetre, until there was sufficient room for Natalie to slip behind it. *Damn but this robe was heavy.* His muscles bunched and sweat formed under his armpits, as he heaved it a little further away. "What exactly are you doing up here anyway?"

"Doing a bit of inventory and seeing if there is anything that could be used in the house. What's too far gone will go in the firewood pile. Then I'm to clean the area. I think Edwina and Dodge may turn the attic into a playroom for the girls. They'll need to build a new set of stairs though."

An inventory. Perfect. All he had to do was get her to share. The kitchen dresser Natalie was so keen to reach loomed out of the shadows. She bent down to wrench open the cupboard doors and all but disappeared inside the opening. Intrigued, Troy took one of the candles and manoeuvred his larger body behind the dresser. Holding the candle closer he was able to partially illuminate the interior.

"Thanks," mumbled Natalie. Objects grated and rattled as she moved them about.

"You act like you're looking for something in particular." He set the candle down on the counter and folded his body lower in order to see what she was up to.

"I am, actually. Old letters, books, newspapers, even magazines. I'm writing a history book on the Lette family and the town in general." With almost all of her upper torso embedded inside, her voice was muffled but still distinct enough for Troy to hear.

"Sounds interesting." That much was true but paper held little value. If some of this old furniture was restored to its original condition, there could be a tidy sum to be made. He craned his neck to try and see inside the cupboard, but her body blocked his vision.

"Here, can you take these and put them somewhere safe? Preferably away from any leaks from the roof." She thrust a hand out and handed him an old teapot then a pile of bric-a-brac in various states of disrepair.

Troy set the candle down and dutifully took each item she held out, then twisted around to place them on the dresser counter. What a lot of rubbish. Cups and saucers, most cracked, a handful of tiny tin soldiers, a biscuit tin, an assortment of mismatched plates, several clay pots, statues, a couple of wine glasses, a wooden box with small gnaw marks along the edges, and a moth-eaten feather boa.

"There's... hang on... " Natalie thrashed about before dragging out a painting in a dull gilt frame. She laughed. "It's so filthy I can't tell what the subject is, although I think it could be a horse." She handed it over.

"If it's an original oil painting of an equestrian scene, might be worth a few bob." Leaning close, Troy puffed out a breath but the thick dust didn't budge. After leaning it against the back of one of the wardrobes, he asked, "Anything else?"

"Some books but they're in bad shape and… oh wow! A gas mask. It might be World War I era. Maybe one of the Lette boys brought it back. You know that they all fought in the war?" Natalie edged out backwards and, with a soft groan, placed a hand to the small of her spine, as she straightened. She lifted up the gas mask. "Check it out."

Taking it, Troy turned the object over in his hands as he also rose to his feet. "This is really something. I know very little about our family history apart from the fact my great grandfather was called Mitchell Lette."

"He had two brothers, Alfred and Gregory, and a sister called Matilda. Gregory and Matilda were twins."

"You're very knowledgeable."

She shrugged. "I'm researching your family for my book."

"Think there's a market for that kind of story? Surely no one would be interested in our family. We're hardly famous."

"You'd be surprised. The two publishing houses I approached told me there is a resurgence in the popularity of Australian history – especially anything to do with the wars. I intend to focus a lot on that aspect, so I need to find as much raw material as possible. You know, stuff like letters, newspapers, that kind of thing. I want to give it a personal twist using the war's effects on families and the town in general." Natalie inspected the collection on the dresser, fingering the pots and a couple of wonky-looking statues. Everything was covered in thick grey dust along with mice droppings. She sneezed and searched in her pocket.

Troy gave her his clean handkerchief. "Old habit. I suffered from hay fever when I was a kid, so I never left home without one in my pocket." Shifting his weight, he cleared his throat. "How are you doing, financially I mean?"

She shot him a fierce look. "I hope you're not going to offer me money. I'm not a charity case. Things are tight but then I'm not alone. Many people are doing it tough these days. I make enough with my cleaning work for Noah and me to get by. I won't deny if the book sells well, the extra money will be a Godsend." Biting her lip, she turned aside. Her shoulders slumped as she picked up the wooden chest.

There was more to it than simply needing additional dosh. "What is it you're not telling me?"

"Nothing." Her voice was sharp, defensive and he had to battle his rising frustration.

If she was in trouble, he needed to know. He could help her. Hell, he wanted to help her and do anything he could to make her life easier. She wore her independence and pride like armour. Maybe if he did a bit of snooping on her account, then he could decide on a plan of attack. He edged out from behind the wardrobes. Snatching up one of the rags they'd brought with them to the attic, he wound his way in and around an old bed frame, a floor lamp, three side tables and a narrow chest of drawers to where rain dripped into a rusty bucket. Natalie followed him and held out the chest. After wetting the cloth, he wiped off decades-old grime and dirt.

"What do you think's inside?" She fiddled with the clasp then frowned. "What a pity. It's locked."

"Not a problem, I'll just unscrew the lock casing." Smiling, he unhooked a screwdriver and a set of Alan-keys from his tool belt and set to work. His mobile rang. But he ignored the sound.

"Not going to answer it?" Natalie tilted her head.

"Nope. If it's important they will leave a message." Sure enough, a text message pinged. From his father. He set his jaw and thirty seconds later, he tossed the hinges aside and winked as he looked up. "Ready?"

"Wait a sec while I wash my hands." She popped the box on top of the chest of drawers before going back to the bucket where she washed and dried her hands then stood with her hands fluttering by her sides.

Troy picked up the torch and shone it over the box.

Natalie opened the lid then drew a sharp breath. "How fantastic! More letters and photographs. Wait! Don't touch them yet. I've got some cotton gloves we can use for the photographs, and you need to wash your hands before you touch the paper." She edged around to where she'd left her backpack, rummaging inside while he made use of the bucket. She handed him a pair of gloves. Sending him a happy grin, she lifted the bundle of letters and photographs. Buried underneath were several brass and celluloid buttons, a yellowed pair of once-white baby booties, a photo-frame, and a collection of copper and silver coins. There was another coin but it was much larger, about three to four times bigger than a regular copper penny.

Troy picked up the bronze disc and held it closer to

the light. He gave a low whistle and met Natalie's excited eyes. "It's a Dead Man's Penny."

"The one sent to the family of men who died during World War I?"

"Yep. The very same."

Her smile spread over her face, lighting up her eyes. "What an amazing find. Edwina is going to be rapt. How awesome would it be if we found a Memorial Scroll too. There's a desk I haven't had a chance to search yet."

"What about those wardrobes and this chest of drawers?"

"Already gone through all of them."

Frowning, Troy turned the disc over in his hands. "I must admit, you've got me keen to discover more about my family."

"You could help me with the research... if you wish," Natalie mumbled as she ducked her head and replaced the items into the wooden box. "This needs a good clean!"

Ignoring her last words, he fastened onto her offer like a hungry tiger. "I'd love to." Almost reverently, she laid the Dead Man's Penny on top of the papers before she closed the lid.

"Great. I'll show this to Edwina later but first, I'm sure I can squeeze behind the dresser and get to the desk. You can be in charge of the torch." Without waiting for his agreement, she hurried behind the wardrobes again. "Light please!"

Somehow, he managed to wedge his larger body in the small space and aim the torch as Natalie sucked in her breath and sidled her way around the dresser. She clambered over an empty shelving unit that stood waist-high.

With the large furniture blocking the candlelight, this corner of the attic was deep in shadow. The incessant drip of water was somehow ominous in the muffled stillness. Troy stood on tiptoe and by bracing his body on the shelving unit was able to angle the torch to give better light to reveal the desk Natalie was after. It was made from walnut darkened with age and looked older than dirt. It leaned heavily to one side and rocked on its spindly Victorian legs when she touched one of the drawers.

Sneezing, Natalie jiggled it open then sighed. "Nothing. I'll keep looking." She wrestled open drawer after drawer. All she found however were some magazines circa 1950 that had been shredded by mice for their nests, an old pipe and more books. After shutting the last drawer, she gave the pipe and books to Troy. He shuffled out from behind the dresser and Natalie followed.

Setting the torch and their recent finds down, Troy lifted a cobweb from her hair and smiled. "You need a shower."

"I do feel filthy," she agreed before blowing her nose on his handkerchief. "Gosh, this dust. Let's box all this stuff up. After we show Edwina the Dead Man's Penny, I'll take the rest home, clean everything up before checking it out more thoroughly. If Dodge hasn't left for work, he can drop the tubs off on the way." She grimaced and slapped at her grubby clothes as the rain found another source of entrance and began dripping onto the dresser.

"This roof." Troy shook his head. "I'll source some tarps and get some blokes to give me a hand."

"The local SES guys will help. I'll give you Roman's

number, he's the captain." She looked at the ceiling. "There's already one tarp up there, but I guess this weather has damaged the roof even more."

"Place is falling down around their ears." He located two large plastic tubs; Natalie must have placed in the attic for just that purpose, and began to fill them with the bric-a-brac.

"Not really. Dodge and his father did a lot of renovating work years ago. Unfortunately, the town was hit by a supercell storm not long after I moved here with Noah. The roof was smashed, and water got into one of the walls, cracking the brickwork. Like so many others in town, they weren't insured. Then the lockdowns hit and tourism dried up. A book deal will help them fix their home," Natalie's voice was sharp as she brought over the teapot to place into a tub.

"Which also belongs to my mother."

"But only a share of it. No one's seen hide nor hair of her or any of your family, apparently for years. And now here you are. I know you overheard us talking in the kitchen."

He clamped the lid over the first tub and snapped the tabs in place. "You're really protective of Aunt Edwina, aren't you?"

"She's been good to me and Noah."

Which brought him back to the thought niggling at the back of his mind. Something was wrong in her life. Was it money or the lack of? Or something else? "Heard anything more from the police?"

"Only that they're continuing their inquiries. Doesn't sound promising they'll find out who knocked Ernest on the head." Natalie walked around the room, snuffing out the candles by placing the ends into the water bucket.

He smiled. That was Natalie alright, always overly cautious.

When she finished, she slipped her pack over her shoulders as he pushed the tubs closer to the manhole.

"This friend of yours, Ernest whoever. Known him long?"

"We met for the first time in person, the other night. He's a nice guy and I like him." Defiance rang in her voice, but he didn't take the bait. He'd check the fellow out himself, see if he really was a decent type and didn't have a criminal record. It was the least he could do for the woman he'd once loved with all his heart.

In the process, he'd discover who had attacked Ernest and why. He'd also finish what he'd started – the reason why he was in Bindarra Creek in the first place.

CHAPTER 7

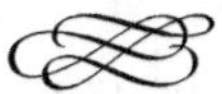

[Extract from The Herald]

SHEER HEROISM. AUSTRALIAN LIGHT HORSE ATTEMPT THE IMPOSSIBLE

Tornado of Fire Defends Eight Fold Turkish Trenches. Soldiers Fight Over Bodies Three Deep. An account by C.E.W. Bean, War Correspondent of Gallipoli. August 15ᵗʰ '15...

The Victorian 8ᵗʰ Light Horse led the charge. (They had drawn lots as to order.) No trenches were gained in this fight, but for sheer self sacrifice and heroism, this charge of the Australian Light Horse is unsurpassed in history. A Cable message received yesterday stated that the 8ᵗʰ and the 10ᵗʰ (Western Australian) Light Horse were practically wiped out in the fighting on August 7ᵗʰ.

Whatever had she been thinking? Inviting Troy to assist with her research was only asking for trouble. Although, once spoken she could hardly take the words back. She kept telling herself the invitation was so she could pump him for more information about why he was really in Bindarra Creek; decide whether he'd been the one who had attacked Ernest. Yet a little voice whispered she was deceiving herself – never in a million years would she allow him anywhere near Noah if she truly believed he was capable of such a terrible deed. Then again, she couldn't deny Troy's reason for being in town was decidedly shonky. It was as if a war raged inside her head. It was enough to give her a resounding headache that refused to budge, no matter how much paracetamol she'd swallowed since yesterday.

Heart fluttering as if she was eighteen again, she rushed around the living room, plumping cushions, straightening the throw rug, before fiddling with the curtains. Much to her son's lively surprise.

"What's got into you, Mum?" Sauntering up to the coffee table he snatched another cupcake and crammed it into his mouth.

"Noah! They're for when our guest arrives."

"What? The Queen?" He guffawed, then choked.

Sighing, Natalie thumped him on the back for a few seconds until he finished spluttering. She returned to her position by the window as Noah threw himself onto the couch. Maybe the time spent with Troy today would alleviate her doubts. Maybe even give her closure from the past so she could move on. Gosh, she hoped so – she couldn't take any more of this confusion occupying her mind. She twitched aside the curtain. Although there were no gardens to soften the aging house, at least the grass had been mown recently. The cloudy sky made the morning darker than normal, and the blustery wind bent the backs of the trees on the other side of the road. A Coke can rattled down a footpath that appeared empty of people – not that she blamed them. The Sunday morning was bleak and cold.

A shadow moved behind the hibiscus shrub that bordered her house from next door. She waited, expecting to see someone walk past her house. Nothing happened. Weird. She tweaked at the hem of her fluffy cream sweater then stood on tiptoe, the better to see further. Whoever had been there, had gone.

"Seriously, Mum. What's up?"

How to respond when she didn't know the answer herself? Or maybe she just didn't want to acknowledge the reason why her belly had turned to quavering jelly. Glad that she had her back to him so he couldn't see the heat in her cheeks, she managed to keep her voice even. "Our guest is related to Edwina and her family." How hard this was to form the next words. She knew her son, knew that he would bombard Troy the moment he stepped through the door. She couldn't risk Troy mentioning it first. She forced a laugh. "It's quite a coincidence actually. He's a friend of your father's from high school."

"He knew Dad?"

The eagerness in Noah's voice was like a freshly gouged wound. "Yes. I met him a few times when I first dated your father, but haven't heard from or seen him for years." *Liar. You more than met him. You had a full-on relationship with him.* Her pulse quickened as Troy's muscular form appeared further along the street. Quickly, she moved away from the window and met her son's gaze. "How are you feeling today?"

He made a rude noise, obviously annoyed she'd brought up *'that subject'* and ignored her question. "I'm not going to my room, so don't bother asking me. Besides, I want to help." As if to prove he meant what he said, he jumped up and dragged one of the plastic tubs closer to the couch and ripped off the lid.

Thank heavens she had already cleaned most of the dust and dirt from the items before repacking them in the tubs. No way did she want to aggravate Noah's sinuses more than usual. "Don't forget, you're grounded."

"Awww, Mum! It was only PE."

"I don't care. Skipping school is not an option. You're not going horse riding or skateboarding with your mates."

"But it's the only pupil-free day this term!"

"Don't care. You should have thought of that before you wagged class."

"Bloody hell."

"And don't swear." A knock sounded and Natalie crossed to the front door to let Troy and his dog inside.

After murmuring hello and giving Chip a fondle about the ears, she took Troy's parka from him and hung it on a hook, pleased when he pulled off his muddy boots and left them by the door. Palms clammy, she introduced him to

Noah and watched the two of them as they greeted each other easily as if they'd known one another a lifetime.

Another twist of the knife. She had to duck her head to hide the tears that burned behind her eyes.

Troy sniffed the air then turned to her with a grin. "Something smells good. I didn't know lunch would be included."

"Oh, it's nothing really. I was going to cook soup for dinner anyway, so I thought I'd get it done early then I would have all day to work on the book." She had to force her hands to remain by her sides instead of shielding her hot face from his penetrating gaze. Smile pinned in place, she mumbled something about checking the stove and walked into the kitchen where she poured a glass of water.

A cold moist nose nuzzled her jean-clad leg and, crouching, Natalie gave Chip a longer pat and scratch. How she would love a dog for Noah, and herself. But vet bills were expensive for someone who lived on a shoe-string. Perhaps if the book sold well and after Noah had had his operation, she could think about a pet. After sorting out a bowl of water for Chip, Natalie switched the kettle on and went back to the living room. "I'll make us a cup of tea, shall I?"

"Maybe later. I'd like to get a bit of a start first." Troy smiled slowly and her tummy flipped as a quiver ran through her. He and Noah knelt beside the open tub, removing each item with careful hands and placing them either on the floor or the coffee table. Two more cupcakes had disappeared, and the plate containing the last two had been popped onto the entertainment unit.

Troy pulled the next item out, a ceramic statue of an Egyptian dog, then cradled it in his hands. "This looks like a nice piece but it's a pity the ears and nose have been damaged. There's also a large crack running along the base."

"Yes, I think the brothers sent a few curios home from Egypt and France. From what I've discovered from my research, they weren't alone. Apparently, it was a favourite pastime of some soldiers to visit the markets and haggle with the traders."

"Is this the only one you've found?"

"No, there's a few others in the plastic tubs in my bedroom." Deciding she'd be better off not gazing into his chocolate dark eyes like she was a starstruck teenager, she knelt down on the rug and shrugged. "I doubt there's anything of value amongst them. Most are made from clay and are in poor condition."

"What do you want me to do with it? We've made three piles – keep, maybe and chuck."

"Maybe. Edwina has already told me she is only interested in the china, but we might find a museum who will be interested in taking it."

"Now this – we should keep." Noah wrapped the feather boa around his neck and leaping to his feet, performed mincing steps around the room.

Natalie and Troy laughed.

"Wish I could have seen the Dead Man's penny," Noah mourned as he tossed the boa on top of the statue in the maybe pile.

"I'm sure Aunt Edwina will show it to you, if you ask." Troy met Natalie's eyes. "I told Noah about all that junk we discovered in the attic. By the way, the roof is now entirely covered in tarps thanks to Roman Taylor and his SES guys. He's a good bloke."

"Yes, he's also Abby's, the Senior Police Constable's husband."

"Is that so?" A thoughtful expression settled on his face.

He was up to something – but what? "If you stay in town for any length of time, you could always join the team."

He grinned and there went that tummy flutter again. Oh God, was she that obvious? Mentally kicking herself, she picked up her notebook and mobile and began to jot down every item. Next she photographed each one, even those they intended to put in the rubbish.

"Always so careful," said Troy, soto-voice. "I like that about you."

"Oh really? You used to find it irritating." She stopped as she caught sight of Noah.

His mouth hung open as he stared at them. Her son was no fool.

Forget Troy. Get on with what you're supposed to be doing! Hopefully Noah will forget everything I just said. One by one she rifled through the stack of old books, reading the spines of those still legible and opening the covers of those that were either too far gone or had no covers at all. Midway through, her hands closed over a leather book bound with the remains of a tatty and faded purple ribbon and wrapped in a grubby lace doily. Her heart stuttered as she opened the cover. "Oh my... you won't believe what I've found. A diary."

"So?" Troy raised his brows as he leaned back against the couch.

"It belongs to Matilda. Gregory's twin. He was one of the Lette brothers who went to war." Catching her breath, she turned a few pages at random and began to read. After a few minutes, she raised her eyes. "There is so much material here I can use in the book. It will give us a fabulous insight into how the family coped during those terrible years." She flicked through more pages, her nerves fizzing at the ink sketches scattered throughout and scrapes of folded paper inserted here and there. "There's a few old newspaper clippings here as well and Matilda has drawn lots of images. Looks like scenes of the farm, the river, the house and some rather good renderings of people she must have known. Possibly her family. This one looks like it's a depiction of Christmas morning." Awed with her find, Natalie closed the cover and hugged it to her chest.

"I bet I know what you're doing the rest of today." Troy laughed and after another two heartbeats, Noah's puzzled expression faded as he smiled.

She knew her son; he was biding his time to ask more questions. Questions, she didn't know whether she would ever be able to answer. Lowering her head, she re-opened the book while Troy and Noah turned their attention to the last tub. The next hour passed with Noah taking over cataloguing the contents and Troy deciding which pile to add the items to, while she read and read. There was too much to process in one day so eventually, she closed the diary. After her guest departed, she'd make notes for her book. With so much material, she itched to start.

She looked over at Noah and Troy. Noah had taken advantage of her distraction as she'd read and wore the old gas mask. He gave Chip a hearty scratch along her back while she grinned and panted. A smudge of dirt adorned Troy's face – right next to his mouth. Then said mouth quirked into a tiny smile as he must have spotted her stare. *Stop looking at his mouth.*

"I've been thinking about all this memorabilia from the war." Troy held up a rusty looking bayonet and scabbard. He indicated the maybe and chuck piles. "There's quite a decent amount here, even a couple of old Women's Weekly magazines dated in the early 1940's. I reckon they could use them in the Lodge."

Natalie frowned. "Edwina is only interested in the china."

Troy inserted the bayonet back into the scabbard before wrapping a thin cloth around it. "I've got an idea that might change her mind. Apart from donating the less damaged items, what about using them to decorate a room at the Lodge? It could be a bedroom or say a small sitting room. I noticed plenty of period furniture in the attic that could be restored and used to give the right historical ambiance of the time."

"Wow, I love it. That's a fabulous idea." Setting down the diary, Natalie picked up the notebook and scanned down the inventory list. "If there are sufficient pieces, we could do two or more time periods. The rooms could be labelled say, something like… the Roaring Twenties."

"Exactly." Troy grinned. "We might be able to scavenge enough curios to have an Ancient Egyptian bedroom. You did say there were more containers?"

Excitement fizzed. Natalie set down the notebook and surged to her feet. "Yes, I've got eight or maybe ten stored in my bedroom. I'll get them."

"Do you think I could help setting up the rooms?" Noah's voice came out muffled from behind the mask. "Sounds like fun."

"Will you take that off? Who knows what germs are living inside it?" Holding out her hand, she gave her fingers a wiggle to get him to hurry up, only half-joking. An infection could lay him prone for weeks and push him further down the elective surgery list.

Troy's eyebrows rose at her sharp tone.

She attempted to soften it with a smile as Noah, a pout marring his face, handed it over. "Can you help me bring the other tubs into the lounge room?"

"Sure." Shoulders slumped, Noah slouched out the door.

"I could help?"

The thought of having Troy inside her bedroom brought to mind images she had believed she'd well and truly squashed. Cheeks burning, she mumbled, "It's all good. You could turn the slow cooker off though, please. We should have something to eat."

"Funny how time gets away from you when you're with someone special."

Their eyes caught and held. Did he mean it? Or was he simply saying something he thought she wanted to hear? There was no deception in his steady gaze. The tiny frown on his brow indicated he could be as surprised as her at his words.

"Come on, Mum!" bellowed Noah from the bedroom.

In a few seconds, he'd be back with them and any chance of talking privately would be lost. She couldn't wait any longer. "Are you really here on holiday to visit your relatives or do you have another agenda? I have to know," she said fiercely.

Her heart sank as Troy turned away and ruffled his dog's ears. Avoiding her? When he looked up again, his expression was stern. "You were correct the other day. Mum wants Fig Tree Lodge sold."

CHAPTER 8

10.30PM, 20TH AUG., 1915.
D. A. LETTE, ESQ.
FIG TREE HOUSE, BINDARRA CREEK.

Regret to inform you it is officially reported your son Lieut A. Lette reported missing eighth inst. Any further particulars will be at once communicated to you.

Colonel Hawker,
Victoria Barracks, Melbourne.

Seething, Troy turned on his side in his sleeping bag, for what seemed like the hundredth time that night. It wasn't the hardness of the ground beneath his body that was the problem. He was used to living rough. No, it was his restless mind, stupidly replaying every word Natalie had spoken, remembering every time she smiled, recalling the way her eyes would light up like sunlight glimmering through leaves. *Right, that's it.* Now he knew he was losing his mind. He was many things, but a poet was not one of them.

He flung himself onto his back and glared into the darkness. Beside him curled up in her warm blanket, Chip snorted, her feet scrabbling in her sleep as if she dreamed of chasing rabbits across the field. The tent flapped as the wind gusted. Troy drew the edge of the sleeping bag closer to his chin. Damn, but it was a cold night. If the temperature kept dropping, he may well decide to take Aunt Edwina up on her invitation to bunk down in the old stables. No longer the cobweb-filled shanty building he remembered from his childhood visit but renovated into a cosy, small private apartment. It was currently vacant due to her son-in-law, Warren and his new wife leaving town after they separated a few months ago. According to his aunt, the wife had decamped to her parents' place with their twin boys, while Warren had retreated to his houseboat on Lake Macquarie. Troy only had a hazy memory of meeting Warren once when he was about eleven years old. He recalled a stocky, strong bloke who had a deep belly laugh.

Yawning, he willed himself to sleep, but a certain brunette's face wouldn't disappear from his mind. It had been easier when he'd been in the Army to relegate her to the past; his career had been full and challenging. Since his discharge, he'd had too much time on his hands while he pondered what to do with the rest of his life. As each day passed, his thoughts had turned more and more to *'what if's'* and wondering where it had all gone wrong. More than that, the burning desire to see her once more had increased in intensity so he'd jumped at his parents' suggestion to check on Aunt Edwina.

What he had thought would be a simple task had turned into something much trickier. No way did he want to be instrumental in removing his mother's cousin from her home. He'd only connected with her a couple of times and yet he'd discovered that he liked her. No, he couldn't leave – not yet. Especially, as he didn't trust the new man in Natalie's life. Unfortunately, there was her repeated questioning of his motives for being in town. It was obvious she believed he was a heartless jerk about to evict an old woman from her home, and boy, did that rankle! Had she invited him over to sort through all that junk so she could interrogate him? There was him thinking that maybe once he'd met her again, he would realise she belonged in the past. That he could move on maybe even meet someone he could share the remainder of his life with. Now there would be no moving on for him until he'd found closure. He had to find a way to shift her from his mind, and his heart. Because as much as he wanted to deny it, his response to her presence grew stronger each time he saw her.

Chip growled. Troy laid a hand on her neck to quieten her as he listened, straining his eyes as he scanned his tent. The front flap had been pulled to the side and the blackness of night was alleviated a trifle by the security light glowing near the amenities block at the top of the slight hill. The light was sufficient to illuminate a dim outline crouched near his tent entrance.

Someone was rifling through his gear.

In an instant, he was fully alert. His fingers closed over the zipper as he kept his gaze pinned on the would-be thief. Getting out of a zipped up sleeping bag fast and without making any noise while hanging onto his dog's collar was a lesson in stealth. It was impossible to disguise the soft zoom of the zip.

The figure turned towards him. Whoever it was, held something in their hand, like a short stick or baton.

A blast of wind slapped the tent flap closed. Abandoning caution, Troy yanked free of the last metre of zip and surged out of the bag as he let go of Chip. His dog bounded forward, snarling, hackles up. Troy snatched his torch and rushed from the tent. Footsteps pinpointed the location of the vague shape as it fled up the hill, Chip barking at his heels. No time to yank on boots. In his bare feet, Troy raced after his dog and the fleeing figure.

He had barely closed five metres before something or someone cannoned into him, knocking him to the ground. A savage kick swiped the side of his thigh, no doubt aiming for his groin. An instinct honed by years of training had Troy rolling out of the way at the last second. Ignoring the flare of pain, he was on his bare feet and hammered out with his fists, catching the assailant in the gut. He smashed another into their ribs.

Lights sprang to life in the closest vans.

A punch landed on his left ear. Head ringing and assailed with instant dizziness, Troy reeled backwards. It took only seconds for him to regain his equilibrium. Even that short time frame had taken too long. The second stranger had disappeared between the maze of caravans, cabins and vehicles.

He'd never find them in the dark.

A door creaked open from a nearby cabin. "You okay, mate?" called a hoarse voice.

He hesitated a beat, then decided the people living in the park needed to know possible thieves were on the loose. "All good. Thanks. But best keep your door locked. Someone tried to steal my camping gear."

"Bloody kids," growled the man before slamming his door shut.

They weren't kids. Troy might not have gotten a glimpse of their faces but there was a big difference between a youth's outline and a fully-grown man. He whistled and Chip came bounding towards him, a happy grin on her face, even if her hackles remained stiff and upright. "Good girl." He patted her and ruffled her ears before returning to his camp to mull over the night's foray. He had learned one important thing; whoever the thieves were, one of them was trained in self-defence. Possibly ex-military – and that begged the question of what the devil they were doing in Bindarra Creek? What had they been looking for? He had little of value with him, merely his camping gear, a couple of spare sets of clothes in a duffle bag, and his car, a beat-up, thirty-year old Holden ute. The would-be thieves had taken no notice of his vehicle. His car keys had been inside the duffle bag which had sat inside the tent. Now the contents were strewn over the damp ground and would need a good wash before he could wear any of them.

Muttering under his breath, he gathered up the soiled clothes and stuffed them into a garbage bag, before tidying up his camping gear and finding his keys half-buried in a muddy puddle. It would be good to see some sunshine and an end to the rain, but the weather bureau had declared La Niña would be hanging around all winter. Still, that meant the white-water kayaking would be sweet – whenever he managed to complete this 'mission'. Things were a lot more complicated in Edwina Lette's life than either he or his parents had imagined.

The wind picked up, and he shivered; just as well he'd worn trackpants and a tee to bed. An Army habit he had yet to rid himself of; ensuring he was ready for anything. His bare toes felt like blocks of ice. He ensured his tent front flaps were snug before he dried his feet. He slipped inside his sleeping bag and pulled the blanket over Chip who had jammed her cold body close. Sleep would be a lost cause. He had a couple of hours before dawn, and he had a lot to process.

By the time a pale sun crept over the horizon, he hadn't come to any conclusion except to wonder whether the thieves were connected with the intruder at Fig Tree Lodge. Of course, the house was full of antiques however there had been no indication anything had been stolen. He needed to check that with Edwina and Dodge.

After a hot shower he rummaged up a breakfast of baked beans for him and a bowl of dry dog food for Chip. He then made use of the laundromat. As soon as his clothes were dry and re-packed, he headed to the office and settled his account. It was time he took up the offer and moved into Fig Tree Lodge.

First, he had a few places to visit.

Fifteen minutes later, he pulled up outside the police station and checked the time. Another ten minutes before opening. He sipped the coffee he'd purchased from the Cyprus Café moments earlier while he waited and lowered the window on the passenger side of the cabin. Chip promptly stuck her head out and sniffed the air, still fresh from the cold night and no doubt brimming with the wonderful scents of the countryside that only a doggy nose could detect. It wasn't long before a police paddy-wagon turned into a narrow driveway and disappeared behind the building.

Troy swallowed the last mouthful of coffee before screwing the lid onto his stainless steel coffee mug. He and Chip exited the ute and headed to the front door which had just been opened by the young male constable. Donaldson, if he remembered correctly.

"Morning, mate. Wondered if I could have a word with the Senior Constable?" Troy gave an easy smile.

The young cop's smooth brown skin broke into a wide grin. "Sure ting. Come inside. Abby's just getting every-ting sorted for the day."

"Are you from Jamaica?"

The constable rolled his eyes as he waved Troy past. "Twas born in St Lucia but been here in Australia since I was ten and still can't shake the accent."

"I wouldn't bother trying, mate. I bet the girls love it."

"I wish!" He extended his hand. "In case you've forgotten, I'm Constable AJ Donaldson."

Troy shook hands and indicated for Chip to wait outside. "Your surname sounds familiar."

"Dad is our local mayor. You may have heard him on our local radio. Tis morning he gave a segment on winter gardening – his new hobby. If you'll take a seat, I'll tell Ab…I mean Senior Constable Taylor you want to talk with her." With another smile, AJ wandered behind the counter to the far end of the room where the policewoman was in conversation with a fair-haired man. They both looked up and gave Troy the once-over. As if satisfied he presented no threat, the male cop turned back to his computer while the policewoman tugged her vest down before marching over.

"Mr Davidson? What can I do for you?"

"Morning. I wondered if there'd been any progress on the break-in at Fig Tree Lodge."

"Oh? Are you asking on behalf of the family?" She waved him to a seat but remained standing, plucking out her notebook and pen as if she was about to interrogate a suspect.

"Actually, yes, since I am family." He leaned back in the plastic chair, deliberately folding his body into a relaxed stance.

"I remember your connection to Ms Lette. Very well. Wait a moment please." She went to a desk and retrieved a folder before returning. After running her gaze over the top sheet, she dragged a rolling chair over and sat. Her stare drilled into him as she spoke. "No fingerprints were found at the scene. Neither did we find whatever was used to cosh Mr Verne on the head. The blood on the step was matched to him, presumably dropped from the weapon on the intruder's departure."

Troy frowned as he cast his mind back to the part he'd

played. "Were there any fingerprints on the books that were on the library floor?"

"None. However, we did find a page that was either torn out or ripped out by accident in the grounds. There was a smudged partial on one corner. We're running it through our data base but don't hold much hope. The sample is too incomplete to be of much use unless we catch the culprit." She lowered her eyes to the file and turned a page. "We canvassed the entire street. No one saw anything that could be helpful."

Troy smiled. "No strangers in town?"

"Well, there is you." Senior Constable Taylor closed the folder with a snap. "A few tourists have trickled in, a couple staying at the caravan park and another lot at the motel. They have been questioned. There are a few campers up in Akuna National Park; there for the white-water rafting I believe. AJ and the Senior Sergeant are heading out there this afternoon. Let's talk about you, Mr Davidson. Where did you get those bruises on your knuckles? Looks to me as if you've been in a fight recently."

Natalie had warned him the policewoman knew her onions. He had to admit he was surprised she'd noticed the minor red abrasions adorning his hands. That would teach him to allow preconceptions to cloud his judgement. He'd thought – remote, small country town would equal slow, hayseed community. He had never been more wrong and realised the longer he stayed, the more he liked this way of life. "That's the reason why I popped in this morning," he said and went on to describe the earlier events.

The Senior Constable sighed and rose to her feet. "Just what I needed before I've had my cuppa – paperwork – not. Okay, let's get your statement down."

He followed her over to her desk where he sat again, in another hard plastic chair while she shoved an A4 notepad towards him. Ten minutes later he was finished, his statement recorded into the computer, and he had signed the printed document.

"Anything else?" She quirked an eyebrow.

"There was something." Heat crawled up his neck at her inquisitive stare. "It's about that bloke, Ernest Verne. What do you know about him?"

To her credit, her expression remained impassive. "Only what he has told us."

"You haven't checked him out, then?" His mobile blared.

Senior Constable Taylor waited.

Troy made no move to answer his phone. Eventually, the call stopped.

"At this stage, no. He is the victim here, Mr Davidson. The medical report is quite specific – there is no way he could have done that injury himself, and it didn't occur by falling over or down the stairs." Taylor linked her fingers together and settled back into her chair giving the impression she wasn't going anywhere until she had her answers. "Do you have reason to suspect him of… well, I guess that's another question isn't it? What do you suspect him of?"

His phone pinged as a message came through. Fishing out his mobile, he checked the ID. His father. Again. Jaw tightening, he met the policewoman's steady gaze. "Nothing. I thought it strange that he arrives in town and soon after is attacked. I wondered whether *he* was the target, rather than simply being in the wrong place at the wrong time." Troy rubbed his bristly chin.

"We're looking into every angle, trust me. We may be country but we're just as capable as city cops."

He fought the urge to squirm under her hard glare. "Of course. I didn't mean to imply otherwise. Please, call me Troy."

"Don't forget, we're also looking into the Army," called AJ from his stance behind the counter where he was tapping away on a computer.

Senior Constable Taylor added when Troy raised his eyebrows, "I'm surprised you weren't aware of this, Mr Davidson, seeing how you are ex-military. A few months ago, the Army began to set up a training facility in the area. There may well be times when the national park is off-limits to civilians while they are running an exercise. This of course means, that we are seeing an influx of soldiers in town."

"No, I wasn't aware. I've not kept up to date with military news. Is it complete?" A surge of interest spiked through Troy.

"No idea, to be honest, but if it isn't, they must be close. AJ is correct; what it means is that we have another pool of people that may have to be contacted. That brings me to my next point." She paused and Troy braced himself.

"The same could be said of you, Mr Davidson. You are a stranger to town. You arrive. Fig Tree Lodge is broken into. Mr Verne attacked. Now you say someone attempted to – exactly what? Steal your camping gear? Is there a connection here, sir?" Taylor checked the time on her watch. "You don't report the incident to us until a good three hours later. Meaning, you have packed up your gear making it impossible for us to gather any evidence. Makes me wonder if you have something to hide."

Troy stood. "I think we're done. Thank you for your time." Shoulders rigid, he marched from the police station. Coming here had been a mistake, because it appeared the police now had *him* in their sights as the number one suspect.

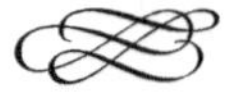

CHAPTER 9

[Telegram]
HELIOPOLIS, CAIRO.
25TH AUG., 1915.

With heavy heart advise Alfred killed in action on eighth. Mitchell.

Ernest couldn't wait to return to Fig Tree Lodge and as soon as Monday's early morning rounds had finished, he pressed the doctor to release him. If he hurried, he could cadge a lift with Ms Lette's grandson when he finished his shift at the hospital. After signing what felt like a zillion forms, he hurried outside and waved Dodge down just as the younger man reached his old Land Rover. "Do you mind?"

"Course not, mate. Hop in." Dodge unlocked the doors.

A sigh of relief escaped as Ernest settled into the seat.

"Rough night?" Dodge queried as he put the four-wheel drive into motion, turning out onto the road.

Ernest snapped his seatbelt on and planted his feet, shod in dusty shoes neatly together on the floor. "Everyone was very kind, but I felt a bit of a fraud taking up a bed when I only had a knock on the head."

"Concussion can be serious. I guess the docs wanted to make sure you were one hundred percent okay before they let you go."

Ernest turned to face the other man. "Have there been any developments in locating the intruder?"

"Nope." Dodge fought back a yawn as he slowed the car for Bindarra Creek's only roundabout.

Tension bled from Ernest's shoulders. He was still safe for the time being. How much longer he had before the police cottoned on to him giving an alias was another matter. If he was lucky, they would do a perfunctory job with investigating the break-in and his assault then move on. That blonde policewoman; she had struck Ernest as someone who lived for the law. Which meant at any moment, she could front up with more questions. Should he fess up to Natalie before that happened? It had all seemed so simple making his plans in his white-walled, soulless apartment. It had never occurred to him that someone could chisel through his armour and stir stupid, weak emotions into life.

Shifting in his seat, Ernest stared out the window as they traversed the quiet streets. He shivered in his thin shirt. Another cold, wintry day had dawned. Leaves and the odd scrap of rubbish blew along the footpath in the blustery wind. Overhead the clouds hung low and sullen, like a sulky child before a tantrum, not that he knew anything about kids. He'd always kept well out of their way – they were as alien to him as a spaceship. No, his interests had always been safely rooted in the past.

The vehicle jerked to a halt, and he realised they'd arrived.

Switching off the engine, Dodge smiled. "There'll be a hot brekkie waiting for us. Come on, mate. I'm starving."

A sense of comradeship enfolded Ernest. He'd been on digs, both small and large. He'd lectured in universities, attended conferences all over the world; and yet never, never had he experienced feeling like he was... one of them.

More than a little shaken and fighting the doubt that seemed to grow stronger each day, he followed Dodge into the warm kitchen, taking care to wipe his damp shoes on the entrance mat. He was welcomed by Dodge's wife, Tessa with a smile and waved into a seat. His stomach growled as aromatic scents of eggs and bacon hit his nostrils. Perfect. For the first time since... well, he couldn't really remember when... he relaxed in the company of others.

Breakfast seemed to go on forever as, no sooner had he sat down, every member of the household had streamed into the kitchen, even the two kids, demanding to know how he was and then wanting to discuss the events of last Friday. As he sipped another cup of tea and nibbled on the last hot, buttered crumpet, no irritation simmered inside. Instead, he felt... content. If they could see him now, none of his work colleagues would recognise him, kicking back, smiling and enjoying the moment.

Eventually, he stirred and excused himself. After a hot shower and a fresh set of clothes, he left the house and stepped out into the cold day. He'd been regaled by Ms Lette of the finds in the attic and marvelled over the discovery of the Dead Man's Penny she'd shown him. He wanted to roam the library where books had been disturbed to see if he could work out what the intruder sought. It would have to wait until later that night. First, he wanted to call on Natalie.

"Good morning!" called a feminine voice from behind him.

Looking around, he found an elderly lady and an equally elderly man pedalling a tandem bicycle. The bike wobbled to and fro over the road as they approached. He jumped out of the way.

"Lovely to see you again, Harold," panted the old man wrapped up in a scarf, a trench coat and checked pants, which looked suspiciously like pyjamas, and who clearly had mistaken Ernest for someone else.

The plump woman had a clerical dog collar around her neck, and they both wore Sea Eagles beanies. They gripped the handlebars so tight, even Ernest could see the gleam of pale bones through their skins.

The female vicar managed a quick smile. "Sorry, we're still getting the hang of riding together, but it's fabulous exercise."

Grinning, Ernest waved them on and watched as they careened down the street. It would be a miracle if they didn't have an accident. He winced as, for one breath-taking moment, the bike looked as if it was about to crash head-on into a telegraph pole. At the last second, it veered to the right, over the footpath and into a ditch where it swayed before slowly sinking to the left. Both riders hopped off and laughed as they pulled the bike back onto the road, before setting off again.

Suddenly, the urge to have a bike of his own was alarmingly tempting. A vision of riding the tree-lined streets of Bindarra Creek rose. Perhaps there'd even be others with him.

Enough of this nonsense. In a few days, he would return to his old life. He picked up the pace and was soon outside Natalie's house. He scowled as he spotted the beaten-up ute parked in the drive. That Troy fellow, if he wasn't mistaken. After brushing down the overcoat he wore, he smoothed back his hair and knocked on the door. Ms Lette had informed him earlier of the time Natalie would be home from her cleaning work; that plus the fact Troy was also here told him she hadn't been mistaken.

Footsteps approached on the path behind him then stopped. Ernest turned around but whoever it was must have gone into another yard. The shrubs growing close to the side of the house rustled. Probably a cat. Even as that thought crossed his mind, his skin prickled. Could someone be following him?

Never a fanciful man, he shrugged it off and gave another knock. His heart skipped a beat as the door opened to reveal Natalie. Her face lit up with a smile so friendly, he could almost feel himself soften inside like ice cream in the summer sun.

"Ernest! How lovely. How's the head?"

"All good." His chest puffed up under the warmth of her concern. "I go back for a check up on Friday, when the stitches should come out."

"That's great. Come on in." Opening the door wider, she stepped back to allow him access.

He entered the living room where that Troy was sprawled in an armchair with a notebook in hand. On the coffee table in the centre of the room was stacked a plethora of items, too many to take in at first glance. There appeared to be no logic behind their placement. He had to restrain his urge to bring some kind of order. Several large plastic tubs, some with lids still on, were placed about the rug in front of the fireplace where embers glowed and emitted a homely warmth. Troy smiled and greeted him in an easy fashion.

Ernest wasn't snowed. He could sense the other fellow's wariness hidden beneath his casual air as they eyed each other off. He took a seat on the sofa and declined Natalie's offer of a hot drink. She knelt on the rug and launched into an account of what had been found in the attic, holding up various pieces for Ernest to examine. His rigid posture relaxed as he forgot all else and became lost in the fascination of looking into the past.

"Now, for the next part of our show." Natalie grinned and despite his hidden frustration, Ernest couldn't help his answering smile. Turning around, she grabbed something from a pile on top of the coffee table then held out a leather-bound book. "Matilda's diary. Remember, Ernest, I mentioned how there were three brothers who fought in World War I and they had a sister? This book is crammed full of rich detail about the lives of their family during that time."

Natalie's excitement was contagious.

He all but leapt from his chair when she waved the diary around and showed him the copious notes she had made from the contents. "That's fascinating." He didn't have to fake his curiosity as he stared at the book in her hand. "I did mention that I was a history teacher."

She laughed. "I knew you'd want to look at it. Ernest, I would really appreciate if you could let me know your thoughts on the points I've jotted down. If you think they're sufficiently interesting for the book." She handed both the diary and her notebook to him. "While you're doing that, how about I get us some juice and sandwiches."

Heart thumping so loud, it was a wonder the others couldn't hear, Ernest set the old book on the chair cushion beside him and using his fingertips, opened the cover.

Troy stirred. "I can give you a hand if you like, Nat?"

"No need," said Natalie. "Stay where it's warm. The kitchen is like an ice box." One more smile shared impartially between the two men, and she was out the door.

Left alone with Troy, Ernest did his best to ignore the other's brooding presence as he began to read through Natalie's jottings, comparing them with the pages she'd flagged in the diary with sticky notes. Taking a pen from the coffee table, he inserted a few suggestions into the notebook.

"See anything of value?" Troy's smooth voice interrupted.

More than a little annoyed, Ernest placed his finger to mark the page and glanced up. "It's certainly an interesting window into their lives."

"I was at the police station, this morning."

"Oh, yes?"

"Have you made your formal statement, yet?"

Scowling, Ernest fought hard to stop the burn spreading over his cheeks. "No. I haven't had time. I was only discharged this morning." Now why the dickens did he feel the need to explain his actions? To *him* of all people!

"I would have thought you'd be keen to have whoever coshed you caught." Troy leaned back and tented his fingers. "Senior Constable Taylor is hot on the case. She's making all sorts of enquiries."

Ernest dropped his gaze to the diary. If that was true, then his time in this small town had to end – soon.

The brittle silence was broken by Natalie's return, bearing a tray which she set down on top of a sideboard. "Let's have some lunch. Ernest? How do you take your tea?"

"White with one sugar, please."

After handing around mugs of tea, she took her own and settled on the floor beside the laden coffee table once more. "Please, help yourself to the sandwiches and biscuits."

Troy stood and moved to the sideboard, but Ernest smiled, saying, "I'll just have the tea for the moment, thank you."

"Just wait until you see what's in this box." Natalie's

face lit up with a broad smile when she patted one of the plastic tubs before sipping her tea.

Sitting forward, Ernest now saw the side had been marked with black texta. *Egypt.* And his breathing all but seized.

Could it be…? Was it…?

Natalie set her mug onto the floor and with a flourish, ripped off the lid as Troy ambled across the room, a plate laden with sandwiches in his hand. Even he grinned, as Ernest all but fell onto his knees and shuffled closer.

"You'll like this, mate." Troy stuffed bread and cheese into his mouth and sank into a crouch.

They all gathered around the plastic box as if it was the ark of the covenant.

Almost as if she was offering up a gift to the gods, Natalie lifted out an oddly shaped item bundled in a thin cloth. Unpeeling the wrapping, she held out her hands with the item cradled in her palms.

"May I?" Ernest's eyes widened and his every nerve tightened.

Natalie nodded, extending her hands and Troy crowded closer. "Please, do. What do you think it is?"

They both waited as Ernest examined the piece with a careful touch. He couldn't believe his luck. The moment he'd set eyes on Natalie's short podcast about locating World War I historical artefacts in some old house, he'd felt a settling of the unrest that had plagued him since childhood. Bindarra Creek. Fig Tree Lodge. That was where the answers lay.

He'd been right.

"Well?" Troy's quiet query dragged him from his internal reflections.

Looking up, he found both waiting as if they were hanging on his every word. Whatever reservations the other man felt about him were nowhere to be seen. He was caught up in the same excitement that welled in Ernest's breast and sparkled in Natalie's eyes.

Ernest's voice shook as he said, "This is a statue of the ancient Egyptian goddess Isis and it's very old. Of course, I would need to run tests, however I believe it dates to the Ptolemaic Period, possibly somewhere between 332 and 30 BC. The reason I'm assigning this timeline is that the statue looks like it is made from a type of glassy ceramic often used in that period, called faience. The pale blue colour of the glaze is another factor."

"It is beautiful," said Natalie. "Isis – what was she known for?"

"Fertility, motherhood, death, healing and rebirth. She was also known as the goddess of magic. Did you know that it's believed Queen Cleopatra identified with Isis, and that she would dress like the goddess when she attended public events in Egypt?"

"Is it worth anything?"

"Could it have belonged to her?" Both Troy and Natalie spoke at once. They paused, looked at each other, and laughed.

Their gazes held – for too long and Natalie flushed when she finally glanced away. They shared a history. Whether it would rekindle Ernest didn't know but he couldn't deny how right they looked together. Something cold and dark slithered into his heart. His lips thinned and he could barely get the words past his clenched jaw. At this rate, he'd be down to his gums in no time. "A collector or any museum would pay handsomely for this piece."

Natalie leaned closer, almost touching Ernest's arm. "There's several chips plus that big crack. And the glaze has faded a fair bit. Might diminish the price somewhat."

"True. But you can't put a price on its historical value." He wished she would move away, especially with that hawk-eyed Troy watching her every move. Ernest was no fool. Even though a romantic liaison had never come his way, his past had sharpened his ability to sense the yearnings of others. There were times in the loneliness of the night when he wondered whether this sense was because of his own well-buried fantasy of something more for himself. By daylight, his inner walls were impenetrable. He needed no one. Natalie might be a nice lady, but nothing and no one had ever come close to being more desirable than his obsession. He focussed on the object in his hands and his chest expanded as he thought of the glory that would soon be his for the taking. All he had to do was dilute their interest in the statue and he was well on his way. "I have a contact or two that may be able to help. Let me borrow the statue while I make some calls. Plus, the piece needs to be dated correctly, and to do that I need to run tests."

"Sounds good, but I don't think it's necessary for you to take the statue – not yet, anyway. Given this is family property and as a consequence, family money on the table, I prefer that we keep it close until we make a decision." Troy gave a pleasant smile, but his expression was guarded.

Ernest bared his teeth. "Then strictly speaking the statue should remain in the possession of Ms Lette in Fig Tree Lodge rather than… where is it you're staying again? A tent, I believe from what Ms Lette has told me. Hardly what I would term secure."

"I've been offered the converted stables at the Lodge. Looks like we're going to be seeing a lot of each other."

Wonderful. Just what Ernest didn't need, macho man, breathing down his neck.

Seemingly oblivious to his and Troy's rooster posturing, Natalie slipped the statue from his hands, re-wrapped it then placed it inside the container. She packed loose rags around it for extra protection, before securing the lid. "I'll speak to Edwina tomorrow. In the meantime, no one but us knows about it so it can stay right here with all the other bric-a-brac."

Ernest couldn't tear his gaze from the plastic tub. "Were you aware that Queen Cleopatra VII was more than just a pretty face? She was a brilliant strategist, spoke nine languages, and commanded armies. Muslim scholars wrote that she was a scholar, a scientist, a gifted philosopher and a chemist. She knew how to build a fleet, suppress an insurrection and control a currency." His voice rang with the vibrancy of his passion. When he stopped, he became aware that the others were staring at him.

"You know a lot about her," Natalie ventured. She patted the tub containing the statue, looking thoughtful, likely remembering his earlier comment about the goddess Isis.

He willed himself to relax, sitting back in the chair and casually crossing his legs. As if his life's work was not mere metres from him. It took all his willpower, not to grab the statue and run. Soon, he told himself, soon he'd have everything he had ever wanted. All he had to do was wait for the optimum time.

CHAPTER 10

[Extract taken from Matilda Lette's diary. Undated.]

These are such hard words to write. I cannot believe it is true and yet the ache in my heart and my unrelenting tears tells me it must be so. Another telegram arrived after lunch from the Melbourne barracks. Alfred is dead. His body lost in a carnage I cannot imagine. My eldest brother. The one I looked up to will never come home.

AFTER A FRIGID DAWN, a pale sun had finally broken through the last wisps of fog making a pleasant change from the past days of wind and cloud. Manning the stall she shared with Mrs Beatrix Fukuka, Natalie eyed her pineapple upside-down cake which had begun to show an alarming tendency to sag in the middle. Her elderly companion's efforts were much more professional; the icing on her light-as-air sponge was picture perfect, and the marzipan flowers adorning each cupcake would have done any chef proud. Still, it didn't matter too much what Natalie's cakes looked like – as long as they sold. She'd gone a little more adventurous than her usual carrot and walnut loaves. Along with the wonky cake, she'd also tried her hand at several small Bakewell tarts as well as three family-sized apple pies. Stamping her feet, she wished more people would show up on the nearly empty main street. As soon as she had sold her quota, she was heading straight to the café for a hot cuppa and scrambled eggs.

The cake and bring-and-buy stalls had been a staple of community life for some time and now ran on the first Tuesday of the month. When the weather was bad, everyone adjourned to the CWA hall. Fingers crossed, today was shaping up just fine. All up, there were seven 'stalls' which were simply trestle tables set up on the foot-path. A couple were lucky enough to have shade pergolas protecting them from the weather. Natalie and Mrs Fukuka were not amongst the lucky. Mostly operated by members of the CWA, the stalls usually made a tidy sum which they donated to whatever charity was flavour of the month. Swing band music blared from the further-most stall. Natalie didn't have to look to know who oversaw that one – Samantha Morgan who was the wife of the police Senior Sergeant, her grandmother Sara Luchetti, and Dulcie Stirling.

At the stall to her right, Mrs Fukuka's husband, Makki, had a wonderful display of their home-made, organic wine, jams and pickled preserves – all from their own quite extensive garden. Last payday, Natalie had purchased a bottle of brandy to enjoy a small glass after dinner now and then. She'd been blown away by the smooth, rich flavour, honey tinged with the tang of blackberries, clover and nutmeg.

"Makki, if you have more bottles of that awesome brandy, can you put one aside for me please?"

"For you, Natalia san, not a problem." The sweet man beamed, his weathered skin crinkling up like crumpled paper, as he plucked a bottle from the table and handed it over.

Natalie paid and stashed the bottle inside her backpack which resided by her feet. She blew on her fingers to warm them. "I've got hot tea in my thermos, would you both like a cup?"

"Oh, please, that would be lovely." Mrs Fukuka gave her trade-mark gentle smile while Makki gave a thumbs up and a wide grin.

After handing out the tea in the enamel mugs she'd brought with her and accepting a buttered scone in return, Natalie sat in her camping chair and took stock of the street. Old Ted and his wife Betty trundled past, so wrapped up against the chill that she only recognised them by way of Ted's new, red walker on which sat their almost as old cocker spaniel, Fernando, snug in a basket lashed to the walker's arms. The dog was well protected against the icy wind in his padded dog-coat. Makki pressed on them a bottle of home-made pickles and another of raspberry jam, while his wife handed them a string bag bulging with spinach and cabbage without asking for payment. It was a well-known fact that the pensioners, like others in town, were struggling with the rising cost of living. Since Ted's hip operation last spring, his gardening days were over.

Natalie slipped one of the apple pies into a paper bag and tucked it in beside old Fernando. She discreetly popped some coins into the tin by way of payment. The pensioner couple didn't like charity. Betty insisted she'd drop a rabbit casserole over to the Fukuka's later that week for them and Beatrix's sister, Mrs Pamela Brown, with whom they shared a house.

Business remained slow as the morning passed but began to pick up closer to lunch time. Natalie sold an apple pie to Cleo Kendall while Ryan Rossiter snapped up several cupcakes and some jam. Just before twelve, Dr Fatima Maloof pulled up in her snazzy dark blue Lexus, wearing one of her colourful hijabs over her black hair.

She rushed over and inspected their wares. "I'll have one of those apple pies, please, Natalie. I will be brave and take the odd-looking pineapple cake." Her dark eyes twinkled, then she turned to Mrs Fukuka and Makki. "Half a dozen cupcakes, two jams and a bottle of your organic tomato and basil paste. Thank you." She paid, loaded everything in her car, then visited another three stalls, before returning to her car with her purchases, and driving off.

"Two years ago, we would have sold everything by ten o'clock," Mrs Fukuka mused as she placed the money into the tin.

"Yes, we need more tourists. But it may be picking up. Look, these guys definitely look like tourists." Natalie pointed at the approaching jeep. A couple of hang-gliders were strapped to the roof and camping gear was stuffed into the rear. Two blokes with fair bleached hair, like surfers, sat in the front, laughing and chatting. Another bloke sprawled in the back with his head lolling against the window, as if he'd had a heavy night. "Hardly the sort to buy cake or china teacups."

Pity the majority of travellers appeared to be campers or young thrill-seekers, which meant they might not spend much money in town, except of course when they visited the two pubs.

An Army truck rumbled past with who knew what packed in crates on its tray. The soldiers in front didn't even glance at the stalls. Perhaps once the new training facility was up and running, their families might move to town. Or at least, the soldiers might come to forage for something different than the food they were served in the mess. At the next CWA meeting she would broach the idea of making crafts for soldiers wanting to send gifts home.

It wasn't until one-thirty, before all the perishables and fresh food had been sold. Makki trotted off and returned a few minutes later with his old ute into which they proceeded to load their tables and pergolas as well as a few crates of the unsold wine, preserves and the bric-a-brac. Mrs Fukuka hopped into the front seat of the cabin. A few of the other ladies including Natalie, hurried off to the CWA hall. She couldn't deny the heady burn of delight when she noticed Troy sitting in his parked car as if he'd been waiting for her.

Upon seeing her, he and Chip climbed out with his dog forging ahead, tail wagging in a frenzy, as if she hadn't seen Natalie in weeks. Her blood surged through her veins, showing no doubt in her flushed face as she waited for them near the entrance.

Troy gave that slow sexy smile of his, and heat fluttered in the pit of her belly. "Aunt Edwina told me you'd be here. Thought I'd drop by and give you a lift home."

"I've got my bike." She indicated her trusty steed propped up against the fence.

"Not a problem. It can ride in the back of my ute."

"I have to help unload our gear first. Do you mind waiting?"

"How about I give you a hand?" He strode over to where Makki's ute was parked and introduced himself to the small group milling about the tray. It wasn't long before Mrs Fukuka was locking the front door of the hall and everyone went their separate ways.

When Troy opened his ute's passenger door, Chip jumped in. A wry smile flickered across Troy's face. "Do you mind sharing the front seat?"

Natalie laughed. "Of course not. It's too cold for her to ride in the back." She slid in beside the dog. After a bit of pushing and shoving to get Chip to shift out of the way, Natalie managed to get her seat belt done up just as Troy finished stowing her bike in the rear. She positioned her backpack on her lap.

"How did you go with your cake stall?" he asked as he settled behind the steering wheel.

"Good. Everything sold, even my pineapple upside down cake. What have you been doing this morning?"

He pulled out onto the road and grinned. "Been spending time with Aunt Edwina. She's quite a character."

A little of Natalie's glow faded. "Have you been badgering her to sell?" *Did I just say that out loud?* She placed her hand over her mouth.

Troy shot her a hard glance over the top of Chip's head. "I didn't mention it. But I did call Mum while I was there, and they had a bit of a chin-wag. No idea what they talked about as I left them to it. I thought it might be nice if they re-connected." His fingers tapped a quick beat on the wheel, and he frowned. "I didn't see Ernest. Thought he might be with you at the cake sale."

"I haven't seen him since yesterday."

"That's a surprise. He seemed very enthusiastic about that statue."

"Well, he would be, wouldn't he? He's a history teacher and he loves all things Egyptian. It wasn't a secret. He said as much on his profile." *Good heavens. Why can't I keep my mouth shut?* Squeezing her eyes closed, she hoped Troy hadn't twigged. A futile hope.

"What profile? Are you talking about social media?" He flicked the indicator on, and they turned into her street.

"Kind of. I met him on a dating app."

He pulled up outside her house and turned the engine off. "That surprises me. I would have thought meeting people through social media would be too much of a risk for you."

"Then, maybe you don't know me as well as you think you do," she snapped and reached for the door handle.

Uncertain whether she was annoyed with Troy or irritated with herself for caring about his opinion, she shouldered her backpack and marched to the front door.

"I didn't mean to upset you." He jogged after her.

"You didn't," she tried for a lofty *I couldn't care less* voice as she retrieved her keys from her bag.

Acutely aware of Troy standing so close that she could feel the warmth of his body and smell the fresh tang of his aftershave, she went to place her key in the lock. The door moved under her hand. She pulled back, saying over her shoulder, "How strange. I'm certain I locked up when I left but it's not even closed. Perhaps Noah has come home early."

"Wait." Troy placed a hand over hers, gently pulling her away from the door. "Let me go first."

"What, you don't think… ? No, Noah is probably home and has forgotten to latch the door." Even so, she stepped aside so Troy could brush past, noting that he placed his elbow on the timber and pushed the door open fully. He waved her back when she went to follow as he walked softly along the short hallway then paused at the living room entrance. His sharp intake of air caused her to forget his warning.

She rushed forward and peered around his bulk. *"Oh no!"* Her heart gave a nervous jump against her ribs. The two armchairs and coffee table were overturned. The floor lamp lay shattered over the rug while every ornament and photo had been flung from the fireplace's mantlepiece and smashed. Their old television had been shoved off the entertainment unit and lay face down. Books had been ripped from the timber bookcase and littered the floor; many with pages torn out. The plastic tubs which had stored their finds from Edwina's attic had been up-ended. It looked as if the tubs had been shaken so that everything inside would tumble out. And there was a massive hole in the plaster, like someone had punched their fist through the wall.

Her landlord was going to have a fit once he found out she'd been burgled. She moved about the room then ducked into the dining room and kitchen. "How strange. I don't think anything has been taken."

Shoving her keys into her pocket, she crouched to pick up the shattered pieces of the Egyptian dog statue. Tears stung and a lump clogged her throat. "I don't think this is fixable." She stared at the destruction wrought inside her living room. "Either way, securing money for the artifacts is no longer an option. We'll be lucky to salvage sufficient items to furnish one room in the Lodge."

"Don't touch anything else. Phone the police while I check the rest of the house. Chip, stay." Turning, he disappeared out the door while the dog padded over and licked Natalie's cheek.

She buried her face in Chip's warm hair, breathing in the doggy scent and gaining a measure of comfort from her wagging tail. After a couple of seconds, she wiped away her tears and gave Chip a *thank you* scratch behind her ears. Shrugging her backpack off her shoulders, she undid the main zipper and searched for her phone. Her fingers brushed over Matilda's diary, and she froze.

What if the intruder had been after the diary? Or the

Isis statue? But why? And who else apart from Edwina and Ernest knew that she had both in her possession?

Oh my... ! The Isis statue!

Forgetting her phone. Troy. The damage in her lounge room. Natalie snatched up her backpack in one hand, launched upright and raced for the outside laundry. Her feet tangled together as she banged open the kitchen door and she almost fell flat on her face. Chip barked and ran circles around her as if she thought it a game. Troy yelled something to her from inside the house. Re-gaining her balance she sprinted a couple of metres to the old shed. Knees like jelly she skidded to a halt outside a door made of planks a good fifteen centimetres thick and which was so old that Noah had speculated the timber had petrified. No fancy twenty-first century lock here. It was an old-fashioned mechanism and the key was the size of a teaspoon. The only copy was on her keyring.

"What's going on? Are you okay?" Troy landed behind her, breathing hard.

"The Isis statue." She inserted the key and turned. The lock clicked free and Troy pushed the door open. Inside the old windowless building was a tub, the washing machine, a toilet in the corner, and four – untouched – plastic tubs. "The top one has the statue in it."

Sagging against the wall, she looked at Troy and gave a shaky laugh. "Thank heavens. At least, some things haven't been damaged. For a second I thought… I mean, it was the craziest idea that maybe whoever broke in had been after the diary and the Isis statue."

Chip padded around the small area, sniffing with gusto at the dust mites.

"If the statue is here, was the diary in the house?"

"No." Straightening, she shook the backpack she still held. "I had it with me. I thought I'd make more notes while I was selling cakes."

"There I was thinking this was a quiet, country town where nothing much ever happens. I was never more wrong." He trailed a finger over her cheek. "You need new locks on your kitchen door. Whoever it was, jimmied their way inside with a crowbar."

"Looks like I need a lot of things. Noah is not going to be happy if the television is broken."

"One thing at a time. I'll see to the security side of things. But first, shall I check…?"

"Yes, please." She held her breath while Troy lifted the lid of the uppermost plastic tub and sifted amongst the contents.

His smile was broad when he looked at her. "Safe and sound."

"I'll make that phone call, and I could really do with a cuppa. What do you think we should do with the statue?"

"I think since no one but you and I know it's here, let's leave it. Besides, you're only guessing that's the reason you've been burgled. I understand there's new people in town living in the caravan park. Others are camping rough in the National Park. People can risk their liberty if they are in need."

"True, and times are difficult at the moment. I never thought of that." Relief flooded through her. What Troy said was logical and made more sense than her fanciful idea. From what Ernest had told her, only a collector or a historian would have any idea of the statue's value. Since the circle of people who even knew of its existence was minimal, the idea that someone was after it was laughable. After calling the police, she tucked her mobile away and locked up the shed. She entered the house to find Troy making tea in the kitchen and Chip watching expectantly.

He shrugged. "I was going to clean up then remembered the police will probably want to see the evidence for themselves. Maybe see if there's any fingerprints left behind. Here, sit down sweetheart, you look done in." He pulled out a chair.

Instead, Natalie turned into his warmth. She dropped her pack on the table and wrapped her arms around his waist, resting her head over the steady beat of his heart. His arms enclosed her. For Natalie, it was as if the years between them had never happened. She was back where she once was; giddy with love and all the delight life could give.

"Natalie." Her name on his lips, said in that deep tone of voice that vibrated through to her soul was all it took.

All those years of loneliness and lost time – suddenly it was too much, and she was tired of pretending. She lifted her face and met his kiss with her own. A kiss of hunger, yearning, regret – and hope. A kiss that took her to heights she'd dreamt of almost every night for years.

They drew apart, and simply stood gazing into each other's eyes.

As if they were dragged from the very depths of her heart where she'd hidden those long-ago dreams, the words whispered past her lips, "Will you stay?"

CHAPTER 11

Fig Tree House,
Bindarra Creek, NSW.
25th September, 1915.

Dear Gregory,

It has been some time since we have had a letter from you or Mitchell. We understand finding time to write must be hard but we worry so. All mother can talk about is having you both home again and often spends time in Alfred's room. Father leaves more chores to me and my days are busy. I often think of you so far away and how different it must be for you now. Spring has finally arrived after a hard winter. I picked some bottlebrush flowers and a sprig from the willow tree near our special place. I enclose them with this letter. I hope they will remind you of all of us waiting for you and give you the strength you may need. May God keep you in his care.

Write soon. Your loving twin, Matilda.

"Maybe you should have our number on speed dial," grumbled the blonde policewoman as she tucked her notebook away. She nodded to her younger counterpart who'd been taking pictures of the damage and dusting for prints, then rose to her feet. "I've never received so many calls from one person! Okay, if you think of anything else, give me a call. Again." She flashed a quick grin. "I'll leave you to clean up the mess."

Her sharp gaze swept over Troy in such a knowing fashion he wondered if she could read his mind. He was glad to see her walk out the door. His palms itched to hold Natalie in his arms once more, not that that would happen any time soon with Noah hovering by his elbow. The boy had arrived home from school a good thirty minutes ago, agog and excited about all the police action in his own house. Probably would be spouting off about the break-in for weeks, if he knew boys. Troy had been impressed when the police turned up a mere six minutes after Natalie's phone call. However, the processing of the scene had taken longer than he'd imagined. He had hoped for more alone time with Natalie before school ended for the day – a forlorn hope as it turned out. If Troy had to spend what little remained of the afternoon washing fingerprint dust off furniture, he didn't care. He'd be in the company of the woman who had never left his dreams.

Natalie entered the kitchen after seeing the police officers off and began to clear the table of the mugs and plates. The tiny shy glances she kept shooting him from under her lashes, sent quivers of anticipation zinging through his veins and heated his blood to fever point.

She'd asked him to stay.

He hoped she meant for the night. All night. In her bed.

Bloody hell. What if she meant he was to sleep on the couch? Well, time would tell and there was work to be done. "Where would you like me to start?"

She huffed out a breath. "I guess a couple of buckets of warm water and some sugar soap. We'll all grab a rag and if we work together, we should have that grey dust gone in no time."

"Ugh. I thought I could hang at the skate park with Drew and my mates?" Noah shoved his hands into his jeans pockets.

"Sorry hon. You do remember you're grounded all this week?"

"It was only PE!" grouched Noah.

"Don't care. I won't change my mind." Natalie waited until Noah gave a grudging nod before walking out the kitchen door. She headed towards the laundry.

The kid dragged out a chair and slumped into it, a sulky pout to his mouth. What help he would be remained to be seen but, so far, he seemed like a good kid.

Troy waited while Natalie unlocked the laundry door and entered. A few seconds later she re-appeared with buckets hanging from her arm, and re-locked the laundry door. She was certainly taking her role as caretaker of the statue seriously.

After snapping on the rubber gloves Natalie gave him, he took control of one bucket, pouring in the sugar soap then adding warm water from the kitchen tap. "How about you and I share a bucket, champ?" He smiled at Noah. Chip looked up from where she lay on the old lino floor and thumped her tail.

"If I have to." The boy hauled himself out of the chair and gave a massive hard-done-by sigh.

Natalie ignored him as she busied herself with the other bucket.

Grinning, Troy tossed the kid another pair of gloves. "Buckle up, buttercup."

"Hey!" Noah reddened as he caught the gloves mid-air.

"Gotta earn respect. Come on. Chip, stay there." Troy carried the bucket into the living room and without checking to see if the kid followed, set to cleaning the heaviest piece of furniture which to his mind, was the entertainment unit.

Noah crouched beside him and worked on wiping the thick finger-print dust from the television. "I hope this thing still works." He cast his mother a grin. "Or we'll have to get a new one."

"Keep dreaming, hon." Natalie smiled back as she cleaned the bookcase.

Troy paused and said, "Don't try to move that book-case, Nat. I'll do it."

"You do realise that I've been moving furniture and lifting stuff for years by myself."

"Not while I'm here."

A rich colour flushed over her cheeks and Troy's heartbeat quickened. When she refrained from arguing the toss, he couldn't fail to notice the interest in the boy's eyes.

"Mum says that you knew Dad ages ago. What was he like? I think it upsets Mum to talk about him too much." Noah lowered his voice and dropped his cloth into the bucket, causing water to slosh over the side. His wringing skills left a lot to be desired as he gave the rag a perfunctory squeeze before slapping it onto the television.

Troy winced as water ran over the screen. "Not too much water, mate, or that telly definitely *won't* work."

Nodding, the boy dutifully scooped up the rag then held it over the bucket and forced out more moisture. This time when he returned to the telly, he soaked up the water residue and made a better job of cleaning. "Do you mind talking about him?"

"Not in the least." Although Troy hoped like hell the kid wouldn't ask any probing questions about him and Natalie. Finished with the unit, he wriggled it into position. "Like your mum said, your father and I were at high school together. We came from different suburbs and attended mostly different classes, but we met on the footy team in our first year."

He leaned back on his heels as he remembered those golden years and smiled. "We hit it off straight away. He was always this super calm, patient guy while I couldn't keep still. But we had lots in common; we both liked the outdoors, playing soccer, or cricket; anything really that got us both out of the house. Your dad enjoyed action-adventure movies, science fiction and horror which meant we often spent a lot of time at the movies. He wasn't a bully but neither did he back down when it was important. He was a good mate," he finished softly.

"I don't remember him at all. There's photos of course; mainly of their wedding and lots of baby photos with me and him. I just wish I could picture him in my mind, or remember us doing stuff together."

Troy rubbed his face. "You know what, mate? I think I've got one of those home movies back at my parents' house. The one class that we did take together was drama – would you believe?"

Noah laughed. "Can't see it, to be honest."

"Yeah, and neither could my parents." Troy grinned. "Your dad and I made this short movie for our final assignment. Was supposed to be a horror story but the kids in our class laughed most of the way through it. We both played starring roles. I was the monster, and your dad was the hero that saved the town. I'll dig it out and send you a copy."

Noah said, "You could bring it yourself."

"I could at that; it's definitely worth thinking about." Troy glanced across the room and met Natalie's gaze.

Noah dipped his rag into the bucket again and wrung out the water. "It would be great to see you again, won't it Mum?"

Natalie blushed and said in a prim voice, "Of course, it's always nice to have visitors."

Her son's cheeky grin broadened. "When did you meet Mum?"

What a loaded question! This time it was Troy whose

face heated as the blasted kid fixed a far too innocent expression on his face.

"Your father introduced us. Now, Noah, if you've finished with the television, how about you start with the bric-a-brac, but first can you please get the broom?" Natalie intervened as she crossed the room and retrieved the wet cloth from her son. She shooed her son out of the room, then turned to Troy. "That was kind of you; about the movie."

"It's not a problem. I only hope I can find it and that Mum hasn't chucked it out. All my old books and trophies from school were boxed up years ago."

"Still kind." She hesitated, licked her lips then added, "Please don't feel obligated to bring it here personally."

"I want to; unless you prefer I didn't?"

His question hung in the air for several seconds before she answered.

"No objections." She spun around as if she was keen to hide her expression, and hurried over to the door, mumbling, "I need that broom."

He cleared his throat. "About tonight…"

She turned at the doorway and smiled. "I haven't changed my mind. I hope you like spaghetti bolognese, because that's what we're having for dinner."

"Sounds perfect."

The next few hours passed in a happy blur for Troy. He couldn't believe how right it felt to be cleaning house, helping prepare a meal and then eating it together with Natalie and her son. It was as if he was the last piece of a jigsaw puzzle that completed the picture of a family of three.

As they laughed and talked around the table, he determined that this time he wouldn't stuff it up. He'd do everything he could to become part of Natalie's life; and that included Noah. He liked the boy; he was kind, respectful and quick to help his mother around the house, even if that help was preceded by the normal teenage whining. His disposition was sunny, seeming not to hold onto resentment in a way that reminded him strongly of John. Noah was also mischievous with a teasing sense of humour that caused Troy to laugh more than he'd ever laughed around kids.

After dinner, they played a couple of rounds of Scrabble until Noah slouched off to bed, after wishing them a good night. Chip, who'd scored the remains of a barbecue chook for dinner, snored as she slept curled up on the rug. The fire crackled and hissed in the hearth, while some mindless sitcom droned away on the television. Troy was in seventh heaven when Natalie snuggled close to him on the sofa. He nuzzled her soft hair. "I can leave if you want."

"No." She shifted then placed her hands either side of his face. "I'd like you to stay the night with me." Her smile shot heat through his body like an exploding grenade.

"Yes, ma'am." He rose to his feet before scooping her into his arms. Biding Chip to stay, he carried Natalie into her bedroom where he made love to the woman he had never forgotten. The woman who had never left his heart.

Later, he couldn't say what woke him. Whether it was his sixth sense honed by years of active duty or a faint noise. Either way, he opened his eyes and tension flooded his system.

Curled into his side with her warm breath fanning his bare chest, Natalie stirred, mumbling, "Wassmatta?"

"Hush." Throwing back the doona, he slipped from the bed and sought his clothes, pulling on his pants and a tee-shirt. He bent over her, pressed her mobile into her hand, and whispered, "Don't make a sound and wait here. I thought I heard someone outside."

Taking care with each step he took, he sidled out of the bedroom and along the hall. A faint light shone through the living room window from the streetlight outside. His faithful guard dog lay sleeping by the fire, deaf to the world. He shook his head and paused to listen.

There it was again. Scratching like metal over metal. The noise came from the front door.

Someone was attempting to pick the new lock he'd installed that afternoon.

Chip finally stirred and padded over to him to sniff his hand. He fondled her ears and pushed her butt to get her to sit. Moving to the front door, he ever so carefully turned the lock and yanked open the door. The form looming on the step reared backwards with a gruff curse before jumping onto the ground and taking off like an Olympic runner.

Troy sprinted after him, Chip barking hysterically in front of him. When he reached the corner there was no sign of the intruder. Probably ducked into someone's yard and was even now climbing over the rear fence.

Pointless to stay on the hunt.

Whistling for Chip to return, he jogged back down the road to find both Natalie and Noah waiting outside the house. Chip bounded up to slather wet licks over the boy's face.

Noah said, "I can't believe you chased away a burglar. That is awesome!"

"I can't believe we have to call the police – again! Abby is not going to be happy." Natalie smiled wryly as she reached for her phone.

CHAPTER 12

Maadi camp,
December, 1915.

Dear Matilda,
    I have to say old girl I sorely am sick to the teeth with all this waiting about. Drills and bayonet training in the heat and the flies. All of us feel the same. Everyone is on edge. We want to be fighting the Jerries, or the Turks and yet the Army has us running about sandhills. Rumours abound and everyone is keen for news of the war. Many have brothers or mates missing in Gallipoli. It puts a damper on everyone I can tell you. I have begun training as a signalman. I think when I get home I would like to work with the Post-Master General. We had a terrible sandstorm last week. A lot of the bivvies blew away and we lost another two horses. Tomorrow will be Christmas Day and have been told to expect a good feed with plum puddings and jam all the way from Blighty. It is strange to not be there with you all to wish you well. I hope you get lots of presents.

Give my love to the old folks and Happy Christmas your affect. brother, Gregory.

One of the hardest things Ernest had ever done in his life was to walk out of Natalie's house on Monday afternoon, leaving the Isis statue stored inside a plastic tub. So near and yet it may as well have been locked inside a burial chamber at the bottom of a pyramid. That Troy fellow had insisted it shouldn't stray far from the Lette family, seeing how they *'owned'* it. As if anyone could or should own a piece of history. In his opinion, artifacts belonged to the world to marvel over and imagine lives so very different from their own.

Later that night he prowled around Fig Tree Lodge's library with no further understanding of what an intruder wanted in a room full of books and little else. Tuesday, he spent poring over his research on his laptop. The problem was he had become so lost in the work, he'd failed to register the passage of time, and night had fallen once again. One blessing he'd finally shaken off that Troy fellow who had disappeared that morning and didn't re-appear at the Lodge until Thursday. When Ernest had phoned Natalie and asked her out to dinner, he had half-expected her to refuse. Now here they both sat enjoying the crisp if rather chilly, night air.

Fairy lights twinkled in the acacia trees scattered between the outdoor dining area of the Riverside Pub and the banks of the Akuna River. Patio heaters dotted about the area helped ward off the cold and, as the wind had dropped, it was very pleasant sitting outside. A waitress appeared at their table and took their order. Ernest aligned the menus together then placed them to the side. He smiled at Natalie seated opposite. With her long, dark hair flowing loose over her shoulders, she looked lovely in blue jeans and a chunky, orange and white flecked jumper. "Thank you for agreeing to see me again."

"No, I'm the one who should be thanking you." She gave a tired smile, as an anxious expression furrowed her brow. "Having my house trashed on Tuesday and then to have someone attempt to break in again during the night… well, I'm a little shaken. I'm sorry I had to postpone our dinner. Wednesday was a write-off, what with the police coming and going. Noah and I needed an early night."

"It's understandable. How is Noah handling it?"

"A lot better than me. I think it's given him certain kudos with his mates. He's at a Scout meeting, and I have to pick him up at nine-thirty. I hope that's okay if I leave a bit early."

"I don't have children, but I imagine parents usually arrange their lives around their kids."

Natalie laughed. "That is definitely true."

"Have you heard anything from the police? Do they have any leads?"

Natalie shook her head, then took a sip of the wine he'd poured out earlier. "Not as far as I can tell. They keep asking if I've had an argument with a neighbour recently.

Or seen any kids hanging about the street." She shrugged and placed the wine glass back on the table.

Lowering his gaze, Ernest straightened the cutlery before positioning his bread and butter plate so it was eight centimetres from the edge of the table. He couldn't imagine anyone having that kind of a grudge against her. Could the ransacking of Natalie's home be connected with his attack? If so, then he could well be responsible. The *'how'* and the *'who'* were the real issue. After due thought, he couldn't see how there was any possible link. It had to be random kids. "Since I heard about the break-in on Tuesday, I've been worried about you and your son. I would have liked to have helped." He scanned her face, trying to read her expression.

"That's very kind of you. But Troy was there." Rich colour bloomed over her cheeks.

Of course – Troy.

Laughter came from the direction of the bar, spilling out across the lawn and floating like the very magic of life in the cool night air. At a nearby table, a young couple toasted each other, their smiles only for each other. Three kids skipped past followed by a couple, obviously their parents, and two smiling, elderly women. Grandmothers or he'd eat his best hat. All around him hummed the essence of living. Never had he felt more remote from the rest of the world.

"You have feelings for him, I can tell." Words Ernest had never meant to say. His hands twisted in his lap as he searched Natalie's face.

The colour in her cheeks deepened and she dropped

her gaze as she toyed with the wine glass. "That was a long time ago."

"True, but now he is here, and your heart has woken." He writhed inside. Who spoke like that these days? He did – apparently, but she didn't jeer or scoff. Or dismiss him. Rather she looked him straight in the eyes and her lips trembled. How he longed to reach across and at the very least, take her hand in his. Instead, he contented himself with pouring more wine into both their glasses.

"I don't know. Truly. I'm so confused. I thought I had it all figured out what path I wanted to take for the future. The type of man I need in my life. I liked everything you'd written in your profile. Then when we met, it seemed to reinforce you were exactly who you said you were, and I was impressed. I like you Ernest, really like you. We seem to be able to talk about anything and I think we have a lot in common. But… you're right in that Troy's reappearance has shaken me."

Her honesty warmed him. That was what had drawn him to her in the first place; apart from the fact that she could be the key to unlocking the final clues he hungered for. However, for the first time in his life, his obsession could wait.

"I realise that I shouldn't be feeling this confusion if I was interested in pursuing something more than friendship with you." She was the one who reached for *his* hand. "I feel like I'm leading you on, and it's not like that because I wanted this, whatever this is between us, to grow into something more. Something special. Now – everything that I thought I wanted for myself, appears to have turned on its head. I'm sorry, Ernest."

This time, he was the one to avoid her gaze. "Doesn't matter," he mumbled.

"That's where you are *so* wrong. It does matter. You matter, Ernest." When she squeezed his fingers, he finally looked up.

That lump of coal in his chest some called a heart, or was it his soul, sparked into an ember of fire.

"Your air of calm and control makes me feel safe. I like how I feel there would be no surprises with you. That's a really big thing with me."

"That's kind of you to say so. But it doesn't sound like boyfriend material." He forced a grin and stifled the strange urge to wriggle on his chair. The conversation had somehow been channelled into more than discussing their future intentions. He didn't like the way it made him so uncomfortable. He was a man who needed to be in control of his emotions. "Seems silly saying boyfriend and girlfriend at my age."

"I know. Makes me feel like I'm mutton pretending to be lamb." Natalie maintained her steady gaze. If anything, her hold over his hand had tightened. "Honestly, I can't give you a definite answer. But you *are* someone I would like to call a friend. I know we feel comfortable together. No matter what happens, I don't want to lose that friendship."

"Friendship," he repeated, his lips closing over the word. Suddenly, he was swamped with an intense loneliness, an emotion he thought he had successfully vanquished a long time ago.

"Friendships are just as important. Probably more than any other kind of relationship, because friends stay with you forever." She squeezed his fingers. "Somehow, I don't think you have many friends. I was the same – until I came here. We're a lot more alike than you think. I sense that you've also experienced disappointment, possibly a deep hurt, when you were very young."

He drew in a deep breath, feeling something tremble inside. "No one has ever said that to me before."

Lowering her voice, Natalie added, "It helps to talk about it, not that I've done much of that myself. It's only recently that I've felt comfortable enough to open up to someone who has become a close friend. For years I kept my issues locked away. I know they're probably trivial compared to what some people have had to live with but to me, they were very real."

"I'm listening, if you wish to share. No pressure." To his intense surprise, Natalie took him at his word.

"My parents had one of those volatile marriages, and I hated every minute of it. Dad was career Army. When he was home, the first few days would be wonderful, then came the drinking, the fights, the accusations. You see, he also wasn't a one-man woman. His excuse was his job; said Mum had no idea what he experienced, of the things he had to do, the things he had seen. Depending on her mood, Mum would either forgive him for his latest fling or scream and throw stuff. They divorced when I was fourteen, but it was a bitter divorce. They even fought over who got our cat would you believe? Of course, there was the argument about who would get me. By the time the solicitors had finished dragging the court battle out, I was eighteen and it didn't matter anymore."

Her words conjured up his own memories, which had

haunted Ernest for years. A strange pain wrenched at his heart as he imagined the child Natalie caught in the middle of two warring adults. "It must have been a terrible time for you. I'm sorry."

"Yeah, me too." Eyes glassy with unshed tears, she gave a short mirthless laugh. "The thing is… "

"Yes?" he whispered.

"My father's excuse was his job. Then when I met Troy… well, he was career Army, too."

"You were afraid history would repeat itself and you would make the same mistake as your mother." Ernest nodded slowly. "I think that's a perfectly natural reaction. I would have done the same."

"Did you?"

More than a little humbled at her confiding in him, he knew he could no longer hold back. "My arrival in this life was an inconvenience for my mother. She was just over forty years old and, on her way to becoming a court judge. Nothing was going to stop her climb to the top, certainly not a baby. She placed me in her father's care, and I rarely heard from her."

"He wasn't a good man." Natalie's words were more statement than question.

Even so, Ernest nodded. "Yes. He considered me to be a weak, cry baby. He believed the only way to make a man out of me, was to flog me for every tiny transgression. I couldn't even make a bed that would meet his exact standards."

"You're a good man and that's in spite of him, not because of him. He probably caused you to avoid becoming close to anyone in case they hurt you. Oh,

Ernest. What a pair we are." She raised his hand to her mouth and kissed his knuckles.

His eyes misted. "The old bastard did give me one good thing – my love for history. He was a light horseman in the Great War, you see and when he was feeling talkative, would go on and on about Egypt and the pyramids."

"Are they… ?"

"Still alive? No. Mother was killed in a car accident when I was twenty-five. *He* died after I turned seventeen. Yourself?"

"Mum lives in Bendigo, and the last I heard from Dad, he was in Darwin living out of a campervan. I rarely see or talk to them."

Ernest frowned. "What about Noah? Surely, they want to connect with their grandson? I take it you, like me, are an only child?"

"Only kid, thank heavens. Mum sends Christmas cards, a birthday present every so often. My father – absolutely nothing. I think they would both prefer to remember neither of us existed."

"What a pity we can't choose our families."

Natalie grinned and released his hand. "I know. Just think of how many less screwed-up people there would be in the world."

"Probably do the entire psychology profession out of a job." He glanced towards the pub. "Ahh, here come our meals."

"I am hungry." Natalie took another sip of her wine while the waitress deposited their plates before walking away. Natalie's smile was like sunshine as she picked up her fork. "We have shared interests and I meant what I said, Ernest. About you and me. About our friendship."

Words failed him, so he simply nodded. She must have understood because she changed the subject and tried her pasta dish.

The remainder of the meal passed in a bit of a daze for Ernest. He'd never, ever mentioned his childhood. Yet here he had opened up to a virtual stranger. The weird thing was, it didn't feel wrong. It felt right and the longer they talked, the more his anxiety settled. He would make the most of this moment. Nothing was going to ruin their time together.

Sipping his wine, he glanced around. His heart stuttered, missed a beat. Or was it several? as two police officers emerged from the hotel and weaved their way through the tables. He'd recognise that blonde hair anywhere. Senior Constable Taylor, and with her, instead of her younger counterpart, was a tall, fair-haired man in his thirties. The male cop had sergeant stripes on his uniform. Both had their flat gazes fixed on him.

They had come for him.

Ernest's throat tightened. Suddenly he couldn't breathe. He sensed Natalie staring at him. Heard as if from a great distance her voice asking if he was alright. He couldn't respond. All he could think was that his day of reckoning had arrived.

Somehow, he'd have to bluff his way out. He couldn't bear Natalie thinking the worse of him. Still his grandfather's long-dead voice wouldn't stop taunting him. Kept telling him what a mewling whiny – useless – waste of space he was; that he would never amount to anything, never achieve glory. Never be worthy of respect. In an instant, his yearning to be liked for himself was locked away deep inside. His chin jutted as the officers reached their table.

"May we?" Without waiting for an affirmative, the male cop highjacked a vacant chair from nearby and dropped into it.

Senior Constable Taylor stood a pace away, thumbs hooked into her utility belt as she nodded a greeting to Natalie. Had she positioned herself deliberately to block any attempt of his to escape?

"Hope we haven't interrupted something." The senior police officer examined Natalie's face before switching his gaze to Ernest's. Like he was determined not to miss any nuance of expression.

Suddenly, bluffing didn't seem a good idea. Maybe if he took control of the conversation, he could steer it into less dangerous waters. Ernest tapped the table with his forefinger. "Good evening, Senior Constable. And you sir, are... ?"

"Senior Sergeant Morgan," declared the officer in a confident tone. No fool here. "During the course of our investigation into your assault, it has come to our attention that you are not who you say you are. Do you care to offer an explanation, sir?"

Natalie shrank back against her chair. He didn't like the frown crinkling her forehead. A little honesty would go a long way here – as long as he picked the right answer that would satisfy both the police, and also not drive Natalie away. Because for once in his life, the thought of returning to the barren, lonely role he had built for himself held little appeal.

"It seems you have caught me out." Ignoring the police, he turned and spoke directly to Natalie. "Verne is not my real name, it's the name of a former colleague who actually *is* a history schoolteacher. My surname is Callen and I'm an archaeologist."

"Why did you lie?"

For the moment, it appeared that the police were content with Natalie asking the questions. Ernest didn't have to try hard to infuse sincerity into his voice. "There were a couple of reasons; the main one being I'm quite well-known in archaeological circles and didn't want attention drawn to my personal life." Thinking hard, he paused. What he had once thought might work as a good reason should he be found out, no longer sounded realistic.

"And the other?"

His mouth dried. Natalie definitely wasn't impressed. Sweat trickled under his armpits. If he lost her… *But think of the prize,* snarled his inner voice – the one that had kept him sane and alive through all the long, dark and painful days of his childhood. Just like that, he snapped back. The real Ernest, the one he was most comfortable with, the one that drove others away. The one that kept him safe.

Ernest Callen: respected and always listened to even if he was never liked. He raised an eyebrow, projecting power into each word, as the new Ernest, fragile, barely half-formed, retired whimpering to the darkest recesses of his mind. "I wanted to be accepted for the man I am, and not for what I can bring to a relationship; a comfortable lifestyle."

"Right." Natalie expelled the word in a loud breath.

He couldn't read her. What the dickens was she thinking?

"Interesting, Mr Callen," drawled Sullivan.

He hadn't bought anything Ernest said. Sullivan had a mocking smile on his face, while Abby Taylor, well, at least she looked concerned as she eyed Natalie.

Sweat trickled down Ernest's spine. He was about to be hung out to dry like a dead fish.

A group of young people crossed the lawn, heading towards the car park. Behind them strolled a man with his hands in his jeans pockets. He stopped and leaned against one of the trees decked with lights.

Even from this distance, Ernest recognised him instantly. Troy Davidson. If only he could remember where he'd seen him before - more importantly, why a sickening coil of unease prickled whenever he was near.

CHAPTER 13

Maadi,
4th March, 1916.

Dear family,

A lot has happened since I last wrote. Our numbers increased with the arrival of the 1st, 2nd and 3rd Light Horse Brigade and the New Zealanders Rifle brigade from Gallipoli. They have formed into the Anzac Mounted Division along with a mob of tommies. These cobbers have seen a lot of action. I can tell by the look in their eyes. Yesterday our squad had a full leave day. Some of the boys went into town to meet up with the native girls. I went for a camel ride to see the sphinx. Its nose is missing but it is still an immense and imposing structure. You would love it, dear sister. I have mailed a few pieces of pottery I purchased in the souk which I think you and Mother will like. You will be pleased to know I passed my signalman training. I have asked for the extra pay to be sent to you, mother. More news. After tucker *tonight Larry came rushing to our tent. Soon we will be on the road to Beersheba.*

With affect., Gregory.

Natalie certainly had a lot to mull over as she performed her cleaning duties at the local caravan park early Friday morning. Even though tourists had been few and far between the past couple of years, the park was close to capacity. With sky-rocketing rental prices and a shortage of houses to let, people from elsewhere had trickled into town desperate for a roof over their heads. The result was there were only three cabins available for any short-term travellers as well as six vacant tent spots. Seeing how many families had to cram into limited accommodation made her grateful for the decrepit two bedder she and Noah rented. It didn't matter that the roof leaked in the kitchen when it rained. Or that the toilet was situated in the laundry shed which was accessed via a short concrete path. Or that any trips to the loo during the night were often a very cold and sometimes wet experience.

As she organised her cleaning products and hurried to the office to sign out, she couldn't help reflecting that she and Noah could be one pay cheque, maybe two at the most, away from the same scary situation. It was enough to give her nightmares. She had to make a go of that book, but disappointment weighed her down like an anchor tied to her feet. The revelations last night about Ernest's real identity had been a hard pill to swallow. She had trusted him; blindly, she realised now.

Baring her soul to someone who had deliberately lied to her had eroded what little confidence she possessed. Even though he had spent the rest of the evening, protesting how his name made little difference to their relationship or how he felt, well – let's just say that it hadn't worked. His voice had rung with distress; the worried expression in his eyes looked sincere but could she really trust her own judgement? In the end, she had allowed him to walk her to her rusty car and told him that she needed time. She'd call him.

The sight of him standing with slumped shoulders and staring after her, had pulled at her heartstrings. She couldn't afford to make another mistake. She had Noah to think of, and both their futures.

Her first attempt at on-line dating had certainly turned into a mess. Which was a pity as there had been a faint, and non-expressed hope, they could collaborate on the book together. Now it was all down to her.

Lastly, there was Troy. Why was it that Ernest's lies had resurrected her misgivings where Troy was concerned? The night they had spent together had been heaven; it was as if the years that had separated them had never happened. Yet, nothing had changed. Despite the intimacy of those magical hours, neither had broached the subject of their past – or the future. Which only made her doubt even more whether she could have one with a man who withheld from her. He wasn't the only one hiding the truth.

She would have to make a decision soon, before her son became too attached to Troy. Maybe today she would find the right moment to speak with him.

No – she'd make the right moment happen. It was time she stopped cowering and owned up to her own mistakes. It would be up to Troy to decide if they could forge some kind of a relationship together.

Instead of returning home, she made for Fig Tree Lodge, thinking that she might browse the library room for any old history books. Hopefully, she could also organise some alone time with Troy.

"Cooee!" she called out as she knocked on the kitchen door before wiping her muddy boots on the mat.

"Come in!" said Kaylee from inside the house.

Shrugging out of her heavy parka, Natalie stepped through the doorway. Her smile withered as she met the concerned faces of Kaylee and her step-father, Dodge. Both were standing by the centre counter and the room reeked of a heavy tension that sent all her nerves on edge.

"Natalie! Is Gran with you?" Dodge pushed past to wrench open the screen door and stare into the yard.

"No. I haven't seen her. I came over to do some more poking about in the attic and maybe a look through your library. I did mention it to Edwina yesterday." She hung her parka over the back of a stool.

"Cuppa? It may warm you up. It's freezing outside." Without waiting for a response, Kaylee poured a cup from the pot on the counter. Her eyes were red-rimmed as if she'd been crying, and Natalie tensed.

Something was wrong.

"What is it?"

"It's Grannie. She isn't here. Dad and I have looked all over the house. Where could she be at this time of the morning?" Tears filled Kaylee's eyes while Dodge shut the door, a heavy frown on his tired face.

"There was no yoga class this morning, so she can't be there. How about I make some calls? I'm sure she can't be far." Natalie placed her backpack on the counter and unzipped one of the pockets.

"Don't bother. I've contacted everyone she knows – which is just about every person in town. No one has seen her since yesterday afternoon." Dodge stood near the window, peering outside, and drumming his fingers on the sill.

Natalie's heart sank and uneasiness spread through her bones. She shook her head as Kaylee proffered the cup of tea. Her insides quivered so badly she thought she'd throw up if she so much as took a sip.

"As far as I can tell from the phone calls I've made, Mrs Miller saw her at three-fifteen yesterday in the cemetery. She had on her pink gumboots and was wearing that puffer-jacket she's so fond of. God – if she's had a fall, or her heart… " Shoulders hunched, Dodge turned away, mumbling, "At least she had some protection from the cold. Last night was bitter."

This was bad. A memory flashed through her mind of Tessa telling her of Edwina's past heart troubles. "You've probably already discussed this but… did either of you see or speak to her after that time?"

Dodge swung around. Leaning against the cupboard he folded his arms, his face grim. "Tessa, Tilly and I were at the shop all afternoon, Kaylee at school. I went straight from there to the hospital to start my shift while Tessa and the girls headed for Abby's place. There was some kind of girly sleepover thing happening last night for Emma Fahey."

Kaylee gave a little smile. "It was fun. There was lots of food. Roman, Drew and Eddie did all the cooking while we sat around playing games and dancing. Weren't you invited, Natalie?"

"Yes, I was but I had a… dinner date at the Riverside pub. Then I've got my work at the caravan park, and I often have to start early. Today, I began at six." Her cheeks heated at Dodge's understanding glance. It seemed everyone was privy to her straitened financial circumstances while those who could offered her as much work as she could take on. The blessings and trials of living in a close-knit community. "I guess I could be the last person to talk to her. That was at ten o'clock last night when I phoned her after I picked Noah up from Scouts. She sounded perfectly normal, but we only talked for a couple of minutes before she said she had to go."

Dodge's head came up and his gaze sharpened. "Why? That's not like Gran to cut short a conversation."

"I'm not sure," Natalie said slowly as she replayed the conversation in her mind. "Oh wait! I think she said there was a knock on the door!"

"Someone else was here. Who would come calling at that time of night?" Dodge prowled around the kitchen, as if looking to see if anything had been disturbed. "Are you certain Kaylee, that you didn't see Gran when you arrived? Anyway, why did you come back alone?"

"I've got school, remember? Mum wanted to stay at

Abby's place for breakfast and to help clean up. Didn't she say?" Kaylee lowered her gaze as she fiddled with her bracelet.

Dodge shrugged, the dark shadows beneath his eyes a testament to a lack of sleep. "Yeah, I forgot about the text she sent. Busy night at the hospital, the fire alarm went off twice. Both false alarms, thank goodness, but it still meant evacuating those we could and waiting until the firies gave us the all clear." He checked the clock on the wall. "I got home about twenty minutes ago, and you about, what five or so minutes before me?"

Kaylee nodded. "Sounds right. What about Grannie's new man? Maybe he came over and they went off to his place for the night."

"What man, Kaylee?"

Confusion clouded Kaylee's eyes at her stepfather's sharp tones. "The bloke she's been seeing the past few weeks."

"Is that where she's been sneaking off to lately? I thought she was hanging out with her friends and dreaming up some kind of crazy scheme." Dodge ran a hand along his jaw. "Okay hon, tell us everything you know about this bloke. Is he a local? Where do they meet?"

Kaylee was already shaking her head. "Grannie was pretty secretive about it all and didn't tell me much. He's not local. Gran did say one time how she loved his posh voice. I thought you and Mum knew all about him." Her voice morphed into a typical teenage aggrieved *'it's not my fault'* tone.

"First I heard about it, and I know your mother would

have told me if she knew. The guy could be Ernest. The time frame fits plus he's got one of those *'born with a silver spoon'* voices." Dodge's voice was harsh as he pinned a glare on Natalie – like this was all her fault.

Her stomach went into free-fall. What if it *was* her fault? She was the one who'd invited Ernest to town. Could the mystery man really be him? He'd acted so keen on *her*. To the best of her knowledge, he'd shown no interest in any other woman and certainly not someone twenty years older than him.

"Ernest was with me last night at the pub." She had left at nine-fifty, which would give him sufficient time to drive back to Fig Tree Lodge and be the mysterious caller. But why knock? He had a keycard.

Before she could speak, Dodge kept going. "Where is he anyway? Shouldn't he be out of bed by now? It's past seven." Raising his head, he glared at the ceiling.

"Maybe he's gone for his morning walk."

"I'm going to check his room." Dodge stalked from the kitchen, his footsteps fading as he disappeared down the hall.

"I'll ring Mum, and ask what's keeping her. She told Dad she'd be home in a jiff when he called to ask if she knew where Grannie could be and that was ages ago." Kaylee plucked her mobile from her school jacket and ran out of the room to make the call.

Left alone, Natalie busied herself by washing and drying the cups. Maybe there was another newcomer in Bindarra Creek. Another stranger. Although, seriously, how coincidental was that? Two strangers! Or maybe Edwina's beau was someone who had visited in the past –

someone like Troy. Not that he could be involved – surely, given she was his relative. However, his probing questions about the state of Fig Tree Lodge and his hints about selling the property had definitely added to Edwina's stress lately. A cup slipped through her fingers, and she just caught it before it crashed to the floor. She didn't want Troy to be the cause of Edwina's non-appearance.

Oh, if only this stupid hope of hers would disappear! If only she could rid herself of her longing for a life with him. He wasn't the man for her. She'd made that decision years ago when she'd married John. Troy took risks. She wanted – no, needed – safe. But despite everything she did to push him from her thoughts and heart, he was the one who haunted her dreams and taunted her with the fantasy of a different kind of life. They were both older. Maybe he had changed.

Hot burning tears crouched behind Natalie's eyelids just waiting for the moment to launch down her face. She pushed them back, and focused on the issue at hand as Dodge strode through the doorway, Kaylee on his heels.

"Your friend is not in his room." Dodge's voice was flat, his eyes cool. "And Troy isn't in the studio apartment."

His expression reminded her that he'd once been a cop. A good one. She shivered as cold air wafted over her face and bare arms. "They've probably gone out."

"Oh Grannie. What if she's had another heart attack?" Kaylee buried her face in her hands.

Natalie hurried over and placed an arm around the

young girl's shoulders. "I'm sure we'll find her. She can't have gotten far."

"You don't know Grannie very well then. She can really move fast when she wants to." Kaylee gave a watery laugh.

Uncertain what to say, Natalie gave Kaylee another gentle hug as Dodge strode to the door. "I'll search the grounds, again. If only old Rufus was still with us. He'd sniff Gran out quick smart." He paused, his gaze resting briefly on the empty dog bed, before he wrenched open the door. "Kaylee, hon, don't worry. Natalie is right. We'll find her."

Natalie snatched up her parka and began to shrug it over her arms. "I'll help look, too." She lowered her voice. "Once we're certain she isn't on the property, I think we should call the police."

"I'm sure Tessa would have told Abby before she left." Dodge looked over at the young girl. "What did Mum say when you called her?"

"She's on her way. She'll be here in a couple of minutes. I told her about Grannie's boyfriend, too. Mum said she'd pass that onto Abby so she can contact the real estate agents about any new tenants." Kaylee fished out a tissue from a pocket and blew her nose. "Can I stay with you? Until Mum arrives?"

Dodge smiled as he stepped outside. "Course you can. Let's go." Holding out his hand, he waited until Kaylee rushed over. "We'll start over near the old stables. Nat – why don't you take the garage area and the front?"

"Will do." Snatching up her pack, she hurried out the door while Dodge and Kaylee took off towards the eastern boundary of the property. As soon as she was out of ear shot, she pulled out her mobile and tried Troy's number. The call went to voice mail. Same with Ernest. Where could they be at this time of the morning?

Five minutes later, she had scoured the garage inside and out and was poking through the shrubs near the fig tree in the front yard when two vehicles entered the drive. One was the old Land Rover belonging to the family with Tessa behind the wheel; the other was a police paddy wagon.

Tessa was out of the car a second after the engine died. Slamming the door shut, she ran over to Natalie. "Any sign?"

"Nothing. But Dodge and Kaylee are searching the backyard now. Maybe… " Natalie bit her lip, unable to continue.

"This is terrible." Tessa covered her face in her hands for an instant in a gesture that mirrored that of her daughter's. Dropping her hands, she revealed a face filled with determination. "Grannie has to be here somewhere."

"Mum!" Kaylee shouted as she sprinted down the drive and into her mother's open arms.

Dodge wasn't far behind her, his face grim as he shook his head in answer to the glance his wife sent him over Kaylee's shoulders.

Giving them some privacy, Natalie hurried to where Senior Constable Abby Taylor was stepping out of the paddy wagon, mobile in hand as she spoke to someone on the other end. Abby's blonde hair was pulled back in a tight bun at the base of her neck. Her eyes were sharp and keen as she swept her gaze over Natalie and then around the property.

Nothing would escape her.

While Tessa comforted her daughter, Dodge retrieved their youngest, Tilly, from the back seat of the Land Rover.

"Give me an update." Abby produced a notebook and pen as Dodge and his family joined them. After both Dodge and Natalie had detailed their earlier conversation, she scribbled down the last few lines and scrutinised their faces. "To summarise, to the best of your knowledge Natalie was the last person to speak with Ms Lette at approximately ten last night and Mrs Miller the last person to see her at three-fifteen yesterday."

"Correct," Dodge agreed as he lifted Tilly into his arms.

With another all-encompassing glance around the small group, Abby settled her gaze on Natalie. "I don't see your guest, here. Has anyone seen him this morning?"

Had there been a slight emphasis on the word *him*? As if his absence was connected with Edwina's? Her belly cramped as Natalie mumbled, "No. He's probably gone for a walk."

When Dodge snorted, an expression flickered over Abby's face too fast for Natalie to interpret. Her hands balled into fists. She wanted to insist that he could have nothing to do with Edwina's disappearance but feared she would only add to Abby and Dodge's suspicions, so she clamped her mouth tight.

"Dodge, do you want to make this official?" Abby

tucked her book and pen away before producing her mobile.

After sharing a look fraught with meaning with his wife, he nodded. "Yeah, we don't want to waste any more time. I thought we'd call in the SES straight away rather than waiting any longer."

"No worries. We'll conduct our own search of the property first. We'd like a close blood relative to provide a DNA sample as well as a hair or toothbrush belonging to Ms Lette and a recent photograph of her. We'll also need your cars, Dodge, so don't go near them until they've been cleared."

"Why the cars?" asked Tessa, frowning.

"To eliminate us as suspects." Dodge fished out his keys. "That won't be a problem and I'm happy to volunteer my DNA."

"Excellent. I'll request a mobile forensic team and get that underway ASAP. Roman is already aware Ms Lette is a possible missing person. He's standing by to organise a search team, as soon as I give him the go-ahead. I've updated Riley on the drive over here. Should we be unable to locate Ms Lette by this afternoon, he'll call in a dog search team – if there's one available. We've got a missing hiker in the Blue Mountains and a boy who's wandered off from a property out near Parkes. Riley and AJ will do the rounds of your grandmother's friends." Abby held up a hand. "I understand you've already contacted them, but you know the drill. All enquires have to be official from here on in. I'll also tell them to keep an eye out for your guest."

Tessa spoke up. "Troy Davidson is also staying here. In the converted stables."

"Oh?" Abby's eyebrows rose. "Anyone seen him this morning?"

"No. I knocked but there was no answer," replied Dodge.

"We'll need to speak to him. If you see him, tell him to come down to the station. I know it will be dumb of me to ask all of you to stay home and leave it to us?"

"Too right." Dodge's jaw jutted while Tessa planted one hand on her hips, the other remained around Kaylee's shoulders. "You know I'm an SES member. No way am I standing on the sidelines."

Abby's radio crackled. She half-turned aside as she clicked the device attached to the lapel of the police jacket she wore and answered in a low voice. Several seconds later, she signed off and looked directly at Natalie who tensed. There was something about the other woman's carefully blanked expression that warned her, whatever she was going to say would not be pleasant.

"Riley has just spoken with the vicar, Mrs Miller. She's added to her account of yesterday and now advises she saw someone else in the cemetery at the same time as Ms Lette. It was Troy Davidson. I understand from the last time we spoke to him that he is related to the family. I also understand that he is a particular friend of yours, Natalie." The Senior Constable produced her pocketbook once more. "Mrs Miller also states that Mr Davidson approached Ms Lette and they appeared to have a heated argument. She states that Ms Lette threw her hands in the air and marched off. Mr Davidson followed. They both disappeared around the back of the church. When was the last time you heard or spoke to him, Natalie?"

All eyes flashed to Natalie who stood frozen in place, a million thoughts whirling through her head, as dread formed and burned like dry-ice in the pit of her belly. Troy. It couldn't be. No, Mrs Miller had to be mistaken. The police had to be mistaken. No way would Troy hurt an old lady. Even as she hugged that thought close, another seared into her brain. She had never really known the man behind the façade he'd presented.

In fifteen years, people changed. Sometimes for the worse.

CHAPTER 14

France,
7ᵗʰ June, 1916.

Dear family,

How is everyone? A lot more quiet then here I guess if life is much the same. We have whizzbangs going all night and day. Makes it hard for a bloke to rest. To top it all off it has rained for several days and the trenches and tunnels are full of mud and water. Makes life dashed difficult at times. Read in a French newspaper today that Kitchener and his staff are lost, the Germans torpedoed or the Hampshire hit a mine. Jolly rum news, made the men quite down. Some good news the Russians had a big victory at Gilicia and took 25000 prisoners! I am in a dugout about half a mile from the German trenches. There is a rumour flying around about something called the big push. Hope its big enough to end this war and we can all go home.

Love to all, Mitchell

Early the next day, Troy caught up with Natalie, and that damn hanger-on, Ernest, down by the Akuna River. No sooner had he spotted them, then so did Chip. His dog scampered forward to happily slobber over Natalie as she crouched down to stroke her head. Petty of him, he knew, but he did gain a certain satisfaction at how Chip growled and avoided Ernest's outstretched hand. Irritation mingled with his growing unease. What a waste yesterday had been. Instead of helping with the search, he'd had to spend the majority of the day answering pointless questions about meeting Edwina in the cemetery. Of course, the cops were simply doing their job, however he'd come away with a bad taste at the back of his mouth. Rolling his shoulders, his gaze swept over Ernest. Someone else the coppers also had in their sights. When he'd finally been allowed to leave, he'd noticed the other bloke waiting to be interviewed. Whatever Ernest had to say must have satisfied the police because here he was – free as a bird and chatting away with Natalie.

A chilly wind sighed through the trailing branches of an old willow tree and sent ripples across the river's surface that was still running hard and fast. If anyone slipped in, they'd have to be a strong swimmer, or they would soon find themselves in trouble.

Every now and then, a voice could be heard calling out for his mother's cousin. The sounds were distorted from the fog that still lingered in the low-lying areas, making it difficult to work out in which direction the noise had come from. It appeared the entire town had turned out in the search for the elderly woman – now that more than a full day had passed and there had been no sign. Police from Tamworth had arrived in the early hours to assist in the search. Senior Sergeant Morgan and the SES captain had delegated the searchers into teams, along with maps and strict times to call in and give updates.

As the hours passed with no sign of Edwina, a sense of desperation had afflicted the community. An elderly woman. The middle of a frosty winter. With more bad weather predicted. The sands of time were running out.

Frowning, Natalie made no move to step any closer. "Troy, you were seen arguing with Edwina on Thursday afternoon. What was that about?"

Troy shrugged, noting how stiffy she held herself. "We went to the cemetery to look at the old family gravestones. Aunt Edwina brought up the subject of Fig Tree Lodge. Apparently when Mum and she spoke the other day, Mum pressed her about selling the property. Aunt was pretty miffed with me, calling me a snake in the grass."

"I'm not surprised." Natalie's lips thinned and she fondled Chip's ears.

"You don't believe I have anything to do with her disappearance?" He gaped at her, feeling as if she'd just ripped out his intestines.

Lowering her head, she avoided his glance. "I spoke to her later that night, remember? No, I don't think you're involved."

The gap between them was widening with every

second. Going by the broad grin on Ernest's face, it was obvious the other bloke had picked up on their discord. "Thank you, I guess," he bit out before adding, "The police were satisfied with my explanation. Afterwards, I joined the search."

"They questioned me too," Ernest admitted. "As I told Natalie, there was nothing I could tell them."

"Where have you been exactly, Troy? I've been trying to call you. You never answered." Natalie's voice trembled.

A sharp pain stabbed through his heart at the sight of her pale face and the anxious set of her mouth. It was clear she was concerned about Edwina. Maybe there was even a tad of worry about him as well. A little of his irritation faded as his gaze wandered over her. It was still early in the morning. Already, the bottoms of Natalie's jeans were wet and muddy bearing evidence that she'd been checking the riverbank and shoreline.

"Missed me, did you?" He tried for a cheerful tone, hoping to bring some light to her shadowed eyes.

To his horror, tears welled, and she sniffed as she pulled out a handkerchief and blew her nose. "I'm just so worried. I know everyone is, especially her family. She's such a kind old woman and she's been good to me. When we arrived in town, she went out of her way to make Noah and me feel welcome, like we were part of the community. Since then, I like to think that we've become friends."

"I'm sure she feels the same way about you, Natalie. Who wouldn't?" Ernest slipped an arm around her shoulders, much to Troy's annoyance.

He shrugged the irritation away. If Natalie gained

some comfort from the other man, then who was he to begrudge it? He cleared his throat and stuck his hands into the pockets of his thick parka, partly for warmth. Partly to stop himself from peeling Ernest away from Natalie who had made no move away from the other man's touch. "After the police finished questioning me yesterday afternoon, I was with the SES. Last night, Roman asked for any suggestions I had about the search, given my Army background. I'm sorry. I should have returned your calls, but it was late by the time I finished."

"Where have you looked?"

He ran a hand over his short hair and grimaced. "Every street. Every building that we could gain access to. We've scoured the churches and the cemetery twice and found nothing."

Natalie turned to look at the river as Chip wandered off to sniff at a tuff of grass. Ernest's arm fell away and he walked towards the water edge, leaving them alone. "What if… ?"

"I've only just re-connected with her. From the little I've seen of her, Aunt Edwina is pretty savvy. She wouldn't go anywhere near any of the waterways given how much rain is washing down from further up-state. She's a countrywoman."

Her shoulders hunched. "What's next?" Her voice was small.

"They're talking about broadening the search onto the properties just outside town. One possibility that's been raised, is she has become confused and wandered away."

"Edwina?" Natalie snorted and faced him, planting her hands on her hips. "I've never known anyone more together than her. She puts me to shame." She licked her lips and shot Ernest a lightning-fast glance. "I've been thinking about the intruder. Plus, there was that knock on the door around ten Thursday night. Could someone have lured her out of the house so they could break in again? Remember; Dodge was at work. Tessa and the girls were at Abby's house. If Edwina left that meant the house would be empty since there are no other lodgers, apart from you. Remind me again, where you were around the time of my phone call?"

"I was out walking Chip. We were gone quite a while as I took a detour past the pub and went in for a beer just before closing time. When we returned, maybe twenty minutes after ten, the lights were out. I thought everyone had gone to bed. I guess the place would have looked empty. What could anyone possibly want from there that's so important?" Dragging a hand from his pocket, he rubbed his bristly chin. He needed a shave but that would have to wait. At least he'd managed a quick shower and a hot breakfast thanks to the CWA ladies who had turned up at the SES building bearing food and hot drinks for everyone to start the day.

"I don't know. I think we or someone should go right through every room in the Lodge. See if something is missing. See if there is something we've overlooked that could be a clue. Don't forget you chased away a couple of people sifting through your gear. There was also the break-in at my house."

"You think all this, including a missing woman, ties in with a petty thief?" He raised a sceptical eyebrow.

Natalie's face flushed and her eyes sparked. "There's

no need for that tone of voice, Troy," she said as if he was twelve years old.

He shuffled his feet.

"No petty thief hits someone over the head. They don't go down into a cellar which hasn't been used for years. They don't check a person's camping gear and not take anything. They don't go sorting through boxes of old junk. They go for wallets, phones, laptops, jewellery. I'm telling you, Dodge or Tessa needs to check the Lodge," she added forcefully.

"Hon, neither of them is going to be pulled away from the search. Dodge has even phoned his dad, Warren, and the bloke is on his way back to town as we speak. I can't see how any of what has happened is connected." He mulled over her words for a moment, then added, "If someone had gotten Edwina out of the house on some pretext, then why hasn't she turned up?"

"They could have bashed *her* over the head and hidden her somewhere. Maybe we should start searching people's houses; like rentals, maybe the caravan park, the motel." Lifting a hand to her mouth, she chewed on a fingernail. "Let's not forget any strange vehicles. We should check those, too."

"That would need a warrant, maybe a lot of warrants and I think could take some doing. Have you mentioned your idea to the police?"

"No, I haven't spoken to them since yesterday morning. I did try to call Abby this morning, but I keep getting her message bank. They could well have already thought of it." She shrugged.

"Well, it's worth mentioning, just in case. We've got

little to go on as it is, and any lead would be useful right about now."

Natalie tugged her mobile from her pocket. "Thank you, Troy. Oh, there's something I need to tell you; it's about…"

"Look who I've found," Ernest called out as he strolled over with Noah by his side.

Chip came racing up from the riverbank, with muddy paws. She promptly jumped up onto Noah and he ruffled her head until she jumped back down again. "Mum? Has Ms Lette been found?"

Moving forward, Natalie placed an arm around her son and hugged him. Even though he ducked his head, he didn't wriggle out of her grasp. "Not yet. What happened with soccer?"

"Cancelled. Everyone's either joined in the search or they're digging up food for the searchers."

"Drew and Ethan not with you?"

"Nah. They're helping at the SES office. What can I do? Ms Lette's a bit scary and a bit of a crackpot. She once told me that Dad would return. But I kinda like her." Noah scooped a stick off the ground and threw it through the air. Chip took off like a rocket to retrieve and return. Noah played tug to wrest it from her jaws.

Watching, a memory struck Troy. "Nat, do you know when the search dog teams are arriving?"

"No idea. But I hope they come soon." Natalie's tired face lit up.

"Chip could be a search dog, couldn't you girl?" Noah smiled.

Ernest made a weird half-choke, half-gasp sound.

"Sorry. Spit went down the wrong way," he croaked as he thumped his chest.

The side-ways look he sent Noah had all Troy's hackles rising but all he said was, "That's something to think about but how about you raise the cops on your phone, Nat, and ask?"

"I'm on it." She walked a few paces away and made the call.

While they waited, Noah played with the dog, Ernest stared at the river, and Troy wondered what the hell the other man was thinking. He had to admit Natalie had made a good point. Hadn't he also wondered if there was a connection between Ernest's arrival in town and the break-in? Actually, two break-ins and one attempted one. His pulse kicked up several gears. There was a connection – there had to be, otherwise nothing that had happened made any sense. If what they suspected was true, Edwina could be in deadly danger.

Her expression grave, Natalie returned, pocketing her phone into her backpack before slinging it over her shoulders. "I finally got through to Abby. A dog rescue team should arrive sometime tomorrow." She paused and looked up at the cloudy sky. "The weather forecast is for more rain, which will make it hard for the dogs to pick up her scent. They've also predicted a possible major storm early in the week, probably Monday. If that hits, then the dogs won't be much help at all."

"Monday?" To give him credit, Ernest looked positively appalled as his eyes bulged and his mouth fell open a tad. "But... that will mean the woman's been missing for four days!"

Troy's gut twisted at the thought. "Let's pray it doesn't come to that and she's found today." He didn't dare mention his personal fears. From his past experience in the Army, when searching for the injured or the lost, the first twenty-four hours were critical for a successful outcome.

Natalie fiddled with the bag straps. "I also talked to Abby about the intruder."

"What's this about?" Ernest asked.

She filled him in on what she'd said a few minutes ago.

"I agree with Troy. I can't see what an ordinary thief or even a kid would want to come back to the house for," he objected, throwing his hands in the air.

"Don't you see… " Natalie looked from him to Troy. "It has to be more than someone after pocket money. There must be something more going on."

Rolling his eyes, the older man tossed his head, scoffing, "Like what?"

"I haven't a clue, Ernest. At least think about my idea for a second!" Her voice rose to such an extent that even Chip sidled away.

His face red, Ernest pressed his lips together before bending over and brushing a minute speck of dust or dirt from his pants.

Was he hiding his expression or maybe he just doesn't like being spoken to like that? Keeping one eye on him, Troy touched Natalie's wrist. "What did your copper mate say?"

"Not much. But she *did* listen and said she'd take it under advisement. Whatever that means," she grumbled.

"Could mean something or nothing. Nat, I've also been listening."

She met his eyes and appeared to be holding her breath.

"Let's go and search the Lodge."

Natalie smiled, and he glowed under her warm approval. The urge to pull her into his arms was strong, but it was hardly the ideal time. What with Noah hanging on their every word, and Ernest being the third wheel. If he really wanted to be honest with himself, there was a wariness in Natalie's posture each time she looked at him. She still doubted him and that was downright depressing. Who knew what doubts that pompous jackass had been feeding her?

A foghorn's shrill blast came from the direction of the main street.

"Maybe it's Edwina! Maybe she's been found!" Natalie cried.

Taking Natalie's hand in his, he broke into a run. She raced beside him along with her son, Ernest and Chip as they tore across the field and along the street. They weren't the only ones who had heard the sound. The pounding of many feet hitting the tarred road and the concrete footpath sounded like a stampede of running with the bulls.

Ernest soon fell behind, puffing and blowing like he was about to have a seizure. Noah had sprinted ahead with Chip while Troy stayed next to Natalie. Outside the IGA store, a crowd of people was swelling as more and more raced up from every direction.

"What's going on?" Troy asked Noah who had stopped and was standing on his toes to get a look over the sea of heads and shoulders.

Noah tried a standing jump. "Dunno. I can't see or hear anything."

Some bloke in front turned around. "It's Bob Westbury, the shop owner. He blew the foghorn. They must have found something."

"Oh, please, please tell me it's Edwina and she's okay." Face flushed and breathing hard, Natalie pressed a hand to her side.

With a screech of brakes, a police car pulled up behind them. The senior cop and Abby Taylor emerged. The horde of people shuffled back to allow them through, parting like Moses and the Red Sea. The chatter and restless surge died down.

Standing near the back of the mob, a bad feeling settled in Troy's gut as the minutes ticked slowly by and there was no announcement. He gripped Natalie's hand tighter causing her to look at him with concern. Something in his face must have alerted her because she sucked in a sharp breath and raised a hand over her mouth.

A hush descended. Then the crowd exploded into a medley of raised voices and cries. The same bloke who had spoken before, met Troy's worried gaze. "They've found the old lady's puffer jacket in a rubbish bin behind the store. There's blood on it."

CHAPTER 15

I had the oddest dream last night. I dreamt we were playing at our special place. It was a bright sunny day and we were children again. We laughed and I remember how happy I felt. Then suddenly it became dark and rain fell but only in the one spot. A strange woman appeared and I felt something bad was going to happen.

The search for Edwina continued throughout the remainder of Saturday but it was hampered by the rain which started around midday and bled from the sky like an open wound. In the end, neither Natalie nor Troy would leave to waste time checking the Lodge – not after

Edwina's blood-stained jacket had been found. Despite the hunt being widened to include outlying properties, the elderly lady's whereabouts still remained a mystery.

Hope was fading fast.

Natalie could read it in the family's grim faces, but they refused to give up; harrying the police and the SES, and demanding warrants be issued so houses could be checked. Together with Sara Pyeon, Chen Wang and Leslie Wolski, Natalie sloshed through mud and rain as they worked their way through their designated sector south of the town. She did what she could, refusing to give in to her aching muscles. When the rain showed no sign of letting up, she sent Noah home, worried that his asthma would flare up from the wet and cold conditions. For once, he didn't grumble. Instead, her amazing child busied himself with making pots of soup for the search teams. Of Troy, she had seen little, although she knew he was one of the last people to stop searching at night. The same could be said of Ernest; he had also stepped up to the mark, albeit rugged up in gear that would have rivelled a polar explorer. He had certainly done his part in helping find Edwina.

They were putting in the hard yakka; she couldn't doubt that, but her unease about their intentions still niggled away at her. Ernest had lied about his name. Troy had lied about why he was in Bindarra Creek. They both professed they had legitimate reasons for their subterfuge. Ernest – his reputation. Troy – his mother. She sensed there was more they were both not sharing. Maybe whatever it was, they thought it was not important or of any particular significance to her. Still the Chinese whispers wouldn't stop, and she couldn't help but distance herself from both of them.

Particularly from Troy and that was probably because, of the two of them, he had the power to hurt her the most.

The hours wore on, darkness fell, and there was no further sign of Edwina Lette. The search was postponed until morning. No one spoke as they left the SES building around eight.

Chen Wang dropped Natalie off at her house, before he made his way home to his wife and son. Where Troy or Ernest had ended up, she had no idea although Roman had mentioned something about the teams they were part of, had yet to return. Feet dragging, a headache pounding behind her eyes like tribal drums, and feeling as if she could sleep for a month, Natalie trudged to the door.

Noah must have been on the lookout for her, because he flung it open before she could insert her key. After she'd kicked off her mucky gumboots, he pulled her inside to the warmth of the lounge room. He pressed her to rest then rushed to the kitchen, returning with soup and bread. "Any luck?"

"Nothing." How to warn a young boy the outcome may not be the one they hoped for? The words stuck in her throat but when he snuggled down beside her on the sofa and slung an arm over her shoulders, she knew she didn't have to say anything at all. After she finished her dinner, they stayed there for some time, gaining and giving each other comfort. When she caught herself nodding off, she blinked and straightened. Cupping her hands over his dear face, she murmured, "Have I told you how proud I am of you?"

He squirmed away but he was smiling. "Does that mean I'm no longer grounded? There's a pupil free day on Monday and if… if we're not needed for the search a few of us were going to the skatepark."

"No way. Sorry, but wagging school is *not* going to get you good marks." She ruffled his hair. "You, my dear son, will therefore remain grounded. Besides, you did say the forecast is for more rain."

Huffing out a breath, Noah rolled his eyes. "It was only PE," he whined. "By the way, I phoned Makki. He came and delivered the soup for us."

Natalie sighed as she pulled off her damp socks and stretched her toes towards the fire. "Brilliant. Thank you so much."

"I really wanted to stay with the SES and Troy's team, Mum."

"I know you did, but organising food for the search teams is just as important as running about in the cold."

Hair standing on end after her tousling it, Noah jumped to his feet and walked to the windows where he drew aside the curtain. "Weather guy reckons it's gonna be a bad night and the storm's gonna be a beauty."

How long could a seventy-five-year-old with a bad heart survive in the middle of winter with no warm clothes? Dread was like a rock in Natalie's belly, but she refrained from adding to her son's worry. All she could do was pray Edwina was under cover somewhere, protected from the elements.

If she was still alive.

"Hey, Mum? I think there's a car out front. Is Troy coming over tonight?" He rubbed the window to get rid of the fog from his breath. "I was hoping to talk to him. I wanted to ask about Dad."

"Come away, Noah!" Natalie said, her heart thumping quick and fast. "No. I'm not expecting him or anyone. Let's get ready for bed. I'm absolutely bushed." She pushed to her feet but instead of going into the bathroom, she hurried through the house checking all windows and doors were secure.

When she returned to the living room, she found Noah had placed the fire-guard in front of the glowing embers. "Well done, hon. I almost forgot." She smiled and kissed his cheek.

Turning, he hugged her tight in a way that reminded her of when he was little. Tears burned but she blinked them away. She had to remain strong for him. For Edwina. "Goodnight, sweetheart."

"Night, Mum." Hands in pockets, he slouched off to his bedroom while Natalie headed for a hot shower.

After turning the lights out, she stood at the front window for a long time, watching the street. Whatever car Noah had seen was long gone, and yet she couldn't rid herself of an edgy anticipation. Whether she was hoping Troy would appear or whether she was checking to ensure there were no strangers lurking about, was something she refused to admit to herself.

Shivering, she eventually stumbled off to seek her bed only to be tormented by fragmented dreams where Edwina ran through the bush clasping the Isis statue to her chest. When she woke at five-thirty, she felt as if she'd hardly slept at all. She had a hasty breakfast of rolled oats and orange juice, left a note for Noah reminding him he was grounded and to stay home out of the rain. After dressing, she tended to the blisters on her feet from wearing the clunky gumboots for two days straight. A car's horn sounded, and she snatched up her backpack, with its fresh supplies of water and a few protein bars, and spare socks. She pulled on her parka and ran down the path in her old joggers.

Another arduous day ensued of fruitless searching. The search and rescue dog team arrived from Sydney mid-morning, and co-ordinated with Roman and the police, before embarking on their own search. Although a couple of degrees warmer, the rain continued to drizzle down, hampering everyone's efforts and just adding to the general air of depression. The police from Tamworth worked under Riley, and Dodge, who were both born and bred in the town, as well as being distant cousins. Several of the outlying property owners had mounted their own checking of their acres of fields and paddocks, most on horseback or quadbikes. Radios crackled and mobiles buzzed competing with the continual hoarse calling out of Edwina's name.

Nothing.

It was as if she had vanished into thin air.

Sunday's search wound up with a rallying pep talk at the SES building by Warren, Dodge's father and Edwina's son-in-law who had arrived sometime during the night before to help. His right hand was held by Tilly, his grand-daughter. The rest of his family stood off to the side, comfort and courage by numbers. Beside him stood Edwina's oldest friend, Mrs Pamela Brown, whose stern jaw and fierce expression dared anyone to voice any doubts about Edwina's welfare. She stood shoulders back and as straight as a board. Any Army sergeant would have been proud of her. She nodded now and then as if to give credence to every word Warren spoke.

Warren finished up by thanking everyone for their efforts and a request for them not to give up. "… if there is anyone who can survive in these circumstances, it's my mother-in-law. She knows Bindarra Creek. She knows the land here, every waterway, every rock, every gully. She's experienced fires, floods, droughts and a town that was on the brink of dying. Edwina's out there, I can feel her waiting for us. I know we can find her."

There was a rousing cheer when he finished and everyone left, promising to return at five the next morning. Yawning, Natalie trudged through the carpark with the other members of her team. Chen, who had volunteered to be their driver, dropped Sara off first, and then Natalie. Next would be Leslie who had fallen asleep. She waved goodbye and walked down the path to her rental. Surely the rain had to stop soon. Pausing, she glanced up at the sky and blinked away the drizzle falling onto her face. No moon. No stars. Just blackness indicating the heavy cloud cover.

Speaking of blackness – there were no lights on in her house. That was odd. She had distinctly told Noah to remain home that day. Anger flared and she shoved the key into the lock with unnecessary force then stalked through the empty cold house to the laundry. After divesting herself of her wet clothes and shoes, she ran a hot shower. Dressed in a tracksuit and with thick socks on her feet, she checked for a note or message. Nothing.

No note on the table, no message on her phone. She dialled Noah's mobile. No answer. Fingers curling tight around her mobile, she fumed as the call went through to voice mail. She knew her annoyance was born more out of her fatigue and panic that they had still not found Edwina. Yet she couldn't control the sharpness in her voice as she shouted down the phone, "Noah! Where are you? Get home, immediately."

While she waited, she lit the fire and stoked it with more timber before prowling into the kitchen where she fixed herself some toast and vegemite. Her stomach had been rumbling a couple of hours ago but now she no longer felt that hungry. Toast in hand, she checked that no one had broken into her house again. The kitchen door was secure, and all the windows were still latched shut. She swallowed the last mouthful and pulled on her gumboots then checked the laundry. It was solid as a rock and none of the tubs had been disturbed. Even so, she opened the container and unwrapped the Isis statue.

It lay cold and somehow alien in her hands. The blank eyes of Isis stared back at her unblinking, as if the ancient goddess was trying to tell her something. More than a little shaken, she re-wrapped the statue with fumbling fingers and stowed it away once more. She couldn't help her sigh of relief once she had the laundry door locked tight and she was back, safe, inside the main house.

I'm just tired. That's all. It's making me imagine things. Leaning against the kitchen door, she reached for her mobile where it sat on the charger. Still no word from Noah. She snatched up the charger and entered the living room where she plugged it into a powerpoint, made another call to her son which went unanswered, and popped the phone onto the charger.

Then she sat in an armchair. Feet planted rigidly together on the rug, her arms hugging her waist, she stared into the fire. A veritable tempest of emotions brewed inside her mind as she rocked to and fro. Where was he? Why wouldn't he call her back?

Leaping to her feet, she paced back and forth in front of the crackling fire. She checked the time. Checked her phone. No messages. Good heavens! – it was close to nine-thirty! She grabbed the mobile again and began calling his friends' parents. Everyone assured her that Noah wasn't there, and they hadn't seen him all day. When she rang Abby and Roman Taylor, they urged her to call them back if her son didn't turn up soon.

She phoned Troy but he failed to pick up so she sent a message to Ernest.

No one got back to her.

Nine-fifty.

The only places open at that time of night were the hotels. No way would Noah be able to pass himself off as an eighteen-year-old. Not that he would do such a thing – or would he?

Edwina had gone missing in exactly the same way. Home alone. Late at night.

Heart racing a million miles an hour, Natalie hurried to the front door and stood on the step, peering up and down the street. No movement. Not even a cat lurked in the shadows. The wind blew a blast of icy rain in her face, and she stepped back then shut the door.

Noah.

She clutched her belly where sickness churned as her panic rose.

Her mobile buzzed. A message. She flew across the room, her hands shaking as she picked up her phone. Not her son. Ernest.

Had to get fuel. Saw Noah with Troy at petrol station café. Want me to come over?

A new kind of panic gripped her, like hands throttling her throat. *Thx Ernest but no. All good. See u tomorrow.*

Noah was with Troy. Neither had bothered to return her calls or even send her a text.

Her anger returned, bubbling to the surface like a volcano about to erupt. She plonked onto the seat and gripped the arms so tight her hands ached. And waited.

Another ten minutes and a car pulled to a stop out the front of the house. She rose, flicked on the front light and opened the door.

"Hi, Mum," Noah greeted her as he trotted up the path, Chip by his side. The dog wore some serious wet-weather gear, a type of oil-skin coat that was fleece-lined with a snugly fit collar and reflective strips.

Behind them strolled Troy, shoulders hunched in his jacket.

Without saying a word, she stepped back for everyone to enter the house. After all the wet shoes and damp coat removing was finished, she marched into the living room and turned to face them. "I've been calling and calling. Why didn't either of you answer?"

"Sorry, Natalie, my phone is flat after being on all day. It wasn't until I stuck it on the car charger that I saw your message. Since we were on the way home, I thought it best if I came in and explained. Besides, I wanted to ask you something." Troy's voice rang with sincerity.

Not that she believed him.

Noah ducked his head and shuffled his feet. "Cause I knew you'd yell at me for leaving the house. I wanted to talk to Troy."

"Couldn't it have waited? What was so important?" she all but roared. "You were supposed to be grounded."

Her son's face flushed red and, raising his head, he glared at her. "Dad. You hardly ever talk about him. About what he was like, about him when he was young. Troy said he was happy to have a chat. I thought once the search for Ms Lette is over, Troy would leave. I was worried he'd forget, and I wouldn't get another chance."

"I do talk about him," she said.

Noah shook his head. "Not really. You only say the usual stuff, like how he was a great dad and how he cared about us." He met her eyes, and her heart sank. "Anyway, I wanted to know what it's like in the Army. I'm thinking of joining when I finish school."

"What!" Natalie struggled to catch her breath. "No way. There is no way you are joining the military."

"You can't stop me!" shouted Noah. "I'm tired of being treated like an invalid. Once I have the operation, I will be fine!"

"This is your fault!" she raged, turning to face Troy. "You've put these ideas into his head."

Frowning, he held his hands up. "Hey! No way. All I did was answer some questions."

"I don't believe you."

His face reddened. "I can't help that."

"You're keeping secrets from me. I know there is more that you haven't told me about why you're here."

"I've told you everything," he snarled.

"Really? What have you told Noah? Did you tell him how you sweet talked me into leaving John to go out with you?" Natalie looked at her son, hating the words pouring from her mouth but unable to stop the flood. Everything was so tangled up inside. Edwina, John, Noah, and her feelings for Troy. Even Ernest. "He's not the hero you think him to be."

Eyes wide, Noah flicked his gaze from her to Troy and back again. "Mum... I'm sorry. I didn't mean to worry you."

"I never said I was any hero." A pulse ticked urgently in Troy's temple as he glared back at her. Nostrils flaring, he took a step closer to her. "You're certainly not as lily white as you pretend to be."

"How... " She raised her hand, but he caught it.

"I know your secret."

CHAPTER 16

Egypt,
November, 1917.

Dear mother, father and Matilda,

Well things are hotting up over here. Our brigade has participated in a number of raids now. We have pushed through Beersheba and on the Hebron road. The country here is terrible. Steep barren hills covered with flat slippery rock and big gorges. Our regiment has been on the move for a few days now and we have had no water for thirty-five hours. I long for a good night sleep and my throat is so dry I can barely swallow. How much worse my poor Blaze must feel and yet he continues to serve me faithfully. Yesterday we were hit by johnny turk. They rained shell after shell. So many dead men and horses. I carnt speak of their wounds and the cries of those still suffering, man and beast, was terrible to hear. We fell back to Beersheba and arrived late this night. I made sure old Blaze was taken care of before I saw to myself. I will write when I can.

Your affect. son, Gregory

Betrayal, hurt, anger and, let's face it, downright outrage waged a war inside Troy's chest as he stared at the woman he had once loved. "You heard me," he repeated when Natalie failed to respond.

Her hands went to her mouth and she gazed wildly from him to Noah and back again, shaking her head. "Please don't," she whispered.

Troy was beyond hearing her plea. She had wronged him. All those years. Wronged him – and wronged his best mate. "I'm Noah's father, aren't I? Not John. Me." Even he could hear the rage in his voice. On the rug beside the fire, Chip lifted her head to stare at them.

"M... m... mum?" stammered Noah. "What's he saying?"

"How could you?" Natalie went to pull Noah into her arms, but he yanked away.

His thin chest rising and falling rapidly as he struggled with the tears filling his eyes. "Mum?" he whispered again.

Her head went up.

Troy had to give her that, she sure had courage. Albeit she didn't often reveal her tough nature to others. He guessed she had had to be strong to pretend all these years and bring their son up by herself. The thought of all the time he had lost gutted him. His son. *He had a son.*

"This is not the way I wanted you to find out, Noah."

She held her hands out in a beseeching fashion. "But, yes, it's true. Troy is your biological father."

"I don't understand. Dad… isn't my dad?"

Natalie shot Troy a filthy glance. "He is and always will be your father in every sense of the word."

"John didn't know either, did he?" interjected Troy.

"That's where you're wrong. I told him everything about us. He knew I was pregnant with your child and wanted to marry me regardless. He wanted to be a father, and he loved you Noah, unconditionally."

"How can I believe you? When you've kept this from me my entire life." A tear trickled down Noah's cheek. He sniffled and wiped his nose with the back of his hand.

"I couldn't find the right words. I didn't want you to think any less of me or of your father – John, that is. When he died, there never seemed to be the right moment." She pressed a fist to her eyes for a moment then allowed her hands to drop by her sides. "When we married, he made me promise that neither of us would tell you until you were older. We were meant to do it together. I know that I should have told you earlier, but it felt like a betrayal to his memory. He left a letter to be given to you when you turned eighteen."

"I thought he died in a car accident? Then how did he know… ?"

"He didn't hon. It was like an insurance policy. I did the same by the way; if anything happened to me our solicitor also has my letter to give to you."

"Mum, you should have told me." After another furious glare at both of them, Noah ran from the room.

The sound of his bedroom door slamming made Chip jump to her feet and woof loudly.

Troy crossed over and petted his dog until she settled down. When he turned around, he found Natalie standing as far from him as possible. For some reason that sight stimulated another round of frustration and anger inside him.

"What made you realise?" she said, her lovely eyes narrowed to thin slits.

"Noah told me about his condition, his migraines, and the constant fatigue he suffers. I also suffered from a frontal sinus osteoma and had surgery to remove it when I was thirteen. It's a genetic condition." Suddenly all his anger disappeared, leaving him feeling utterly exhausted. Not because of the past gruelling days. "Plus, when I learned of his birthday, I did some maths."

"This doesn't change anything between us; or you and him."

"You can't keep me away from him, Natalie. I have a right to play a part in my son's life."

"So you can turn him into another adrenaline junkie – like yourself? I… I can't lose him, Troy." Her hands fisted.

"Still determined to tread the safe and narrow? That isn't living, Natalie. It's wasting your life."

"That's something we'll probably never agree on. But Noah – he is different. I want a different life for him than… " Her voice trailed away as she sought for a tissue then blew her nose.

"He'll choose his own path and there's nothing you can do to stop that."

"After you've poisoned his mind, filled his head with the fantasy of playing a hero."

Troy paced in front of the fire. "Is this what it's all about? After all these years, you still haven't forgiven me for the career I chose? At least give me the courtesy of explaining why you hated the military." Turning, he moved forward intending to hold her hands, but she shifted out of the way.

Natalie licked her lips and sent an agonising look towards Noah's closed bedroom door. To her credit, this time, she didn't leave him with no answers. With a sad sigh, she sank onto an armchair and told him about her childhood. About her father and all the fights. About how both he and her mother blamed his career for his drinking and the other women. About the hurling of furniture and how she'd hide in her bedroom and wish herself far, far away.

When she finished, Troy plopped onto the sofa and stared at her glumly. No wonder she'd been unable to commit to a life with him. In her eyes, he'd probably been the embodiment of her father.

"I was terrified that I would repeat the same cycle. I couldn't live the rest of my life like that," she admitted in a low voice. She explained how he never kept in touch with her, and how her mother rarely contacted her or her only grandchild. "Mum saw me as the reason why she stayed with him for so long. She resented me. I think that's why we don't speak."

"It's all a bit of a mess, isn't it?" Resting his arms on his knees, he allowed his shoulders to slump.

She nodded, tears brimming from her eyes and mopped her face with the tissue.

Her distress twisted his heartstrings. Although he believed he was the one who'd lost out all these years, he couldn't quite stifle the need to give her comfort. His voice came out gruff as he said, "Look. It's late and we'll both be back at the SES headquarters before dawn. I'd like to talk again with Noah, if he agrees. But not now. Let's leave the hard stuff for a couple of days."

At that, some of the fire returned to her face. "You're talking about custody or access."

"Geeze, Nat, you're not making this easy." He ran a hand over his jaw.

"Being a parent isn't easy. That's one thing you will have to learn. Another… " She rose to her feet and lifted her chin. "… Another is that if you decide to be part of his life – and that's only if it's what Noah wants – you can't walk away."

There it was – the other white elephant that had been lurking in the room ever since they'd met again. Because he had walked away. He hadn't fought for her, hadn't demanded she give a reason why he wasn't good enough to marry. Instead, he'd told himself some cock and bull about her having a better life with John. That his mate was the better man. He wanted to shout that he wasn't perfect, that he'd made a mistake, but he worried that the words would come out all wrong. Anyway, judging by the set of her mouth and her distant expression, she'd pushed him back into the past.

This time, he was damned if he would stay there when it came to a question of his son. What they needed at the moment was time for everyone to process all that had been revealed and for the emotions to settle.

Natalie walked to the front door and threw it open.

Talk about a hint.

Snapping his fingers for Chip to follow, he went and tugged his boots back on. Then lifting his jacket from the hook on the wall, he met her guarded gaze. "If you have no objections, I'd like to phone Noah tomorrow and apologise for the way I acted tonight. I intend to ask him if he'd like to meet with me again and talk."

"Right."

He went to walk out the door but paused on the threshold. "You should have told me, Natalie. Even if you didn't want me in your life, I had the right to know I had a son." Without waiting for her response, he headed for his ute, ushered Chip onto the front seat and slipped behind the steering wheel. Although he told himself not to, he looked in the mirrors as he drove away.

But she was gone.

All in all, the day had been one of extremes. The downright misery of being unable to locate Edwina, followed by the news he had a son and then to be hit with the turmoil of Natalie's past. A whirlwind *of 'what if's'* and *'she should have'* and *'I should have'* pounded through his head. Beset with conflicting thoughts, Troy arrived at Fig Tree Lodge and turned off the engine. After giving Chip time to do her business, he let himself into the converted stables with the key card he'd been given. The lights were on in the kitchen area of the main house. He couldn't imagine anyone over there getting much sleep these days. Since he'd grabbed a hamburger at the service station when he'd met Noah, he didn't need any more food. A hot shower and fresh clothes made him feel a little more human but hadn't washed away his confusion. Eating away at the back of it all, was the knowledge that he hadn't exactly covered himself in glory. He'd acted like a total ass. He'd been mean and spiteful, lashing out at Natalie for everything he'd missed in Noah's life; but knowing, deep down, she'd been right about his job. He wouldn't have given it up even for his own child. If he had, he would have regretted that decision.

After feeding Chip, he fell into bed. Tomorrow, he'd think more about the situation but now, well, now he had a phone call to return. The first time he rang the number, no one picked up so he tried again. This time, it was answered. Placing his elbow over his eyes, he said, "It's me. Listen, there's been a few developments I haven't told you about; the first one being – they found Edwina's coat."

CHAPTER 17

[Extract taken from Matilda Lette's diary.]
28th April, 1918.

My hand is shaking so hard I can barely write. Len from the Post Office walked the Herald to our house this morning. I knew as soon as I saw his face, the news would be bad. There was a report on raids in Egypt with a list of casualties and losses from a place called Jordan Valley in which the 1st and the 2nd Light Horse Brigades took part. I recalled Gregory writing that his 6th LH Regiment had moved under the 2nd LH Brigade. My heart all but leapt from my chest when I read private Gregory Lette was wounded and transported to Heliopolis hospital. Poor Mother has taken to her bed. Father has disappeared to the farm. We await with equal parts hope and dread for advice from the War office. I am writing this note in church and will spend the remaining day praying that God will watch over my dear brother's recovery.

The rain raged all night and into the next day; a consistent drumming on the roof of Fig Tree Lodge that sounded like the beating of military drums during a funeral march. With a storm forecast to hit the area that afternoon or early evening, a touch of desperation tainted the air of the SES headquarters that morning as new search areas were allocated to the teams who had braved the foul weather.

Personally, Ernest held out no hope whatsoever that the old lady would be found alive. Before he'd headed out, the police had cornered him to ask another round of the same questions; why lie about your name, what are you really doing in Bindarra Creek, do you know who attacked you and why; and on and on. There had been a speculative expression in Senior Constable Taylor's eyes that worried him. How deep was she digging? She'd even mentioned Natalie's idea that everything was related and asked for his opinion. As if he could answer that! There'd been that one strange moment when he'd been tempted to mention the Isis statue, and the odd feeling he'd had that someone was following him. But when it came down to it, he really had little more to add to what the police already knew; apart from his reasons for being in town, of course. He shuddered. This town, these people, they were getting to him. The sooner he was back on his home turf, the better.

Everyone was requested to meet back at the SES headquarters at lunchtime for another briefing session. Shivering despite his weather-proof clothes, Ernest poked amongst wet bushes and leech covered foliage as he and the other members of his team worked their way through their designated area. Nothing. He could have told them that; it didn't matter wherever she was - the old woman was long gone.

Silent and with their heads hanging down like old dogs, they stumbled back to the SES building. Cold and with wet feet where the rain had saturated his shoes, Ernest parted ways with his team. The air conditioners were running at full speed but didn't quite alleviate the chill in the air. At least hot food was on offer, courtesy of the members of the community who were unable to partake in the physical searches. After a bit of wandering around, he finally managed to spot Natalie. Maybe he could convince her to allow him to borrow the statue. All he needed was to dream up a good pretence. He called her name and pushed his way through the tired crowd to reach her side. Her pale face and the unhappy droop to her mouth worried him. What the dickens had happened? Was Edwina's probable fate getting too much for her? Or was it something else?

"What's wrong?"

She turned to face him, a small smile momentarily brightening her face. "It's been a difficult few days."

"Did I… is Noah alright?" Now where did that concern for some kid come from? Really, he hardly recognised himself, the way he was carrying on; as if he cared about some missing woman, and he was part of this community.

"He's fine. Not talking to me at the moment, after…

yesterday. The weather is so miserable, I kept him home from school." She pushed her dark hair away from her face and there was a sadness in her eyes, that spoke to him on a level no one had ever touched before.

He cupped a hand over her elbow and steered her over to a private corner. "Here, take my coat. You're shivering."

"Thank you. But what about you? It's so cold and I can't seem to keep warm."

"You've been doing too much. How about I run you home and you stay close to the fire the rest of today?" Hauling off his polar coat, he placed it around her shoulders.

"I can't – Edwina." Her voice broke and she looked away, lips trembling.

"At least, come and have something hot to eat." He was about to lead her to a table when a loudspeaker squawked and Roman Taylor mounted the podium to cancel any further search efforts for the remainder of the day.

When he finished, people began to disperse.

Natalie grasped Ernest's arm as if to hold him in place. "We can't stop."

"Seriously? You've seen what it's like outside and the BOM predicts this afternoon is only going to get worse. Everyone needs to rest. You need to rest. Then first thing tomorrow morning after the storm has passed, we can begin again."

"Do you think she can survive a storm after being out in the cold all this time?" The gravity in her eyes almost undid him.

Ernest cleared his throat and twiddled with the folds

of his thick scarf. "We can hardly see two metres in front of us at the moment. Think about how difficult it is going to be in the middle of a storm. We could walk right past her and not realise. The authorities have called it, Natalie. If we go out there, they may well have to send someone out to look for us. That's a waste of manpower and time."

"I guess you're right." She looked around at the rapidly thinning crowd then quickly jerked her head away, a rich flush mounting her cheeks.

I just bet I know who has caused that! Scowling, he nodded a curt greeting as Troy together with his blasted dog, joined them.

"I can give you a lift, Natalie," said Troy. Interestingly, he had black shadows under his hollowed-out eyes and the set of his face was grim. Even the normally annoying, energetic Chip seemed tired or depressed. She only managed a half-hearted tail wag before dropping onto her belly and placing her nose on her front paws. The dog coat she wore appeared to be saturated.

Natalie held up a hand. "Thank you, Troy, but I've accepted Ernest's offer. However, I don't want to go home. Since the search has been postponed for the rest of the day, I think we should check out the Lodge's library. Remember what we spoke about the other day?"

"Still chasing that old chestnut?" Troy sounded resigned as if he knew better than to argue. "You're right though. We should rule it out, just in case there is a clue we haven't spotted."

About to voice his own objections, Ernest paused. This could be his last chance at getting his hands on that statue.

If Natalie refused to hand it over, then maybe he could wheedle its whereabouts out of her. "An excellent idea."

The irritation on Troy's face was balm to his soul and he resisted rubbing his hands together.

"I'd love a shower first," said Natalie.

"Not a problem. I'm filthy myself, so I won't come in. Come on, I'm parked over here." After giving Troy a tight smile, he led Natalie out of the building and into the bleak day. They ran through the rain to his car, having to jump over the widening puddles. Mud splashed up the sides of his heavy-duty drill pants; not that it made much difference. They were all but ruined after slopping about in soggy fields and drenched bushland.

Fifteen minutes later, Ernest, with Natalie beside him, pulled up outside Fig Tree Lodge. The house was ablaze like a lighthouse beacon in the cold, grey day as if to show Edwina the way home. He parked as close to the house as possible, then found an umbrella to give Natalie a modicum of shelter as they hastened to the front door. After using his keycard, he shook the rain from his brolly and left it on the veranda. They both kicked off their damp shoes and Natalie remained in the hallway while he went to find Dodge to explain what they wanted to do.

Although Dodge didn't think much of the idea, he had no problem with them checking out the library, even told them to go through the entire house if they wanted to, so Natalie headed there straight away to wait while Ernest changed out of his clothes and wet socks. He pulled on a pair of loafers over his frozen but dry socked feet, tugged his sweater over his neatly pressed pants, smoothed back his thick silver hair, and padded down the stairs to the library. Upon entering, he discovered Troy had already beaten him to it.

The library was icy cold as if no one had been in there for some time. Even though Natalie had on a thick knitted jumper and jeans, she rubbed her arms as if she couldn't get warm. She wandered around the library, inspecting the titles on the myriad of books that were stuffed on the shelves. She looked over to Ernest and gave a weary smile. "I bet I know why it's so cold in here; and why I had that weird feeling we were being watched the day you were attacked. Matilda."

"What? Great Aunt Matilda? Isn't she dead?" Troy snorted as he inspected the book titles on the highest shelf.

Privately, Ernest agreed with him, not that he intended to say as much. Instead, he was content to remain quiet and listen. You never knew what interesting titbits you could learn by being a wallflower. If he was lucky, he'd work out what the dickens had happened between the two of them. They were both as stiff as a thousand-year-old mummy. Anyone with two eyes could see they looked right together. Not that he intended to tell either of them. He fingered a book on the mechanics of a steam engine while wondering whether he could just simply slump in a chair and stay there for the rest of the day. The hard work on a dig was nothing compared to what he'd endured lately searching for that dotty old lady.

"Yep. Edwina swears she haunts the house and appears when someone is in trouble. Someone connected to the family." Natalie smiled.

Ernest set his jaw. "You're telling me you believe in ghosts?"

"I keep an open mind." Natalie drifted over to the corner window which looked out over the lush gardens and where an old armchair had been placed with a small round table next to it. She placed a fingertip to the lamp adorning the table. Lace doilies abounded, over the head of the chair and along both arms, as well as beneath the lamp base. "I bet this was a favourite spot of hers. I can almost see her sitting here reading when the winter sun comes through the window."

"Ignoring your ghost for the moment, I wonder what the intruder was looking for in here." Troy turned around and leaned against a bookcase. "You do realise, it could have been Ernest who was in this room."

Ernest met the other man's ironic gaze.

"Yeah, I'm talking about you," drawled Troy.

"Rubbish. I've already given details of my whereabouts that day and I don't intend to repeat myself." Ernest glared back.

"Exactly. I can't see him damaging a couple of books as well as leaving the French doors open. Or somehow magically coshing himself on the head." Natalie planted her hands on her hips as she fired back. "Ernest is a scholar, an academic, books to him are like… I don't know… gold."

A warm glow settled around Ernest's heart. Maybe he *would* sit for a while. Choosing the most comfortable looking armchair, he settled back to watch and listen.

"You can't see how the timing is too coincidental? He

turns up in Bindarra Creek, your house is trashed, Edwina is missing. Don't blind yourself because you… like him. He could be involved." Troy did a lot of finger stabbing in Ernest's direction as he spoke.

"I don't believe it." Natalie's voice shook but there were shadows in her eyes that told a different tale. She had her suspicions where he was concerned. Pity. "He came here to meet me."

In a matter of seconds, Troy crossed the room and took her hands in his. "I'm not saying he isn't interested in you. Anyone with eyes can tell he's got it bad."

Feeling as though he had turned invisible, Ernest leaned forward so he didn't miss anything.

Natalie tried to pull away, but Troy wouldn't let her.

"You deserve someone special. I'm not convinced he is that guy."

The words burst from her lips as if she couldn't stop herself. "What? And you are?"

"I wish I was, but we both know that ship has well and truly sailed."

She wrenched her hands away and stomped over to stand beside Ernest. "You need to tell him about your name."

He had hoped that little gem would stay between him, the police and Natalie. Oh well. "For personal reasons, I used an alias. I'm an archaeologist and my surname is Callen."

"I knew you couldn't be trusted!" Troy burst out.

Dodge and his father, a grey-haired fellow called Warren, surged through the door. "What's going on in here? We can hear the shouting from the kitchen." Dodge looked at everyone in turn.

A second later, Tessa and her two daughters followed. The littlest girl immediately raced over to pet Troy's dog. The teenager who looked like a carbon copy of her mother, flopped into a chair and rubbed her red-rimmed eyes, while Tessa stood beside her husband. Ernest gained the impression that these two were more than a couple, they were equal partners. How strange, that he'd learned more about life in this small town, than anywhere else he had lived. In a calm voice, he summarised everything that had been said, even fessing up to his lying while Troy fairly simmered with anger in the corner.

Dodge said, "Both Abby and Riley must think you're okay, otherwise you would have been run out of town. Moving on to Natalie's idea that the break-ins and Gran's disappearance are connected. What did the police think about it?"

"Took it under advisement, and I'm quoting." Natalie hugged her waist.

"Mmm." Dodge shared a glance with his wife. "And you think there's answers in this room?"

"We've looked but haven't come up with anything, apart from talking about the ghost," Ernest said. "I have come round to Natalie's way of thinking. The answer could lie in the past."

"Matilda?" Tessa gaped at him. "Or do you mean someone in Grannie's past?"

"I miss her, Mum," burst out Kaylee and her mother hurried over to pull her into her arms. They snuggled together on the armchair.

Something strange happened. The open grief in the kid's eyes made Ernest look inside himself, and he didn't like what he saw. He paused. If he continued, there would be no going back. If there was a connection, then he had to speak out. The old bird's life was on the line. "No, I'm talking about someone else. Another woman. Someone probably just as special as your grandmother. Cleopatra, Queen of the Nile."

Everyone gasped. They had obviously never expected him to say *that* name.

"She's a fascinating woman, no less because her tomb and that of Mark Antony's has never been found." He rubbed his chest as a short pain squeezed his heart. His breathing faltered.

"Ernest? Are you okay?" Natalie leaned close.

"Yes, yes. A little heartburn." He rushed into speech as the pain intensified and black spots swam in front of his eyes.

"I'm confused. I have no idea what's going on here," muttered Dodge while his father shook his head. "What has this got to do with Gran?"

Ernest raised his voice. "As I was saying, even though she was a Roman prisoner, she somehow managed to escape and outsmart her enemy. When she committed suicide, she was determined, you see, that her and Marc Antony's remains would remain hidden from her conquerors forever."

"You're looking for her, for both of them, aren't you?" Kind, caring and smart – Natalie was no fool.

Ernest nodded slowly. "Remember I told you that since I was a child I've been fascinated with Egypt. The reason why I chose archaeology as my career – and my life's work."

"Which is to find their tomb," Troy interjected in a hard voice as the Lette family stared at him and Ernest.

The restriction in his chest eased and he shrugged, as he suppressed the relief he hadn't been about to have a heart attack. "What of it? Every man has to have a hobby. You can't deny I've been helpful to you *and* Ms Lette. Without my guidance, neither of you would ever have known the true value of the Isis statue, as well as all the other pieces you found." He turned to Natalie. "Do you recall when I told you it's believed Cleopatra fashioned herself after that ancient goddess?"

Natalie nodded.

"I trust the statue is safely under lock and key?"

Before she could respond, both Dodge and Warren burst into speech, demanding to know what they were talking about. Evidently, the wily old lady hadn't kept them up to date with the finds in the attic. While Natalie attempted to answer their questions, he fought his frustration and kept his attention on Troy. He was the one to watch.

Troy's expression ironed out as he tented his fingers and stared back at him.

Just in time, Ernest snatched back his gasp of surprise. *I know who he reminds me of!*

His mobile trilled. Pausing, he glanced at the caller ID and his gut went into freefall. More than a little bewildered, his hand hovered over the phone. It couldn't be a coincidence.

Snatching up the mobile and ignoring Natalie's query,

he raced from the room. His pulse fairly galloped through his body, as he leaned against the hallway wall and stared back into the library. With his gaze fixed on Troy, he answered the call. The voice on the other end sent another searing pain arcing through his chest.

"I know what you're up to, and I want in."

CHAPTER 18

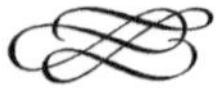

HELIOPOLIS, CAIRO.
2nd May, 1918.

Dear Matilda,

I write this from the hospital. My luck ran out a couple of weeks ago in the Jordan Valley. Valley is such a pretty word, makes me think of green rolling hills, shady trees and mobs of roos. This valley was no such thing. The heat was like being inside a fire and the sunlight blinding. The dust is so fine a small breath would send it swirling in the air to choke your throat. In the day were sandflies and at night mozzies. Mountains of sand and rock are the valley walls. It is a terrible place. The 2nd LH were on the right and hit with heavy artillery by the jerries and shelling by johnny turk. We were overrun but somehow counter attacked. A shell exploded under my poor Blaze. He fell and did not rise again. At first I did not feel any pain then I saw the piece of metal sticking out from my belly. Charlie Law and Tag dragged me behind the lines. I remember little until I woke here. The fever is the worst of it.

Dear sister I fear I will not walk as I carnt feel my legs or feet. I have placed my trust in God's hands.

Tell mother to not worry. I am treated well and the doctors and nurses work hard to save us all.

I send my love to you and father, and especially to mother. I miss you sister and pray I will see everyone at home once more, Gregory.

"NOAH! I'M HOME." Natalie dropped her damp parka by the front door, calling out as she toed off her soggy shoes and pushed inside the cold, gloomy house. She should have braved her blisters and gumboots when she'd come home to change earlier. Her joggers were not up to the task given the crazy wet weather showed no sign of easing any time soon. Then again, she didn't normally spend day after day out in the elements searching behind bushes sloshing through puddles and around houses for a missing, elderly woman. The weather was bitter, with stinging rain and a wind that cut right through to the bone. The clouds remained low and heavy with moisture; and the weather bureau kept issuing warnings of a major storm system heading their way. Every minute Edwina remained unaccounted for, meant her chances of surviving another night diminished. The authorities had deemed the current circumstances too difficult if not downright dangerous for the search to continue that day.

Shivers racked her aching body as Natalie removed her key from the lock and closed the door. Troy was still parked in his ute out the front of her house. Was he waiting for her to turn and wave? Truly she didn't have the energy to think about their shattered relationship. Her focus had to be Noah. She'd hoped that he'd had time to think through the shocking revelations of yesterday and was willing to sit and listen. There was so much to say, she wasn't certain exactly where to begin. Perhaps starting with an explanation of her own childhood might help him understand the difficult decisions she had made.

Stepping into the living room, she switched on the light. The harsh single globe did little to warm the frigid room and she hurried across to stack a fresh pile of wood in the fireplace then set it alight. Strange that Noah hadn't done so already but once he had his headphones on, he became blind and deaf to the rest of the world. She knew he was home as she'd spotted the faint glow of light shining through his bedroom curtains when Troy's car had pulled into the kerb.

The fire crackled into life. She pulled off her wet socks and draped them over the edge of the coffee table to dry. Her stiff bare feet curled into the thin carpet as she stood enjoying the first wafts of warm air over her tired body. Soon the fire would warm the entire room. She couldn't wait to sit in an armchair and toast her toes. Pushing hair from her eyes, she entered the kitchen, intending to prep for dinner; after which she'd spend time working on the book and checking over the catalogue of the items from the attic. She had to keep busy because if she stopped, she feared she'd give into the depression crawling the corners of her mind.

She began to take the vegetables to roast out of the refrigerator and lay them onto the counter. Despite all the re-hashing of everything that had occurred, little had been resolved. When she'd left with Troy and his dog, the Lette family were searching the house, again, for anything that could indicate Natalie's suggestion was correct. She was positive the Isis statue was at the heart of the matter – but the *who* was the problem. Ernest had disappeared, presumably to rest; so she'd accepted Troy's offer to drive her home.

It suddenly struck her how silent it was inside the house – like she was the only one breathing. She drank a glass of water before checking the clock over the stove. Two-thirty. Feeling as if she was wading through quicksand, she went to Noah's bedroom. The door was closed. No sounds came from inside. That wasn't unusual. If he had his headphones on…

After giving a short rap, she opened the door, but his room was empty. His school backpack sat on the floor, the flap folded back and a textbook stuck halfway out. The old laptop they both shared sat on his bed, the screen blank.

"No, no, no, no, no," she chanted under her breath as she charged back into the kitchen. Then stopped. There in the centre of the dining table was a piece of white paper propped up against the fruit bowl. Not an envelope, just a single sheet of paper.

'Mum. Mobile coverage down. Gone to the cemetery to visit Dad. Don't worry. Will be home for lunch. N.'

Her heart stuttered when someone pounded on the kitchen door. Paper in hand she crossed the room and opened the door.

Troy stood shaking water from his wet hair. Beside him, his dog imitated his actions, sending droplets cascading over the floor and the bottom of Natalie's legs.

"May we come in?"

Remembering their altercation of the previous night and Troy's actions, a bad taste filled her mouth. Not budging from where she blocked the doorway, she said, "What do you want?"

"I wanted to talk – to both you and Noah, if he's home and agreeable." Troy peered over her shoulder. "Do you mind asking him?"

Her gaze shot to the paper bunched in her hand. "No, he's gone to the cemetery."

"In this weather?" Troy jerked his thumb at the rain pouring from the laden sky. "How about I go and pick him up?"

The alternative was seeking her son out alone, which wasn't particularly inviting. A little company would be nice; and it didn't mean she actually had to talk if she didn't feel up to discussing the heavy stuff right now. Making a snap decision, she snatched her coat off the hook and rammed a beanie over her hair. "No. We'll go together but in my car," she said as she thrust her bare feet into her damp shoes.

Turning, she grabbed her keys and all but pushed Troy and his dog out of the house. She tugged the hood over her beanie and, head down, splashed down the path to where her old Toyota sedan was parked beneath the carport.

"I didn't think this old girl actually worked. Every time I see you, you're either on your bike or walking." Troy shooed Chip into the rear before sliding onto the passenger seat.

With a creak like the cracking of old bones, Natalie slammed her door shut and started the engine. As she reversed down the drive, she said, "That's because it's not registered. I couldn't afford to get new tyres and pay for the rego, so I let it lapse for a while."

"Is that because you're saving for Noah's operation?"

"Yep. Got it in one." The gears crashed as she jiggled the car into drive. "Sorry about all the noise. It hasn't been driven much lately." She tossed him a quick grin. "Only when I'm certain the cops are well out of the way and won't do me for driving an unregistered vehicle."

His eyes widened and he smiled slowly. "I'm impressed. That's quite a risk for you."

"I did tell you – I'm not the same person."

"Neither am I."

Their eyes met and held for a long, breath-taking moment, until she wrenched hers back to the road. "Keep an eye out for him, please? He may already be on his way home. If so, he'll be on his bike. I'm okay with you talking to Noah, by the way. But only after I've had my session with him first."

"What are you going to say?" Troy rubbed condensation from the side window.

She chewed her lip and squinted as she leaned forward to peer out of the misty windscreen as the wipers worked overtime. "Gosh. This rain. It's so hard to see." She slowed as she neared the round-about then picked up a little speed as she turned into Main Street. "Don't worry. I'm not going to rubbish you or anything."

"I didn't think that you would – you're not the spiteful type. So you're going with the honest approach?"

Flicking on her blinker, she stopped and waited until a fuel tanker zoomed past, going way too fast for the crappy conditions, before turning onto Church Street. "Yes. Total confession time. I'm hoping that he'll come to accept that although we both may have made mistakes, it was only with the best of intentions."

Troy grunted, his gaze apparently glued to the passing scenery.

Not that there was anyone walking or riding down the road. The streets were deserted, although a couple of vehicles had passed them going in the opposite direction. Some kind of dark-coloured SUV, followed a few seconds later by a jeep.

"Why the cemetery?" Troy asked.

"He sometimes goes to talk to John." She applied the brakes to slow down at the Willow Drive intersection but didn't stop. "The cemetery is on the left. Even though he's buried next to his father in a Sydney cemetery, I had a memorial plaque placed in the grounds. Somewhere for us both to visit when we needed to."

Troy turned around and frowned at her when she turned into Wattle Drive. "Aren't we close to the SES?"

"Yes. The cemetery is opposite the carpark. You can't see it though, due to the trees planted along the boundary.

I'm going to park outside St Ignatius church. Here we are." The car jolted forward then shuddered to a halt.

They sat for a few seconds while the rain hammered on the car roof. "Can't see him," shouted Natalie. "I'm going to check." Pulling the hood back up over her beanie, she zipped up her coat and cranked open the door.

"I'm coming with you." His jacket already on and done up, Troy clapped a damp baseball cap onto his head and followed. Chip leaped out but stayed close to his side, tail down and sending both of them reproachful looks now and then. No doubt she was also tired of running about in the rain, even though she wore her fleece-lined oil-skin coat.

The ground was sloppy, full of puddles. With the familiarity of having visited plenty of times over the past few years, Natalie wound her way around the old head-stones and newer grave sites. Water sloshed over her joggers, saturating the bottoms of her jeans. The chill began to seep into her bones, setting her teeth chattering. The hood was already damp. It wouldn't be long and her coat would be soaked. At least the hood's overhang protected her face sufficiently that she could see where she was going. She quickened her pace hoping to warm herself up. Then almost fell flat on her face when she tripped over a fallen branch that had been hidden in a puddle. So much for thinking she was on the ball.

Troy's arm came around her waist. "Steady on," he said in a loud voice. He flicked on his phone torch to give them more light.

Nodding, she lessened her strides a trifle and indicated

with her wet hand the row where her husband's memorial plaque was placed. No one was there.

Troy leaned closer. "We must have missed him."

"Maybe. We didn't pass him on the road though. Let's check the entire cemetery and if the church is unlocked, I think we should look inside there too."

He nodded.

By the time they'd conducted a complete circuit of the cemetery, Natalie was shivering. Alarm bells were going off like firecrackers inside her head. She told herself not to worry, that she was being silly, that the last time she'd gotten all het up about Noah's non-appearance he had been with Troy.

But this time – Troy was with her.

Hot nausea roiled in a belly that fluttered with so many nerves she felt like she must have swallowed a flock of birds.

Troy tried the church doors, but it was locked down tight. They stood on the step under the portico, a brief respite from the onslaught of rain and icy wind. A wet Chip huddled close to their legs.

"He's not here," Troy stated. "Check your phone again, maybe he's sent you a message. He could be at a mate's place."

Natalie was already shaking her head. "I know he's angry and hurt with me, but he knew how worried I was last night. He wouldn't do that to me again."

"I'll take your word for it."

Fingers stiff with cold, she located her mobile in an inside pocket and held it close to keep the rain from the screen.

The message icon was lit.

"It's Noah. It has to be." Breath whooshing from her mouth, she quickly opened the app. The phone wobbled in her trembling hand as she re-read the text hoping that she'd had some kind of mind warp.

She hadn't.

'Bring statue. Wards Gully. Thirty mins. No cops or N's dead.'

Leaning over her shoulder, Troy sucked in a sharp breath. "I don't believe this – what the devil is going on in this town? Can you tell who sent it?"

Tears welling in her eyes, she stared at Troy. She had the oddest sensation that she stood on the edge of a precipice. *One wrong move.*

"Troy." Reaching out, she bunched a fistful of his coat in her hand. "The ID is blocked," she croaked, struggling to fill her lungs with air. It was as if someone had punched her in the throat. She tried again, "Troy. Look. The message says it was sent fifteen minutes ago."

"Bloody useless network," Troy bit out. His face filled with a purpose that should have frightened her. Instead, it not only comforted her but infused her own wilting courage. "The statue?"

"Locked in the laundry."

As one, they turned and raced back to her car. Chip, picking up on their urgency, bounded ahead.

"I'll drive," stated Troy as he wrenched open the driver's door.

Natalie handed him the keys and shoved Chip into the car, before falling onto the seat. She'd barely shut the door before Troy was hurtling out of the carpark. She gripped the seatbelt as they roared down the street. "I'm guessing whoever it is, cornered Noah in the cemetery. Probably thinking they could force him to tell them where the statue is and then when he tells them that I have the only key, they use him as collateral."

The old sedan tore through the round-about.

"Do we tell the police?" she asked, as a few seconds later Troy pulled up outside her house.

His face when he looked at her revealed the same indecision that she felt. He stretched out his hand. "Honestly, I'm in two minds about it – but – your call."

She placed hers in his, linking their fingers together for a brief moment. "I say we take the statue to Wards Gully now. We don't wait for the police, but I *will* phone them and let them know what's happened. They can meet us there."

"I was hoping that's what you'd say. I'm with you, Natalie. From here on in, I'm walking beside you." Raising her hand to his lips, he kissed her cold skin. "Let's go. Where's this Wards Gully?"

They were out of the car and sprinting around the side of the house towards the laundry building.

"It's a section of Bindarra Creek, over Swallows Bridge way. There's a decent rock pool with a lot of boulders on the banks and in the creek itself. Passageway is via a narrow dirt road called Diggers Lane. With this rain, the road may be in a crap condition."

"We'll take my ute, then."

Natalie had her keys out already and jammed them into the lock. She yanked the door open, crying, "Normally, it takes a good fifteen to twenty minutes to reach Wards Gully. Troy! What if we don't get there in time?"

He pushed past her to rip the lid off the top box and drag out the statue. "We will. Whoever it is, wants this bloody thing and wants it bad. They will wait. And we – *we* will find our son."

CHAPTER 19

2.00AM. 29TH AUGUST, 1918.

D. A. LETTE, ESQ.

FIG TREE HOUSE, BINDARRA CREEK.

Regret to inform you it is officially reported your son Private Gregory Lette has passed and is now in God's care. My condolences to you and your family.

Colonel .... [name illegible]
Victoria Barracks, Sydney.

Icy rain plummeted from the cloud-laden sky in bucketloads although the thick foliage of the old willow tree cushioned the onslaught a tad. The heavy droplets plopped onto

Troy's hair and already soaked shoulders. He wiped the moisture from his face with the back of his hand, his body rigid as shock rippled through him. Merely three metres away, a man stood holding a knife to Noah's throat with an arm welded across the boy's chest to keep him in place.

Time slowed like an old newsreel making Troy doubt the evidence in front of him. However, there was no escape from the terror widening the boy's bulging eyes or his sheet-white skin. Or the tiny pricks of blood sliding down Noah's neck.

The dread that had been prowling around the edges of Troy's mind these past days, morphed into harsh reality. His instincts that something bigger, something darker was about to occur hadn't been wrong. What *had* been wrong was the direction he'd thought the danger would spring from. Never had he imagined the danger would come from his own family.

Feeling as though his world had splintered apart and he was the biggest fool on the planet, Troy croaked out, "*Dad?* What are you doing here?"

Beside him, Natalie emitted tiny sobs interspersed with gasps as if she struggled to fill her lungs with air. Or more likely to stop herself from rushing forward and throwing herself at the bloke to save her son. He snapped his fingers around her wrist and gave her a warning squeeze. Now was not the time for heroics. Her entire body was so tense Troy suspected at any moment she would forget caution – an action that could cause his father to make a fatal move. One slip of that blade and nothing any of them could do would save Noah.

"I got tired of you pussy-footing around." His father shot fury from his eyes as he glared at Troy.

"*What?* I don't understand. Troy… do you know this man?" Natalie clutched at Troy's arm.

"I've got no idea what's going on. But, yeah, I hate to admit it, but this is my father, Mark Davidson." Chip gave her wet coat a vigorous shake and whined as she picked up on the menace tainting the air. He indicated for her to stay behind him.

Natalie wrenched her hand free and flung Troy a hate-filled glance. "I should never have trusted you again. Noah… oh please… don't hurt him," she ended on a sob.

"Please, believe me. I had nothing to do with this. I didn't even know he was in town." Troy glanced at Natalie, and her despairing expression cut him to the core. "I'd never hurt or cause Noah to be harmed in any way. Natalie… please… "

Catching herself on a sob, she nodded as she brushed tears from her cheeks. "I want to believe you."

"You *can* trust me… "

"Spare me the hearts and flowers," his father sneered. Noah must have attempted to lean away or maybe he shivered, because Mark shook the arm he held. "Keep still, you little shit."

Troy could see his son's weather-proof anorak where it lay tossed in a puddle, the sleeve almost ripped in half as if the garment had been ripped off in a struggle. "For heaven's sake, Dad. I don't know why you're doing this but leave Noah alone. He's a good kid, he doesn't deserve to be hurt."

He slipped one hand behind his back and made two

hand gestures – *back away, circle round*. Chip melted into the melee of sweeping willow branches while Troy took a step forward only to freeze once more as the soggy mud squelched underfoot.

Stealth wasn't an option while they stood so close to the banks of what had two weeks previous been a placid creek. Both the river and the creek it fed into were swollen from the torrential rain that had occurred further north and now in this area. Water cut into the creek's edges as the level rose higher and higher. Soon, the creek would be lapping at their feet. There had been no sign of the police when they'd arrived at Ward's Gully. No time to wait for them to turn up, that's if they'd even received the multiple messages Natalie had sent on their drive to the creek. No calls would go through, and with the intensity of the storm cell ravaging the area, it was doubtful her messages had been received.

That meant – it was down to him and the woman he loved to save their son. If Troy had thought it was a nightmare before, now it was worse than anything he could have ever imagined.

Darkness infused his father's face as he snarled, "Don't move, or this kid will pay the price."

Troy balled his fists. "Bloody hell, Dad. Why? What's going on?"

"The Isis statue – that's what I want. I know that woman with you must have it hidden somewhere. I searched all over her house but couldn't find it. Then I decided I needed to up the ante." Mark Davidson all but spat the words. "What? You think I sent you here on some kind of holiday? You were supposed to get me an inventory of what's in that house. As well as convince the old bat to sell-up. But no, instead you fail to deliver. Loyalty to our family obviously means nothing to you." His face twisted into an expression Troy had never seen him wear before – the real man behind the polished façade was finally revealed.

It was so sickening, a tremor shuddered deep inside Troy. He'd faced enemy fire many times. Never had he experienced such a gut-wrenching fear. If Noah was harmed… there would be nowhere Mark Davidson could hide. Troy would hunt him down and make him pay.

There had to be some way to reason with him, because when it came down to it, Noah had to live. All those wasted years when he'd never known he had a son. Now he had an opportunity to be part of his life. Unfortunately, that life could well be cut short by the man Troy had looked up to and held on the highest pedestal since the moment he'd drawn breath.

Mark shuffled sideways, dragging Noah with him. The knife never wavered from its position. "Tell me where it is, and the boy won't be hurt."

"I'm sure we can work something out. Let Noah go and we'll talk." Troy held his hands out.

"Stop treating me as if I've lost my marbles! I know exactly what I'm doing." Mark bared his teeth in a brutal grimace. "It's all your mother's fault. She's the one who wants, wants, wants. Nothing has ever been enough for her. She's the reason I'm up to my neck in debt. She's the reason I funnelled my clients' money into my own accounts." He barked a harsh laugh. "*She's* the reason I went to bed with criminals. They sent me a hit list and my name's at the top." Mark grimaced, his eyes flickering shut for a brief moment.

Maybe now was the time. Troy took a sideways step as Chip wound through the drooping branches. She was almost in position – a few more steps and she would be a metre or so to the right of his father. Close enough to launch at him. Cold sweat beaded Troy's forehead. Lightning flashed across the dark, green-tinged sky then thunder rumbled. The storm was about to unleash its fury any moment now.

"Don't go trying any of your army tactics on me. I won't hesitate to use this blade. I've got nothing left to lose."

"He's your grandson!" blurted Natalie. She brushed aside a swaying branch of dripping leaves when it slapped against her. "I was pregnant when I married John. I never told Troy that he was the father but it's true. Surely you won't hurt your own flesh and blood?"

"As if I care! About you. About my wife or my own son! Don't you understand, you stupid cow? *They...will... kill...me.* I need money to start a new life far away from here. And you, you dumb twirp, you have the means I need. It's a no brainer. Statue – kid's alive. You've got ten seconds to tell me where to find it."

Keep him talking, anything to delay his actions until Troy could work out a plan of attack. "If you're in trouble, maybe I can help."

Mark gave a derisive laugh that sent the hairs on the back of Troy's neck prickling. "What? You can bail me out on an Army pension? Hah! I owe millions to that shark. Millions to a hell of a lot of people who entrusted me with their life savings. And whose fault is it?" Spittle formed at the side of his mouth.

"Not Mum's. Not mine. And certainly not your innocent grandson. Come on, Dad. Put the knife down and let Noah go. We'll work something out." Softening his voice, he took another two steps while gesturing for his dog to *get ready*. If only she remembered her training and didn't bark, they might have a chance.

For a few seconds the banshee howling of the wind dropped while the washing-machine churn of the creek raged on. A distant shout cut through the dense bushland causing everyone to jump. Was help on its way or something worse?

"Five, four…"

"Wait! I've got it." Ignoring Troy's outflung hand, Natalie pushed past him, shrugging the backpack off her shoulders. She pulled out the Isis statue and dropped the bag to the ground. The statue wobbled in her shaking hands as she lifted it high.

Mark licked his lips, shifting the knife a tad from Noah's throat. "Give it to me!"

"Let him go first," Natalie begged. "Please."

Shifting from foot to foot as if he was weighing up options, Mark arrowed his glare onto Natalie before snarling, "No, I've got a better idea. I don't trust either of you to not do anything stupid. Both of you, get walking."

Troy didn't budge. He held his index finger up then twisted his hand palm down and Chip sat. "Where?"

"Just get moving if you want this kid to live. Head west. There's a track running alongside the creek, follow it."

Jaw tight and battling his rising frustration, he splashed through the puddles and helped Natalie to her feet.

"And keep that dog of yours under control. Don't underestimate me, Troy."

Wordless, Troy scooped up the backpack, and motioning for Chip to fall in behind, he took Natalie's hand in his as they trudged forward through the relentless rain. He held back dripping branches and steered her over the boggy path which meandered around trees. The scrub grew thick and close, muffling the rush of the nearby creek and blanketing all other sounds. Shouts for help wouldn't travel far and even if he was able to send a message without being seen, it was doubtful there was network coverage in such dense bushland. Worse, he had no idea if the police had received their desperate messages for help.

They were on their own.

Ideas and plans of action flashed through his brain only to be discarded. With Noah's life on the line, this time he had to take the cautious route. He still found it hard to believe he was trapped in a situation that never in his wildest dreams he'd imagined he would encounter. His father – *his own father* – threatening to kill because he was in debt to loan sharks.

The last time he had seen his father in Sydney, there had been no hint anything was wrong in his parents' insulated, upper-class world. Like every other time they'd met, Mark had smiled and oozed self-confidence as impenetrable as a nuclear bunker. His mother had swanned off to lunch-dates with friends, wearing enough diamonds to dazzle the sun. Now Troy wondered how much of it was fake.

Had she known? Was she privy to his father's ruthless behaviour? Did she condone it? The possibility that both his parents could descend into such lawlessness shattered his heart. His life was a sham. "I'm so sorry. I've been feeding him information about what's been going on here. I had no idea he was even in town."

Tears slipped down Natalie's cheeks but there was little he could do to comfort her. He didn't dare do more than squeeze her fingers. Not with his father following behind and holding a knife to Noah's throat.

Troy was ready. All he needed was an opening, a slip of inattention, anything that would cause his father to shift that bloody knife away from Noah. Although what he intended to do was still something he couldn't decide.

Overhead the clouds roiled, and thunder rumbled followed by a crack of lightning so loud Natalie stumbled. The wind whipped through the trees in renewed frenzy, scattering leaves in all directions. He caught a whiff of sulphur. That storm was too close.

Shivering, Natalie twisted her head around to look at her son who staggered in Mark's fierce grip. "It's okay, hon. Everything's going to be okay."

His father hooted with laughter as they emerged into a small clearing edged by a thorny blackberry bush and the creek, which had breached the bank not far from where they all stood. The water swirled around the roots of a massive old willow. The tree's branches leaned out over the turbulent surface. The billowing wind lashed the creek into frothing waves that could rival an ocean.

Beneath the swaying willow tree branches was a make-shift shelter. Rain pelted onto a tarp tent rigged over a low-lying branch of the tree and anchored in place with ropes and tent pegs. In the shadowed interior, a slight figure lay curled in the foetal position on the hard ground.

"Oh my... is that... *Edwina?*" Natalie surged forward, but Troy tightened his grip on her hand. She flung him a fulminating glance.

He shook his head and didn't let go.

Mark bellowed, *"Don't move!"* at the same time as Noah cried out.

Chip growled, her hackles stiff and her body angled towards the bush. Sobbing, Natalie clutched the statue to her chest.

Troy slipped an arm around her cold shoulders as they turned to face Mark and his captive. He leaned close to her ear. "Someone's coming."

Footsteps thudded and a man burst through the scrub. It was Ernest, panting as if he'd run a marathon. His wide-eyed gaze travelled from Mark to Troy and back again.

"What are you doing here?" snapped Mark, yanking Noah closer to his body.

The kid sent pleading eyes towards his mother, but Natalie stared at Ernest as if she couldn't believe what she saw.

Ernest lifted a hand in the air then bent over like he struggled to catch his breath.

"You know each other?" *I knew he wasn't a man to be trusted.* If only he stood closer then Troy could have punched him in the face for the hurt Natalie must be feeling at his duplicity.

"Ernest?" whispered Natalie, her voice trembling as she scrubbed tears from her cheeks.

His father snorted. "How do you think I knew about the amulet? I knew Ernest was onto something when he disappeared to this dump of a town. I've been following his exploits for years. I always hedge my bets both ways. You, my dear son, were supposed to sniff out what the old bat was up to while inspecting the house. I expected Ernest to find the blasted thing, and then I'd do a deal with him. Instead, this stupid woman got her hands on it. Can't work out where she hid it, though. I searched every-where in her house."

"You were the one who tore my house apart! My land-lord is threatening to sue if I don't repair the damages." At least her voice had firmed and no longer held the threat of tears. She sent Troy a glance he couldn't read.

"As if I care! I've got more important things on my mind like getting the hell out of this place before those goons catch up with me." Mark turned to the other man. "Well? I told you to stay at the house."

"I've been looking everywhere for you. As soon as you phoned me, I knew you had to be the one behind it all. No way was I going to wait and allow you to steal the statue for yourself." Gulping, Ernest straightened and avoided looking in Natalie's direction. His face was pale beneath his tan and a pulse ticked erratically near his temple as he peered into the shelter. "My God! Is that Ms Lette? I think she needs a doctor." Eyes rolling like a terrified animal, he flapped his hand towards the tent.

"Thought I could get her to talk. But the stupid woman refused to co-operate. Kept yabbering on about someone called Matilda and saying the devil was close." He snig-gered. "Now she doesn't say anything at all. That's why I needed this kid."

"What do you mean she won't speak? What have you done?" Ernest shook his head wildly. "My God, Mark! Don't tell me you've murdered her!"

CHAPTER 20

[Extract taken from Matilda Lette's diary]
4 September 1918

We have no word from Mitchell for months now. Every day we wait. And wait. But nothing comes. After chores I rode Barney to our special place. I hoped – maybe there where we spent so many happy days I would feel my brothers beside me. I could pretend that the war had never happened. I was wrong. Alfred and Gregory are gone. Truly gone. Mitchell could be lying wounded or dead as I write. I have never felt this alone.

The storm erupted in a crescendo of howling wind. Cringing, Natalie raised an arm over her head while cradling the Isis statue close. "Murder," she repeated.

Edwina couldn't be dead. She couldn't! Or was Ernest talking about her son? Did he believe Mark Davidson intended to kill her boy? *Noah. Please no. Not him, never him.* Sickness rose, strangling her voice and burning her throat. Stupid, useless tears brimmed behind her eyes, and she shook them away.

"Give me the statue!" shouted Mark.

"Let the boy go. You don't need him. No one needs to get hurt." Ernest snuck a sideways peek at Troy before reaching out towards Natalie.

She shook her head and stepped backwards. He was in league with the enemy. Something else she had difficulty in processing. She'd thought he was a friend. Had, when she first met him, considered he could be someone she could grow old with. How wrong she'd been to try for happiness. She'd brought evil to a town that had welcomed her and Noah. A community that had made them feel they belonged. Her gaze darted once more to the still figure and she had to choke back another sob.

Thunder cracked across the sky. The rain increased in intensity, smacking onto trees and the surface of the creek, as the temperature dropped further. Wind whipped through the willow tree's branches. With the day darkened prematurely by the heavy cloud cover, it was hard to see what Davidson was doing and whether Noah was unhurt. Her son's face shone pale and blood trickled down his neck.

Teeth chattering, she wished she could offer Noah her jacket but was loathe to do anything that might antagonise that lunatic.

Twisting around she checked the creek, and her belly

clenched. The level was rising. She turned back and stumbled over a tree root. Her hand braced against the trunk. Balance regained, her fingers trailed over the bark. She could just make out faint initials. *AM* - maybe a *S* or *O* then another *M*. There was another smaller set higher up and even more indistinct. Wiping her hand over her damp pants, she noticed Chip.

The dog remained rigid and still stared into the bushes. Was someone else out there? Could the police have received the message and be on their way?

She cut her gaze to Troy. Ignoring the rain shooting like bullets from the sky, he had his head tilted like he was straining his ears to listen. Maybe someone *was* close by – someone who could help, or at least provide a diversion. Maybe if she kept playing for time…

Mark ordered, "Get that statue off her, Callen. Break it open. I've got to see the treasure hidden inside."

As if she needed any more evidence they *were* in this debacle together! Had to be if he knew Ernest's real surname. Her disappointment cut deep. Not budging an inch from her relative protection beneath the branch, she held the statue out in front of her. If he wanted it, he'd have to come to her.

Mumbling something that could be an apology but was hard to discern over the clash of the storm, Ernest approached. He kept his head down, hidden under the hooded polar jacket he wore. Probably couldn't look her in the eye, the traitor. He took the statue and turned it over in his hands then frowned.

"What? What the devil is wrong now?" barked Davidson.

Ernest looked over at the other man and yelled, "Was it you who hit me over the head?"

"Huh? Why would I do that?" Mark switched his gaze in a nervous manner about the clearing.

"Well, someone did."

Noah's lips were blue. He was shivering so hard it was visible from where Natalie stood. His thin tee-short was soaked through to the bone, as were his mud-coated jeans. They had to do something – soon – or he might catch pneumonia. As if to amplify her thought a wheezing cough came from the direction of the tent.

Natalie almost sagged to the ground, so great was her relief. The old lady was still alive – but for how much longer was the question. She'd already been out in the middle of winter for several days and nights. It was a miracle she had survived this long. However, the ferocious storm could well prove the final straw.

She shot Troy a glance filled with fear and determination, hoping he would interpret her intention. Ensuring she remained beneath the sliver of protection the branch provided from the deluge, she inched her way forward.

She had to get that knife off Davidson. Or at the very least trick him into moving it sufficiently away from Noah's neck to reduce the threat when Troy made his move. Whatever that might be. Because every sense she possessed told her Troy was waiting for the optimum moment. No way would he stand by and allow her son – *their son* – to be hurt or killed.

With that sudden realisation every shaky nerve settled inside, and a sense of calm flooded her. She believed in Troy. He was nothing like her father. The restless energy

Troy had possessed when young was gone – replaced with a steadfastness she knew would hold firm through whatever life threw at them. She trusted him and the strategic skills he'd learned over a lifetime of fighting an enemy. She trusted in her own maternal instinct to protect. And she knew that together they would both do everything in their power to save their son.

Ernest had yet to obey Davidson's latest demand. He still scowled and fingered the statue. Was something praying on his mind? Natalie hadn't missed the expression of dismay on his face when he'd seen Noah. Or herself for that matter. "You know who attacked me. You were there that day. I bet it was you who wrecked those books in the library."

Davidson rolled his eyes and yanked Noah a bit closer. "So? I tore up a couple of books. Big deal. But yeah. I wanted to talk to you. Let you know I was in town, and I was not going away. I thought since I was there, I'd rifle through Edwina's desk. Then I decided instead to keep a close eye on you."

In her peripherals, Natalie spotted Troy signalling his dog. She took another cautious step. *Keep him talking. Distract him.* "No one else was in the house. We know because Troy and I both checked. It had to be you who hit Ernest."

"Don't be stupid. It was a warning. I'm guessing one of the loan shark's goons followed me to the house. Probably thought Ernest was me and decided to send a message."

"That makes sense. There was only the single bulb over the stairs, it was pretty dark in the cellar and we both have grey hair. Plus I had my back to the doorway. It wouldn't be until I fell to the floor that whoever hit me would have realised I wasn't you." Ernest ran his finger along the crack in the statue. Rain drummed on his anorak as lightning flashed through the clouds.

Two seconds later, there was an almighty bang that made her heart leap, her hands going to her ringing ears. The air crackled with electricity and her hair frizzled. The stench of burning hit her nostrils. Water flowed over her joggers and lapped around the tent pegs where Edwina lay so still. The creek was rising fast.

"We need to get out of this storm," she whispered; and they needed to move Edwina to higher ground, or she could drown at their feet.

No one was listening. Ernest and Mark were busy glaring at each other, suspicion etched in their faces while Troy gave off an intense vibe, like he was about to explode at any moment.

Fury bounced off him in waves as he ran a hand along his jaw. "Bloody hell, Dad. What have you gotten yourself into?"

"Me? I'm just like anyone else these days. Out for as much money as I can get."

"Even if you have to rob others?" Troy sneered.

"Get on with it, Callen! I want out of this dump within the next hour. All those times I listened to you brag about the treasures in that lost tomb, and how you'd be the one to discover it. Looks like it will pay off big time for me." A smirk spread over Mark's face. "Got me a passage to South America on a freighter leaving Newcastle harbour later tonight. Those idiots watching the airports are going to look stupid when the boss realises I am gone."

"You'll leave Mum to face the fall-out alone?" Shock resonated in Troy's voice, and he reeled backwards as if he couldn't believe what he had just heard.

The man was a total scumbag. He didn't deserve to have a son like Troy. Or a grandson as wonderful as Noah.

"Smash the bloody thing!" Spittle flew from Mark's mouth as he ignored his son. He was losing control.

Lifting the statue above his head, Ernest slammed it against the trunk of the tree, shattering the ancient ceramic into pieces. An object roughly sixty millimetres in diameter fell into the straggling grass growing around the tree roots. Mark crab-walked Noah closer as Ernest scooped it off the ground and then stared into his palm.

"Well? Is it…?" Mark demanded eagerly.

Face paling into grey, Ernest rolled his eyes towards Natalie before facing Mark. "It's a rock. The amulet is gone!"

"*What!*" Mark's scream bounced around the clearing, cutting above the roar of wind and rain. He pointed the knife at Natalie. "You! You did this! Where is it? Or I swear…" The knife was jabbed against Noah's neck again. More blood flowed down onto the neck of his tee-shirt.

Eyes bulging with terror, Noah mouthed, '*Mum*'.

Her pulse thrummed as fast as the falling rain. Sweat beaded on her forehead as she battled the rush of panic fogging her brain. "I haven't got it, on my son's life…" she shrieked.

Troy bounded forward as did his dog.

"Get back!" Mark slashed the knife down over Noah's

chest. Blood spurted staining the boy's tee as he cried out and went to clutch the gaping wound.

Natalie's heart juddered. Her breathing seized. "*Noah!* Stand still. Troy, please. Don't! Please stay where you are." Mingling with the downpour it was too hard to tell whether the cut was fatal. But it *was* long and looked deep.

His face a warzone of frustration and anguish, Troy grabbed hold of Chip's collar and dragged her to a halt.

Wildness entered Mark's face, his lips drawing back into the snarl of a cornered animal. He shifted his hold over Noah and yanked his chin high leaving an expanse of exposed skin.

Any second and her son could pay the ultimate price.

Chip erupted into a volley of barking. Were the police on their way?

Bellowing obscenities, Mark swung the knife back and forth perilously close to Noah's vulnerable throat while Troy shouted, trying to break through his father's madness.

Dizziness assaulted Natalie's mind. A cold like nothing she'd ever experienced before swept through to her soul. She staggered and fell to her knees into muddy water as the world faded into grey. Out of the mist, a picture emerged.

Sunlight? In the middle of a storm? Sunlight sparkling like ribbons of gold thread through the wispy leaves of a young willow tree growing on the banks of a slow-moving creek. Two bare-footed boys dressed in grubby shirts and old-fashioned britches wrestled and laughed as they rolled over the grass. Nearby, four horses grazed and snorted, their bridles jingling with every movement. Natalie knew they were making noises and yet she could hear no sounds. The long drooping willow branches lifted in a gentle breeze revealing a younger brown-haired boy with a knife in his hand carving something into the trunk. A girl in a long dress sat cross-legged in the tree's shade. She held a leather-bound book in her hands and her long brown hair was tied back with a purple ribbon. She looked up – directly at Natalie – and smiled.

Vicious pain stabbed through Natalie. *Breathe. Breathe,* screamed her inner self. She sucked in a deep lungful, the pressure in her chest eased and the image vanished back into the shadows of the past.

Her world crashed down around her.

Troy pleading, Mark screaming, the dog barking and Ernest... Ernest had aged ten years as he stood trembling, his eyes vacant as if he stared into a nightmare only he could see.

"I know where it is! Shut up! Everyone just shut up!" Whirling around, she fairly flew the few steps to the old willow tree. Her fingers slid over the ragged bark, searching, searching. There. The initials. Not an *O* or an *S* but rather *AMGM.* Alfred. Mitchell. Gregory. And... Matilda.

This had to be their special place. Where they'd played, dreamed of adventure and the lives three of them would never live.

Chip's barking morphed into low growls. Mark fell into blessed silence as Troy reached her side. "What are you looking for?"

"There were some initials here. I think I saw a small hole dug into the trunk too." She found the opening, a circle which the bark had almost grown over, and began to feel around the edge.

"Yeah. I see it." Troy moved closer until he pressed against her back, his warmth easing a little of the chill wracking her bones. He shifted her hand aside. "I'll check. May be snakes inside."

Snakes. She hadn't thought about that and waited, heart thumping like crazy as Troy slipped his fingers, then his arm into the narrow opening, ripping off shreds of brittle bark. The wind tore through the surrounding bush, bending trees and cracking branches as the rain continued to pelt from the angry sky.

"Have you found it?" shrilled Mark so close that Natalie started.

"Not sure. There is something in here… Wait… " He withdrew his arm and stepped back. In his hand was a wrinkled scrap of kangaroo hide wrapped around a roughly circular item. He looked at his father. "Let Noah go and I'll give it to you."

Mark shook his head. "Could be nothing. No. You hand it to me, or I'll kill the boy."

"I don't think you will."

Natalie whispered, "Troy, what are you doing?"

"Don't test me!" roared Mark.

Troy peeled away the wrinkled hide. "You want it? Come and get it."

Natalie crowded close and for a couple of seconds even forgot the threat to her only child as she drank in the sight of the object he held. Even Ernest snapped out of his fugue state to shuffle over. He gasped and held out a hand. "This could be the amulet. May I?"

"Knock yourself out. But don't take one step towards my father without my say so."

Ernest nodded as he very carefully examined the piece. "The outer is solid gold moulded to represent the wings of the bird, possibly a falcon. The wings are studded with gems, possibly precious and they are surrounded by thin circles of enamel. I think maybe, amethysts, peridots, pearls and carnelian. The centrepiece is a scarab beetle that appears to be carved out of an emerald and it looks flawless." His voice rose and with each word he spoke, colour returned to his grey face. Whatever had been eating away at him previously, had obviously been forgotten.

"There's two large garnets or rubies; one is attached to the top of the scarab, presumably meant to represent the head of the beetle, and the other which is slightly smaller is held by the back pincers. The front pincers hold a large diamond which represents the sun god Ra rising in the sky to cast his power on the woman bold enough to wear such a stunning piece." He raised his head and met Natalie's stunned gaze. "The scarab beetle was a favourite form for amulets throughout Egyptian history. It was modelled after the scarab-faced god Khepri who represented the rising or morning sun in the ancient religion. By extension, he also represented creation and the renewal of life. Hence why the scarab beetle is often found in mummy tombs."

"Forget the history lesson! Bring that bloody thing here!"

Mark was closer than she'd realised. So close that five steps and she would be able to touch her son. She wanted to scream, to rant, to pummel the monster until he was nothing more than dust. Instead, she had to stand and wait. Do nothing. But soon…

Ignoring Mark, Ernest turned the piece over and stared at the underside. His mouth moved like he was reading to himself, then he raised the amulet so they could all see the tiny engravings of hieroglyphics.

"Finally." The word burst from Ernest's lips like a thunderclap.

Three fair-haired men burst out of the bush. Two were armed with pistols.

Everything seemed to happen at once.

As he bounded forward, the lead thug levelled his gun towards Mark. His familiar-looking bleached blond hair was plastered to his skull by the rain. One of the hang-gliding tourists - but none of them were real tourists.

The other armed man swivelled his gun, directing his aim at Natalie.

Dragging a struggling Noah in front of him, Mark advanced on Ernest who had turned so white he looked as if he was about to collapse.

Troy dived to the right, taking down the armed thug who'd threatened Natalie, with a rugby tackle. They slammed into the mud. Barking as if she'd tear the flesh from his bones, Chip launched herself onto the man at the rear. He went down screaming in a tangle of man and dog.

A gunshot exploded. Bark ripped from the tree next to her. Almost deafened, Natalie's ears rang with white noise as she staggered forward trying to get to her son.

Noah. Noah.

Swearing, and using Noah as a human shield, Mark snatched the amulet from Ernest's limp grasp. He began to walk backwards, his arm clamping Noah in place even though Noah wrestled desperately to free himself. Three more bullets cracked in rapid succession, snapping leaves and branches as Lead Thug closed the distance.

Splashes, thumps and grunts came from where Troy fought for supremacy on the muddy creek bank. He couldn't help her.

Couldn't help Noah.

Lead Thug was so close now, Natalie could see his picture-perfect teeth curled into a snarl. She read the intent in his eyes.

Mark had planted Noah between him and the killer.

The soggy ground sucked at her feet as she hurtled as fast as possible towards her child, but it was like wading through wet concrete.

Noah's eyes met hers. He gave a sweet smile and mouthed, *'It's okay.'*

The gun fired again.

Natalie screamed as the force of the impact punched her son off his feet. His arms flung into the air. Blood spurted from his chest.

He hit the ground and didn't move.

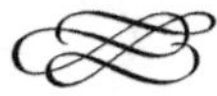

CHAPTER 21

[Extract taken from Matilda Lette's diary. Undated.]

Glad tidings! Mitchell is home. He is so gaunt and frail and needs his walking stick as his leg wound gives him much pain. His eyes are hollow and sad. He sits on the porch doing nothing but looking over the grounds. He will not speak of what he has seen. I want to help but all I can do is pray he can find some peace and he will heal. There is no peace for me. I want Alfred and Gregory to come home. I want my world to be as it once was and will never be again. I remember how I thought they were off to a grand adventure that would last only months. I envied the places they would visit. How foolish I was. After chores today I rode to our special place again. There is nothing left but ghosts. I will never return.

The small figure lay ominously still while rain streamed from the heavy grey clouds and mingled with the growing pool of blood. His son. His only child – a child that Troy never knew he'd fathered until recently. It couldn't end like this – not here, not now. Not when he'd just been gifted another chance at a different kind of future.

Natalie had reached Noah's side and crouched beside him. Blood flowed over her hands where she held them against his upper chest.

Mark was shouting at Ernest to '*get a move on*', urging him to follow as he fled towards the scrub. Shots exploded into the leaves and trees, as Lead Thug attempted to bring Mark down as if he was shooting at a wild dog.

Breaking into a shambling jog, Ernest kept turning around as if he couldn't compute what the hell was happening.

Chip's barks were sharp and ferocious while the thug she had pinned to the ground, screamed for help.

All the while, the blood poured from Noah running over the sodden earth like a river. It seeped into the creek's quickly encroaching waters eating its way further up the slope towards the tent where another victim of his father sprawled, unmoving. There was no mistaking those pink gumboots. Edwina Lette.

A fist plowed into the side of Troy's head. Shards of pain splintered over his skull. Another fist found his kidneys. He grunted as agony exploded. Another punch on his ear and yet another slammed into his gut. The dizziness fogged all thought, but years of training held him fast. He fought for his life, his son, and that of the woman he had always loved.

His strength was failing. He sought an opening and found it, chopping his rigid hand into his opponent's throat. The thug choked. Loosened his bear grip. Troy took immediate advantage, hammering blows with one fist as he groped amongst the mud and weeds for something. Anything.

His desperate fingers closed over a sharp rock. He smashed it against the thug's head, followed that up with a savage kick to the bloke's knee with his steel-cap boot. Heard the crack of bone. The thug dropped to the ground.

His breath whistling in and out of his straining lungs, Troy spat a globule of blood onto the ground. He sent another kick into the fellow's inert body. No response. He was out for the count.

Lightning flashed, a brilliant arc that sizzled with energy and was blindingly bright. Thunder shattered the sky. Troy swore he felt the earth shake beneath his feet. He blinked away the black spots dancing in front of his eyes, making the scene in front of him blur and shake as if in a blender.

His father was nowhere to be seen. Neither was the Lead Thug, who must have chased after him into the bushland.

Distant shots cut through the rampaging storm.

Shouts rang through the bush. *"Over here!" "This way!"* Rapid horses' hooves thudded against the earth. Whoever they were, they were closing in on their position.

Help? Or more criminals to contend with? He didn't know the answer.

The thug Chip had taken down, sobbed and sloshed through the swirling edges of the creek. Chip growled and shook him by the ankle.

Instead of escaping with Mark, Ernest, wearing nothing but a singlet was bent over Noah and pressing his shirt against the boy's wound. His hoodie was draped over Edwina. He must have also propped her against the tree, before returning to do anything he could to help Noah.

Wiping rain, blood and sweat from his eyes, Troy stumbled forward only to stop short as footsteps pounded. He cast around for a weapon.

Too late.

Lead Thug burst back into the clearing, leading with his gun and screeching, "Where is he?" Bullets whizzed in all directions, cutting down bark, exploding leaves as he sprayed the air with gunfire.

A dog yelped, a high pitch howl of pain. More shouts came from the surrounding bushland. Louder.

Arms outstretched, Ernest flung himself over Natalie and Noah, sheltering them beneath his body.

Roaring, Troy launched himself at Lead Thug. A bullet sliced across his upper arm. He buried the pain. Grabbed the gunman's wrist, but it was slick from the rain. He tried again, this time latching hard. He forced the gunfire off to the side, away from the others. Using all his weight, he heaved into Lead Thug, trying to push him to the ground. He kicked out with his foot. Missed. Stumbled in the mud and muck. Blackness was sucking him down. If he caved, his son, Natalie, hell all of them, could die. He let fly with his fist but again, missed his mark.

His face twisted into a caricature of death, Lead Thug kneed Troy in the groin. Sickening, white-hot agony flared through his body. Despite his mind screaming at him not to fall, he felt his knees give way. Lifting his head a fraction, he saw the gun muzzle swing through the sheeting rain towards him.

A loud thump. Lead Thug's expression smoothed into one of astonishment. The gun slipped through his fingers as his eyes rolled up into his head. Another whoosh and thump as the branch came down again on Lead Thug. He dropped like a stone.

Ernest, wheezing so loud he sounded like he was about to have a heart attack, dropped the stick he held then collapsed beside the unconscious gunman. Blood was pouring from a hole in the back of his singlet.

"Natalie! Noah!" Troy's hoarse voice cracked as he fumbled to pick up Lead Thug's gun.

Feeling as if he was being gutted alive, his gaze fixed on where they lay so still. Natalie stirred, lifted her head and met his eyes. Mouth trembling, she nodded then turned back to their son. Sobbing, she begged, as she pressed her blood-soaked hands over his chest while trying to shield him from the icy rain with her body, "Noah, please. Open your eyes. Come on son, please don't leave me. *Noah!*"

Blood running down his back, Ernest shot Troy a glance fraught with horror and crawled closer.

Troy's throat clogged as hopeless despair cut deeper than any wound. His face, paper-white, his lips blue, Noah barely breathed. Limbs shaking and with sickness still churning in his gut, Troy shrugged out of his wet jacket and placed it over the boy, hoping it would provide a little warmth. His son. He was meant to protect him, keep him safe, it didn't matter that he hadn't known he was a father. He was still responsible. He placed a gentle hand on Natalie's wet shoulder, ensuring the gun he held was pointed away from them.

"I never meant… please, forgive me," croaked Ernest.

Troy's aching fist curled. Planting one on the older man was a waste of energy. His conscience would be his burden and that was enough. Besides, in the end Ernest had risked his life to save them. From behind Troy came a loud splash.

"Troy… your dog!" Ernest yelled.

How could he have forgotten his loyal pet? He lurched to his feet, spun around. He staggered towards the churning water.

Saw one of the thugs thrashing in the creek where the rain pelleted down like a volley of bullets.

Saw Chip, her paws flailing the roiling waters as she desperately tried for the bank.

The thug went under. He failed to surface.

The current surged carrying Chip further away from the shore. Her already soaked coat would drag her down.

Hooves pounded like an advancing train. Senior Constable Taylor, looking like a bushranger in her oil-skin riding coat, galloped into the clearing. One quick all-encompassing glance was all she needed. She set the biggest horse Troy had ever seen towards the raging creek. Without hesitation horse and woman plunged into the water aiming for his struggling dog.

"Come on, Chip!" he begged.

Leaning over, Taylor grabbed hold of Chip by the scruff of the neck then hauled her over the saddle. The big horse turned, his powerful legs scrabbling for purchase through the force of the water and the softness of the muddy bed. Another mighty heave, and horse and rider surged out of the creek and up the bank.

Troy hobbled over and retrieved his shivering dog. Together they staggered back to Natalie and Noah where Chip pressed her cold body against the boy's and licked his face.

"Mum?" Noah's eyelashes flickered as Senior Constable Taylor shot a flare into the sky.

CHAPTER 22

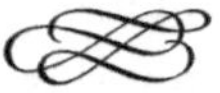

[Final extract taken from Matilda Lette's diary.]
January, 1919.

There was a memorial service at Church this morning. The grief and sorrow filling the pews is unbearable. So many of our lost boys will never come home. During the service, Mother could hardly stand, and Father also. He swayed back and forth like he would fall at any moment. He was at the pub all night and already looks like an old man. I saw Dot, she wore a black dress and is very thin. I want to speak to her but the words wont come. After the service, I went with Mitchell to lay bush rosemary and bottlebrush flowers on the fresh graves. Fourteen of our men went to war. Six came home to be buried beside family and friends. Only three came home alive. I think of all those lying cold and still in soil so far away. Those who will never return. Like my two dear brothers. My throat is so tight. My chest burns from the tears I have shed. I cannot eat or sleep. I mourn for Alfred, but more so for Gregory. He was the better half of me. I am broken.

[Inserted with this final entry was a newspaper clipping announcing the arrival of the Spanish Flu on Australia's shores.]

INSIDE THE HOSPITAL WAITING ROOM, Natalie hugged a blanket over her shaking body and paced the tiled floor. She kept her gaze fixed on the closed doors that led into the ICU; somewhere in the rooms beyond, her son was fighting for his life.

The past hours had been a frantic hive of activity. One minute they'd been in deadly danger and the next the police had arrived, along with several members of the Sullivan and Morgan families on horseback. AJ had led the paramedics, Colm and Chandra, to the clearing. They had instantly leapt into action, stabilising the injured and organising their transport to the hospital. In the meantime, the police had arrested the thugs in the clearing and organised two search parties; one to look for the bloke who'd been swept away in the creek. The other, with Abby in charge, to search the bushland for Troy's father.

Those on horseback had set off immediately leaving Natalie to follow the wounded to the waiting ambulance. She'd wanted to travel with Noah but there wasn't sufficient room once the paramedics placed an unconscious Edwina into the rear. Riley and AJ had loaded a bleeding

Ernest into their paddy wagon, and both vehicles screamed towards the hospital, lights and sirens blaring. Natalie had followed close behind driving the ute with a bruised and bloody Troy and a sodden dog with an injured leg in the seat beside her.

When she'd arrived at the hospital, the building and carpark were ablaze with lights and buzzing with people. There'd been no shortage of hands to assist everyone inside and help with dry clothes, blankets and hot food. Most had been weeded out by Riley and AJ into the main waiting areas, leaving only herself, Troy, and Edwina's immediate family crammed in the area outside the ICU. Troy had been administered first-aid by Shawn Hills who had then been whisked off to help in the emergency department. Opal Flannigan and her husband, Grady, had taken Chip to the vet's for treatment of her bullet graze and monitoring over the next few hours.

Face drawn, Dodge kept pace with Natalie as they traversed the room, round and round. His father had Tilly asleep on his lap while talking in a low voice on his mobile. Tessa and Kaylee were squeezed into one armchair with their arms wrapped around each other. Although Troy was updating Riley and AJ on the events of the afternoon, Natalie could feel his eyes on her every move. Both officers frowned as they listened.

Natalie didn't blame them; after all, the whole situation seemed incredible now that she thought about it properly. The Isis statue hadn't been the magnet that had pulled two obsessed men and a bunch of would-be killers into their orbit. It had been an amulet that may contain vital clues to Cleopatra's final resting place and a treasure trove of precious artifacts and jewels.

An amulet that had fired an unhealthy obsession in Ernest and galvanised a desperate Mark into taking deadly action.

Maybe the amulet was cursed; the odds were the thug who'd fallen into the creek was drowned, both her son and Ernest had been shot while Edwina had hyperthermia and possible pneumonia – both dangerous illnesses for a lady of her advanced years. Three lives on the line.

An amulet of death.

Natalie still couldn't rid her mind of the dread that it was all her fault; it had been her idea to write a book. She was the one who'd broadcast the idea all over the internet. Stopping, she buried her face in her hands as a huge sob exploded from her soul. Arms pulled her close to a warm solid chest.

Troy. Leaning against him, she allowed her emotions to flow until she was drained.

He soothed her back with slow, gentle strokes and she lifted her head to meet his worried stare. "I brought this madness here."

He shook his head. Strain remained etched deep into the lines on his face where blue and black bruises had formed. A white bandage was wrapped around his upper arm and there was a deep cut above his right eye that had required three stitches. "You're not responsible for other people's actions."

"And you're not responsible for your father's." She stroked his cheek with her finger. The bleakness in his eyes wrung her heart. "You thought you were helping your family out. That's all."

"Can you forgive me? For everything? My career choice, my not fighting for you when we were young? For the way I acted the other night?"

"Neither of us acted well the other night," she admitted wryly. Then leaned up to caress him tenderly on the lips. "I'm not letting you get away from me this time. Whatever the future brings, we will face it together."

"That's my idea of a good plan." He grinned before claiming her with a kiss that told her – hell, yeah, he was there to stay.

The double doors burst open, and Dr Frobisher marched through with a colleague by her side. "Mrs Wasson?"

Her pulse rocketed and she gulped as she shifted out of Troy's arms. "I'm here." She gripped his fingers tight.

"This is Dr Patel, a specialist surgeon who flew in earlier from Newcastle." She lifted the clipboard she held. "Your son, Noah, is out of danger. We've removed the bullet and don't believe he will have any lasting damage to muscle or tissue. No bones were affected by the impact, which is another blessing. Give him a few weeks, and he should be back to his normal self."

Natalie sagged against Troy who slung an arm around her and buried his face in her hair, whispering, "Thank heavens."

Dr Frobisher held up a hand when Riley went to speak. "The bullet has been put aside into an evidence bag for any further testing that needs to be performed, Senior Sergeant."

"Can we see him?" asked Natalie.

The doctor smiled. "Soon. It may be up to an hour before he comes to. But only immediate family is allowed and no more than two at a time."

"That's perfect. There's just the two of us." Natalie squeezed Troy's hand.

"I'll request a nurse to come and get you when he wakes. Now." Frobisher consulted her board again. "Any relatives for an Ernest Callen?"

"None." Natalie lifted her chin defying anyone in the room to naysay her. "But I'm a close friend. How is he?"

"He was lucky. The bullet grazed his back. I guess with the rain the wound may have looked worse than what it actually was – you can go and see him if you wish. I want to keep him here a couple of days to monitor his heart."

Riley rose to his feet. "I need to speak with him asap."

Dr Frobisher's mouth thinned. "Very well. But he doesn't need any more stress and you have five minutes only for questions." She looked at Dodge and his family and smiled. "And lastly, but never ever least, Ms Lette is going to be fine. Her temperature is back within normal range, and I can't hear any fluid build-up in her lungs. She's been given an antibiotic injection and has had a chest scan which was clear. The cut on her leg isn't deep but we need to make sure it doesn't get infected. However, I don't see why she can't be discharged. She must be kept warm. Also, someone must stay by her side for the next twenty-four to forty hours to monitor her breathing."

"Me! I'll look after Grannie!" Kaylee jumped to her feet while Dodge and Warren clapped each other on the back.

Tears flowing down her cheeks, Tessa smiled. "Trust

me, none of us will let her out of our sight for a long time."

"That's fine then, but I want her back here first thing tomorrow morning for re-assessment. We may need to run more tests."

Dr Patel lifted both hands in the air. "Never have I seen such a constitution. Anyone else would have perished. But no, this elderly lady, she is strong. Like a bull elephant."

Kaylee giggled. "I can't wait to tell Grannie you called her an elephant and a male one at that."

A perplexed frown knit his forehead and he stared at the ceiling. "She tells me there is a surprise waiting for me at home."

Natalie burst into laughter and after a second, so did everyone else, much to the evident confusion of the visiting surgeon.

The tension in the room evaporated as joy and hope bloomed. Her own heart brimmed over with gratitude as she addressed the two doctors. "I'll never forget the wonderful care you have given my son. Thank you." Still holding Troy's hand in hers, she turned to the others. "Thank all of you for just being here with me."

Tessa came over and hugged her. "We're the ones who should be thanking you." Her teary gaze sought and found Troy. "Both of you. Dodge and I, we know how hard you have worked to bring Gran home to us. We'll also never forget."

"I second that." Dodge held out his hand to shake Troy's. "Good on ya, mate. By the way, congratulations."

He winked at Natalie whose face heated as everyone looked at her and Troy then grinned.

Before anyone could move, an elderly lady in a wheelchair was pushed through the double doors. The clean tracksuit she wore swum on her frail body and a white bandage peeked out from where it was wrapped around the lower part of her left leg. "I keep telling them I can walk on my own two feet, but they won't listen."

"Grannie! Grannie!" shrieked Kaylee all but leaping into Edwina's open arms.

"Bloody hell, Gran! You gave us a fright." Dodge was next in line to give her a hug.

Laughing and crying, Tessa knelt beside the wheelchair and kissed the gaunt, wrinkled cheek.

Eyes suspiciously overbright, Warren leaned over so Edwina could plant a soft kiss on Tilly's face. "Now this calls for a celebration. I'll head home with this little one to the Lodge and get everything all warm and toasty. I'll tell Mum's friends the good news before they storm the building demanding answers." He winked. "I'll also offer a lift to Mrs Brown and anyone else who cares to join us."

"Tell Pam I want a bottle of that brandy and one of Beatrix and Makki's latest sherry. Oh, and get me a hamburger and some fries from the servo. I could eat a horse." Edwina smacked her lips.

"That doctor said you were like an elephant." Kaylee kept her hand on her gran's shoulder as if terrified she'd disappear if she removed it. She giggled even though she had tears running from her eyes.

"The man must have mistaken me for someone else.

But I am fit. I'm thinking of taking up pole dancing. I've heard it does wonders for the figure." She smirked.

Natalie snickered then blushed when those needle-sharp eyes swept over her and Troy.

"Knew it. Told that boy his father would come home." She pulled the blanket up closer to her chin. "I hope he's doing well. Ishya here's been gabbling on about Egypt and armed robbers. Must have missed quite a doozy when I was having a nap."

"A nap!" exploded Dodge. "The doctor believes you've been unconscious for at least twenty-four hours." He ran a hand over his hair. "God, Gran. We've missed you. We thought…"

"Pwush. Us Lettes are made of strong stuff, and don't you forget it boy." Edwina paused and adjusted her blanket with a shaking hand. Red, raw welts marred the skin of her wrists where she'd been tied with rope. "I was lucky that moron kept me trapped in the boot of his car for so long before dragging me into the scrub."

"That explains how we couldn't find you if you were being moved around inside a car." Riley smiled. "I can't tell you how glad we are to see you in one piece, Ms Lette. We have a lot of questions, but they can wait until you've rested."

Edwina frowned. "It's all a bit hazy. I think the bottled water he gave me was drugged cause I kept falling asleep. Said he'd throw me into the creek if I didn't talk. Hah! Little did he know that I can swim like a fish. Is today Saturday?"

"No, Grannie. It's early Tuesday morning, about six

am. You've been missing for so long." Kaylee wiped away fresh tears.

"No need to fret, I'm here now. Where's Pam? I want that brandy."

Dr Frobisher slapped the clipboard against her pant leg as she attempted to gain control. A useless feat as Natalie knew from experience – Ms Edwina Lette had always been a law unto herself. The doctor raised her voice. "Ms Lette must be kept quiet. That means – no excitement."

Grinning broadly, Dodge offered his hand to her and Dr Patel. "Don't worry. The celebration will be low key, and I'll make sure it's short, but Grannie would want her mates as well as her family around her."

"Too right, I do. Mush, Ishya, I've got a party waiting for me." Edwina made shooing motions with her hands while the nurse pushing the wheelchair giggled.

"I give up. Remember, she must be back tomorrow morning for a check up." Frobisher handed over a business card. "Any concerns, you can call me on this number."

"Thank you." Dodge turned to Troy and Natalie. "You're both welcome to join us."

Natalie shared a glance with Troy then smiled. "We'd love to, but we're not budging from Noah's side for quite a while. Could we look in on Ernest, first?"

"I'll get one of the nurses to show you the way. Afterwards, you can wait in the corridor outside the post-op observation room, if you choose. The seats are awful, but you'll be as close as possible to your son."

"Sounds great."

The two doctors disappeared through the double doors again. Everyone else began to talk, grabbing their coats and hovering around Edwina as she was wheeled out the door. Eyes burning and her throat tight, Natalie waved until she could no longer see them.

Before she had time to do anything else, Shawn Hills re-appeared and ushered her, Troy and Senior Sergeant Morgan to a ward. "I'll leave you to it but will come back in a few minutes. Mr Callen needs to rest."

Ernest lay with his eyes closed, partially propped up by a mountain of pillows as well as the incline of the hospital bed. An IV line was attached to his arm and his face was pale. As they approached, he opened his eyes and managed a wan smile. "Natalie. I didn't expect to ever see you again."

Dropping Troy's hand, she moved and sat in a chair, drawing it close to the bed. She gave his fingers a gentle squeeze before letting go. "Friends, remember?"

His voice grew gruff as he mumbled, "I rather thought my actions would negate our friendship. How is Noah? And Ms Lette?"

"Out of danger and resting." Riley Morgan cleared his throat and produced a notebook and pen. "You have a lot of explaining to do, Mr Callen."

"I know. And I'm sorry." He looked at the Senior Sergeant. "Has Davidson been found? The amulet?"

"That's a no to both – at this moment anyway. The storm isn't doing us any favours with communication, thankfully it's easing. Trust me – Davidson will be found." Taking another seat, Riley flipped open the cover and poised his pen above the page. "Let's start at the beginning. Which to my mind, is your relationship with Mark Davidson."

Ernest sighed, his mouth drooping. "I met him at a fundraiser for one of my digs years ago. Since that time, he dropped in and out of my life, and donated money for two of my excavations. Until he phoned me – was it really this morning? – I didn't realise he was involved."

"Yesterday now. It's almost six am," Troy said from where he stood behind Natalie's chair.

"I had no idea he was your father. Nor did I know he kept such close tabs on my work." Wincing, Ernest shifted his position. "Where was I? Oh yes. The phone call. We were all in the library discussing Natalie's idea that Edwina's disappearance, the break-ins and my assault were connected. I had to explain to the old lady's son-in-law and grandson and his family about the statue. Apparently, she hadn't told them of its value." He went on to tell Riley about the historical significance of the statue and the amulet that had been hidden inside.

Natalie remained silent as Ernest spoke and Riley scribbled away in his notebook. None of this was new to her or Troy, and they'd already connected what few dots remained. Now she stirred as her mama bear instinct growled into life. "Why didn't you tell anyone? Warn them? We might have been able to stop him before Noah or anyone else was hurt."

Ernest looked a little shamefaced. "Because I didn't trust Troy. It had just struck me why I thought he was familiar – he reminded me of his father, of Mark. Then I remembered how suddenly he had popped up in town. I thought they were working together to steal the amulet."

"That makes sense." Riley sent a narrow glance across the bed towards Troy. "Keep going, Mr Callen."

"By the time I got off the phone with Mark, both of you had left the Lodge. I didn't think either Dodge or Warren would believe me since Mark is a relation. As a consequence, I did the only thing I could think of; I tried to contact the police."

Natalie sucked in a breath and all her defensiveness subsided. Her instincts about Ernest had been right all along – he was fundamentally a good man. He just needed a true friend to dig him out of his troubled past. Happiness surged through her as she smiled at him and picked up his hand. Troy squeezed her shoulder as if giving his support.

Ernest shrugged then bit down on his lip. "The storm made it impossible to raise anyone. I left multiple messages then set off in my car to try and locate Mark. He hadn't told me where he was staying. He'd actually phoned to gloat that soon he'd have the Isis statue. That he'd beaten me to it. He told me he had an enemy looking for him in town, which was, according to him, his reason for hiding in the shadows. And that he'd worked out what make of car they drove."

Troy's hand left her shoulder. She turned around to find him pacing up and down, head down so she rose and went to him, slipping her arm through his.

"I couldn't find him. So instead, I looked for his SUV and the Jeep he told me about. I came across the Jeep near Swallows Bridge, saw some tracks and tried to follow. By this time, the storm had hit, and I lost my way in the bush.

It's only by pure chance that I heard Mark shouting and stumbled across you."

Troy stopped moving and stared at Ernest. "And then you did everything you could to delay my father as long as possible until help arrived. I have to admit there was a moment when I thought you were in cahoots with him. You risked your life to protect Natalie and Noah. You saved me by knocking that moron on the head with a tree branch. I owe you, mate, and I'm sorry I ever doubted you."

Ernest shook his head. "No, I don't deserve your apology or your gratitude. I came here with every intention of stealing the statue for myself. I wanted that inscription, and I was prepared to deceive Natalie to obtain it."

Natalie went back to the bed and smiled down at him. "What matters, is that in our hour of need you chose the right course of action. The honourable course. Ernest, you chose friendship over deceit and glory. I hope that you will always be my friend."

He rolled his eyes and huffed, but he couldn't hide the shy pleasure lighting his eyes. "What happens now, officer? Will I be charged?"

Nurse Shawn appeared in the doorway and tapped his watch. Frowning, Riley held up three fingers. Shawn shook his head and didn't budge from the doorway.

Riley scratched the side of his face as he tucked away his notebook. "Okay, I think we've got enough for today. However, we're sure to have more questions, Mr Callen and a formal statement will be required. As for being charged," he paused and rose to his feet. "Withholding

information might be the only thing I can come up with –
but we'll get back to you tomorrow. Goodnight." After
giving a brief smile to Natalie and Troy, he departed.

"We'll leave, too." Natalie bent down and planted a kiss
on his cheek. "We'll visit you again later in the day."
Taking Troy's hand, she left the room with him and
hurried down the corridor to find their son.

The nurse on duty beckoned them inside and met
them just beyond the doorway. "He's awake and asking
for you."

Natalie choked up. Troy's hand gripped hers so tight
her fingers went numb. She didn't care. She knew he was
experiencing the same mixed feelings of elation and relief.
Knees trembling, she looked across the room and saw
her son.

Face as white as the sheets he lay on, and with
bandages over his shoulder and chest, he looked older, a
wounded warrior. Natalie had the odd sensation she was
glimpsing the wonderful man he would soon become.

Already he was smiling that sweet, cheeky smile and a
little colour seeped into his cheeks as he spotted them.
Then he was back to looking like he always did – her son,
her precious boy. "Hi, Mum. Where've you been? I want
to know everything that happened. I heard Troy kicked
some serious arse and Chip fell into the creek."

"Noah." Sobbing, she ran across the room and tenderly
cupped his cheeks. She stroked the hair from his forehead
while he sniffled and pretended he was all macho cool.
"Oh sweetheart. We've been so worried."

Noah peered over her head to Troy and his smile
turned shy. "Yeah?"

"Both of us," said Troy. "Your mother has asked me to stay, and I said yes."

"I'm glad." Noah held out his hand slowly. "Hi, Dad."

Blinking furiously, as if he had tears in his eyes, Troy gripped it. "Hi, son." He dropped a kiss onto the top of Natalie's head.

There was so much more to say; so many things to be discussed. She knew that together they would work it out. As a huge smile spread over her face, she snatched this moment, memorised it and held it tight in her heart. The moment the three of them became a family forever.

The End

<u>About the Bindarra Creek Series</u>

Welcome to Bindarra Creek, a struggling country town where people work hard and love deeply. Set in the picturesque tablelands of New England, Australia, Bindarra Creek is a fictional, rural community full of romance, intrigue, adventure, drama and suspense.

There are several multi-author *'series'* set in our small town of Bindarra Creek all written by best-selling Australian romance authors.

Our first series, **A Bindarra Creek Romance,** was released during 2015/2016.
A collection of short romances, **Bindarra Creek Short & Sweet,** were released in January 2019.
A Town Reborn series was released during 2019/2020.
Bindarra Creek Mystery Romances were released during 2022/2023.
Bindarra Creek Christmas Romances came out in December 2022.
Bindarra Creek Small Town Christmas romances are duc for release December 2023.

All books are available as ebooks, some are available also as paperbacks.

Every book can be read as a stand alone, however reading the series as a whole will give you more insight into our fictional community as the town continues to grow and change. There is drama, suspense, mystery and just simply feel-good clean and wholesome romance.

For more info on Bindarra Creek Romances, visit www.bindarracreekromance.com

ACKNOWLEDGMENTS

My heartfelt thanks to Erin Moira O'Hara who not only kindly shared her own personal letters from that period, but also critiqued my manuscript.
Thank you to my editor, Susanne Bellamy for her thoughtful suggestions and editing skills.

Thank you to Annie Seaton for all her hard work in designing the covers for this series and thank you to Patti Roberts of Paradox Book Design for my new cover.

A special thank you to my fellow members of the Bindarra Creek Romance series - it's been an absolute pleasure.

In the spirit of reconciliation, I acknowledge Aboriginal and Torres Strait Islander peoples as the First Australians and Traditional Custodians of the lands where I live, learn and work. I pay my respects to elders past and present and thank them for their ongoing custodianship of and care for the country I live and write on.

In order to achieve authenticity with the historical accounts of Australians during the World War I years, several books and websites were researched.

I thank and acknowledge the following:

Books

Bradley, Phillip, *Australian Light Horse, The Campaign in the Middle East, 1916-1918,* Allen & Unwin, 2016

Carthew, Noel, *Voices from the Trenches, Letters to Home,* New Holland Publishers, 2002

Dapin, Mark (Editor), *From the Trenches, The Best Anzac Writing of World War One,* Viking (Penguin Group), 2013

Websites

Anzac Portal Australian Light Horse in World War I taken from https://anzacportal.dva.gov.au/wars-and-missions/ww1/military-organisation/australian-imperial-force/australian-light-horse

Aussies in Maadi (Meadi) Camp, Egypt 1914-19 taken from http://diggerhistory.info/

Smythe Family History Australia taken from http://www.smythe.id.au/

www.ingramcontent.com/pod-product-compliance
Lightning Source LLC
Chambersburg PA
CBHW072353110726
47909CB00003B/689